FALLING EMBERS

ROMEO ALEXANDER

ROMEO ALEXANDER

Published by Books Unite People LLC, 2023.
Copyright © 2023 by Books Unite People
All rights reserved.

This book is a work of fiction. All resemblance to persons living or dead, is purely coincidental.

Editing by Jo Bird
Beta Reading by Melissa R

ISAIAH

Legs comfortably wrapped around a wooden post, I leaned forward to gaze out over Fairlake. Sitting atop the steeple on the roof of the fire station gave me a good view of the town below. It was the tallest building around since the small town wasn't exactly known for its towering skyscrapers, which meant I had a positively breathtaking view.

The sun was already rising, pushing away the darkness and filling the sky with an aura of red and pink. I adjusted my position as a warm breeze blew past me. Taking a sip from my coffee, I smiled as I listened to the birds continue the song they'd started an hour before human eyes could even see the sun beginning to peek over the horizon.

"Hey! Isaiah, you up there?" a shout came from below.

I peered over the edge to find Zach standing in front of the fire station, a bushy brow cocked as he caught sight of me. Smiling, I waved to signal I could hear him.

"You know the chief is going to have your ass if he catches you up there again," Zach called with a shake of his head.

"Chief doesn't come in for a couple more hours," I informed him. "I made sure to check."

"Yeah, well, he just texted to say he was coming in early to deal with a couple of things. Which you'd know if you had your phone," Zach said.

"Aww crap," I muttered, putting the top on the thermos so it wouldn't spill on my way down. "I should probably come down, huh?"

"Well, if you don't want him to see you on the way over, yeah, probably a good idea."

"Loud and clear."

Unwinding my legs from their anchor, I swung myself around. Holding tight, I secured the strap on the thermos through the loops of my pants before clambering down. I knew the path up to the top like the back of my hand and climbed down with ease, feet and hands finding the necessary footholds to get down the sloped roof. It was considerably more treacherous to do it during rainy days and in winter, but even then, I'd got pretty good at maneuvering around.

Once I reached the flat part of the roof, I used the sturdy lattice built on the side of the firehouse. The chief had decided it was a good idea to give us all something to do whenever we weren't out on a call, which in a small town like Fairlake, was pretty often, which meant using the patch of dirt beside the fire station as a garden. It was growing pretty well now it was early summer, and I was careful not to tread on anything as my feet hit the soil, and I stepped away.

Zach was waiting for me when I rounded the building, already shaking his head. "One of these days, you're going to fall and break your neck. Then everyone will feel bad, but then pissed because you don't listen."

"I know how to listen," I complained, unhooking the thermos from my pants. "But c'mon, I've done that dozens of times. If I haven't fallen and hurt myself yet, I'm not going to."

"Christ, you sound like my kids," he said with a roll of his eyes. "All it takes is one little mistake one time, and boom, you're dead. With our job, you should know that better than anyone."

"Thanks, Dad," I said with a chuckle.

"At least I'm not the chief. You'd be looking at a good half-hour lecture."

"Eh, I could probably cut that in half. It just takes an apology and agreeing with everything he says."

"Right," Zach said with a roll of his eyes. "And the fact that you can pull off a sad face that would make Bambi green with envy has nothing to do with it."

"I do not," I scoffed, giving him a swat. "Now, if you're done treating me like a little kid, I'd kinda like to get some food."

If I had to list my favorite reasons for working at the fire station, the food would definitely make the top five. Someone on shift always knew how to cook, which guaranteed no matter who was assigned to it, the food was bound to be delicious.

Zach rolled his eyes once more. "Fine, I made some stew last night. Should still be bubbling away in the pot."

"Ooh, your venison stew?" I asked, eyes going wide.

"That's the one."

"Time to go fill myself to the point that I can't move then."

Zach smirked. "You really think buttering me up will make me forget I had to save your ass from a chew out?"

"Is it buttering you up if I'm speaking the truth? Because, uh, you know I love the shit out of your venison stew."

"Go get your damn food," he said with a grumpy wave of his hand.

I thought it was a pretty valid question, but I wasn't going to argue when I was about to get fed. Zach had grown up in a hunting family, had taken to it with a passion, and loved to incorporate the game he caught into his meals. Combined with the fresh food from the garden, usually stored in the walk-in freezer, it meant delicious, homemade meals.

Walking in, I waved as I passed through the truck bay and spotted the blond twins Larry and Terry. As usual, they huddled together, voices so low only the other could hear. That was pretty normal for them, leaving the rest of us to wonder just what they were always talking about. Considering they were pretty good at talking to us when we were around, we didn't let it bother us too much.

"Yo," I called out to them.

"Hey," they called back. I didn't know if it was a twin thing, but they tended to speak as one. Thankfully it was only the occasional word or phrase, otherwise, it would be downright creepy rather than slightly unnerving. "Alright?"

"You guys are lucky you're fun to look at, or I'd ask the chief to ship you off to a horror set," I said with a shake of my head. They both chuckled, Terry rolling his eyes and Larry winking at me. I suspected they both liked to flirt occasionally, though only Larry was honest about it.

There wasn't a single person in the station who didn't know I was gay, and not one of them cared...as far as I knew. I was sure the chief pulled new people aside to warn them. Not that he felt they needed to be warned, but the man had a protective streak a few thousand miles wide. He treated each of us like his own kids half the time, protecting us and giving us hell when we screwed around too much. He wouldn't admit it, but when Zach joined up, he was the one who informed me the chief had told him about me and watched Zach's reaction.

Probably looking for the tells that meant the chief would have to unleash on him.

I stopped by the locker room to drop off my jacket. After depositing it in my locker, I sidled up to the sink beside the shower room entrance. I peered at my reflection, reaching up to swipe at the slightly long, soft brown hair that had blown all over the place from the morning wind. There wasn't much I could do about the bright pink spots that had formed on my cheeks from the chill, and I could only hope they faded by the time the Chief got to the station.

"This is definitely the face of someone who wasn't climbing buildings," I told the reflection, grinning at myself and practicing my innocent expression. I might be over six feet tall with broad shoulders, but I had the face of an innocent librarian. There was a slight softness to my features I could use to my advantage when I needed to pretend I was not up to mischief.

It was just unfortunate that it didn't work on people who knew me well.

Assured that I was put together, I left the locker room to head to the kitchen. I stopped and beamed at the large man bent over one of the counters, poking at the stew. "Laurence, I really hope Zach doesn't catch you screwing with his stew."

The behemoth of a man jumped like he'd been goosed, whirling around on me. "Jesus Christ on a cracker, Isaiah, you scared the bejesus out of me."

"I'm stealthy," I said in a low voice, waving my arms around in a horrible interpretation of a ninja.

"A brat is what ya are," he grumbled, turning to look at the stew. "It looks different than usual. Hope he didn't put anything funny in it."

"Probably just the normal arsenic and angel dust," I told him, walking up to nudge him aside, which was easier said than done. I wasn't the smallest person in the world, but I was the smallest in the station, and Laurence had always been the biggest by a wide margin.

Until the latest addition to our crew, anyway.

"I hope you know that anytime your daddy told you you were funny, he was lying because he loves you," Laurence said with a frown. "Like, what is this?"

I peered into the pot and snorted, picking up a spoon to scoop out the lump he was questioning and showing it to him before popping it into my mouth. "It's mushroom, Laurence. Everyone knows he uses cream of mushroom as the base for the stew."

"Why's it so big, though?"

"Probably made it from scratch. Don't be such a baby."

The irony that I, at the ripe old age of twenty-eight, was teasing a man who had just turned forty about being a baby wasn't lost on me. From Laurence's scowl, it also went unappreciated.

"Well, if you won't take any, then I will," I told him, giving him another bump with my hip as I retrieved a bowl from the cabinet and began ladling myself some stew. "There any coffee?"

"Like we don't live off that shit around here," he muttered, gesturing toward the pot. "Just made it like twenty minutes ago. You working with The Shining today?"

I had to actively resist the urge to snort and risk the stew in my mouth shooting out through my nostrils. "If Larry and Terry didn't work with you last night, it looks like it. And you know when they hear you say that, it just makes them wanna be even creepier, right?"

"Like they already aren't creepy enough as it is," he snorted, getting a bowl out of the cabinet as well.

"I didn't look at the schedule," I admitted while I refilled my thermos before slapping it back on my hip so I could eat my stew in peace. "I should probably go do that, though. I just knew I had to be in this morning."

"Chief's probably gonna slap you with another double," Laurence chuckled.

"Thrills and thrills galore," I said with a roll of my eyes. "I should probably go see, or I'll forget."

"Eh, you're probably stuck with The Shining or Maurice, haven't seen him around for a while, the lazy ass," Laurence grumbled.

"He's been out for cancer treatments," I reminded him.

"Lazy ass," Laurence muttered.

"Right, because you didn't tell the chief you were taking over half his shifts if he needed the time."

"Lazy."

I snorted, shaking my head and taking my bowl with me. There was no point trying to get Laurence to budge, the man was as stubborn as he was large. Everyone knew he was as big a softy as the chief, he just liked to complain a lot.

Before heading toward the office, I heard a familiar gruff voice and made my way out front. The chief and Zach stood outside, peering up at the roof.

"Morning," I called as I pushed the door open, slightly worried that Zach might have snitched on me.

"Isaiah," Chief Borton said, barely glancing at me. "Maybe you can solve a little mystery for me."

"Sure, what's up?"

"Maybe you could tell me why I can see what looks like a set of keys hanging off our steeple. See, Zach here doesn't seem to know, and you're the knowledgeable type."

"Keys?" I asked in a high voice, looking up. I gulped when I saw what was indeed a set of keys hanging from the steeple. Even if there was a chance they might be someone else's, I could see the tiny palm tree keychain a cousin had brought back from Hawaii. It was cheap and cheesy, but it was rainbow-colored and made me laugh.

"Well...those do seem to be keys."

7

"We covered that much. Now I'm just wondering how they might have gotten up there," Chief Borton added, his brow rising ever so slightly.

"That," I said, glancing between him and the keys, trying desperately to think of *something* to say, "is a mighty fine question. A mystery for the ages."

"And if I'm not mistaken," he continued, looking utterly unamused by my attempt to buy time, "they appear to be *your* keys."

"Do they?" I asked, voice cracking slightly. "Isn't that a strange coincidence?"

Behind him, Zach buried his face in one of his big hands, slowly shaking his head. There was absolutely no way the chief was fooled in the slightest by my act. My only hope was to double down and pray that, eventually, he decided it wasn't worth trying to squeeze the truth out of me.

"I'm sure it would be equally strange to point out that you don't seem to have your keys on you," he said, narrowing his eyes.

"Seems I misplaced them."

"It seems you've found them."

"Have I?"

"It's too early for this," the chief complained, rubbing his brow furiously. "Just...go get your keys. Consider yourself working a couple of extra doubles this week, and while you're at it, think long and hard about what else might happen if I continue to find you breaking workplace safety protocol."

"Right, yeah, of course," I said, quickly agreeing to his admonishment and the punishment. If Borton chose to give you a dirty look and throw out punishment without chewing your ass out, you accepted it without argument. I was pretty sure the only person who could match his ability to bitch someone out for extended periods was my mother.

"Good," he grunted, heading toward the front door. "That means the rest of the week, by the way."

"Yeah, sure," I said, this time with a little less eagerness than before. I had plans for the weekend, but clearly, that wasn't going to happen. "Of course."

Zach waited until the chief was gone before scoffing. "Seriously, how the hell do you manage to get away scot-free?"

I gave him a disbelieving look. "You call that scot-free?"

"A couple of extra doubles…for the next four days? And without being chewed out? I'd call that pretty much scot-free. If it were me, I'd be dragged into his office wishing for death."

"Maybe it's because I'm so likable that it's impossible to yell at me?"

Zach rolled his eyes. "What, *now* you're willing to accept that?"

I shrugged. "If it gets me out of trouble, screw it. Why not?"

Shoving another spoonful of stew in my mouth, I could only stare back at Zach with what I hoped was innocence. Glancing over my shoulder at the sound of someone approaching, I perked up when I saw a familiar figure jogging in our direction.

"Hey, Bennett," I called as the man grew close enough and pulled his earbuds out. "Earlier than usual, aren't you?"

Bennett, as always, grinned as he slowed to a walk. "Heya, Isaiah, Zach. I got woken up early, so here I am."

"Did you now?" I asked with a smirk, looking him over. "Speaking of which, how's Adam doing?"

Bennett's eyes widened slightly, but other than that, his expression didn't change. "Fine, as far as I know."

"As far as you know," I said, taking another mouthful. Adam was Bennett's childhood best friend who'd returned to

Fairlake a few months before. The guy was a little too serious for my taste, but I knew he was important to Bennett. I also suspected there was more than friendship between the two of them, even though Bennett had been uncharacteristically silent on the matter.

"I guess I'm too early for my normal peep show," Bennett said, looking at the closed bay doors. "Feel like taking your shirt off for me, Zach?"

"My wife is already convinced you or Isaiah are going to try to cart me off from under her nose," Zach said with a snort. "I'm not adding fuel to that fire."

"Don't worry, after a weekend with Bennett, you'd want him to give you back," I told him with another bite.

Bennett laughed. "I'm probably too much for you, Zach, in a lot of ways."

Zach sighed. "I'm not even going to try to guess what you mean. I don't *want* to know."

Bennett winked at me. "Long day for you?"

"Longer since I got busted for climbing on the roof again," I said, pointing toward my still dangling keys. "Betrayed by my own novelty key ring."

Bennett let out a laugh. "Boy, you really need to learn to cover your tracks."

"Weren't you recently busted by your chief for trying to set up a paper football tournament in one of the interview rooms?" I asked.

"I'm not quite sure what you're trying to say."

"I'm saying you're a dirty hypocrite."

"Nah," he said, practically beaming. Not that he wasn't usually happy. Bennett was probably one of the perkiest people I'd ever known. But lately, I'd noticed a distinct glow about him, even as he pretended there was nothing strange or new in his life. "Alright, I should probably head back. I have a few things I need to do before I start my shift."

"Things," I said, voice dripping with meaning.

Bennett sighed, jamming his earbuds back in and resuming his jog. For the past several years, there'd been very few days when he didn't go for a morning jog, even in the dead of winter. I'd watch him pass from a front window, waving and wondering if something was wrong with him.

"Just so you know," Zach said, watching Bennett jog around the square in the center of town. Most of the municipal and government services buildings were built in a square around the biggest park in the city. Fairlake had started as a small town, but they had built it with purpose from the center out. "There's still a running bet between the guys about whether or not you and Bennett have a thing going on."

I rolled my eyes. "We went on a date once…and shared a guy once."

"That…kind of splits the difference, doesn't it?"

"Good, then nobody wins, and all you nosy bastards are assholes for taking a bet. Just because two gay guys live in the same town doesn't mean they're an item."

"You literally just said you went on a date and shared a guy."

"Yeah, and where could two gay guys in a small town get the idea that's something they should do instead of, ya know, trying to be friends first?" I asked with a raised brow, leaving out the fact that I knew Bennett had slept with another guy in town and my suspicion that he currently had something going on with what *should* have been his straight best friend.

This town was a lot gayer than people gave it credit for.

"Why do I feel like no matter what I say, I'll end up feeling like the ignorant straight guy who's saying offensive shit?" Zach asked with a frown.

I laughed, reaching over and punching him on the arm, nearly upsetting the bowl of half-eaten stew in my hand.

"Every single one of you is a bunch of boneheads who say stupid shit all the time. If I was going to be offended, I would have reported all of you years ago."

Zach snorted, rubbing his arm. "Well, what about Larry? He would've been my backup pick."

"Back up? Wait, wait, are you trying to hook me up with Larry?" I asked in shock.

"I mean, Terry doesn't seem to be all that into it when you hit on them," Zach said, rubbing his jaw.

I stared at him. "Are you serious? Larry acts like he likes it because he likes the attention, not because he's secretly imagining what I'd look like under him...or on top of him."

"Hmm, I guess he has already seen you naked, so you'd probably know if he was into you."

"Uh, why?"

"Well, naked and all that. If he was into that, pretty sure he'd, you know, show it."

I gave him a disbelieving look. "I've seen every single one of you naked and haven't popped a boner. What the hell!"

"Well," Zach said, now squinting at me. "I suppose that's kind of the point then, isn't it?"

"Uhhh, I don't know how to tell you this, Zach, but I definitely thought I'd died and gone to heaven the first time I walked in here and saw some of you guys...well, for the first couple of months," I told him, scooping the last spoonful of stew into my mouth.

"I'm old enough to be your dad. What the hell?"

"Unless you had your first kid at eight, then no, you're not. Also, 'daddy' gay is a whole thing, just so you know."

"I don't know what that is, and I'm not sure I want to."

I gestured to him with my spoon. "Tall, kinda buff, a little round in the middle but thick in the arms. Some gray popping in, a little wrinkly—"

"I'm feeling a little self-conscious," Zach said with a frown.

I winked. "You're aging like fine wine, trust me. The point is…what was the point?"

"Something about you drooling over all of us when you first showed up," Zach said, looking just as confused as I felt.

"It wasn't drooling. And I think this was about you trying to hook me up with Larry," I said with sudden outrage. "Why are you suddenly playing matchmaker?"

Zach shrugged, looking unbothered by my outburst. "Like you said, you're one of only a couple of gay guys in town. It's not like I get to see you date or even talk about dating."

"Since when do we talk about our dating lives around here?" I asked incredulously.

"Well, I mean, Laurence, me, and the chief don't really have to," he said, holding up his left hand where a small band caught the sunlight, "since we're always talking about our wives. We all know Maurice is outta the game right now, and the twins are always being seen with some girl or another. The only ones we don't know anything about are you and Julian."

The name sent a jolt through me, and I tried to hold back a grimace. "Yeah, well, no one knows anything about him."

"He is pretty tight-lipped about himself," Zach agreed, but I could see he was watching me closely.

Tight-lipped was putting it mildly. I was pretty sure Julian hadn't said more than a handful of sentences to me since he arrived a few months before. He had been a transfer from another station, but that was all the chief said, and he refused to elaborate further. Like a pack of gossips, the rest of the station had been abuzz over the reason for his transfer, and the ideas varied from the illegal to the mundane.

All I knew was the guy didn't seem interested in dealing

with anyone. He did his job and clearly knew what he was doing, but other than that, little was known about him. I knew he matched Laurence for the station's biggest guy, and he looked like he was carved from marble, probably from the extensive time he spent in the station's weight room.

Zach squinted at me. "Do you...do you have a thing for him?"

My eyes widened, and I jerked back in surprise. "W-what? No! What the hell, Zach?"

His brow quirked, and I could see the hint of a smile forming on his face. "That was...a very quick response. You sure about that?"

I absolutely was not sure, but I'd been working at the station with these guys for too long. Much like the entirety of Fairlake, the firefighters at the station were a pack of gossiping, nosy busybodies. If they got even the slightest hint that I was interested in someone, it would spread around the entire station.

Was I attracted to Julian physically? Damn right I was. The man was gorgeous, and I'd seen how much he could lift, which I found impressive and arousing in equal measure. That he was only the second redhead I'd ever met, with possibly the most interesting shade of green eyes I'd ever seen, certainly went a long way toward helping my interest.

He was also one of the most terrifying people I had ever met. His silence certainly didn't help make him any less unnerving, especially in a group of men who were usually pretty chatty. What sold his terrifying status was that the man just...glowered, no matter what he was doing. And while I couldn't prove it, I'd swear his scowl grew worse whenever I was around, especially if I tried talking to him.

"Yes, I'm sure," I told him with a huff. "The guy can't stand me."

"How the hell can you even tell? I don't think he likes anything."

"Well, you ever see that look he gets whenever I'm around? Yeah, that's how I know."

"Pretty sure he looks like that whenever anyone talks to him...or breathes around him."

"Yeah, well, it looks three times worse when he's paying attention to me."

Zach cocked his head. "That's all in your head. Are you getting sensitive on us?"

"Eat shit," I told him, slapping my empty bowl in his hand. "Say that shit again, and I'll teach your daughter how to access your bank account."

"You wouldn't dare," he growled.

"Maybe I would, maybe I wouldn't," I said, knowing full well I wouldn't do anything of the sort. I might be aware of a few unorthodox means of gaining access to people's infor-mation, but I wasn't going to pass that information along to a teenager. "But if you don't want to find out—"

"This feels like blackmail."

"I think it's technically coercion. I could call Bennett and ask if you like?"

"What, so he can back you up somehow?"

"Perish the thought."

I yelped as Zach managed to loop an arm around the back of my neck and pull me close. Squirming, I slapped at him as the full-grown man actually shoved his knuckles into my skull and rubbed them back and forth vigorously.

"Ah! Quit it, you giant fucking oaf!" I complained as he dragged me toward the front door. I flailed as he did so with seemingly little effort, pulling me inside where everyone else was already coming over to discover the source of the noise.

"Keep doing that, and you might turn him on," Terry called out.

"He does look like he likes it," Larry added, as helpful as ever.

"What is wrong with both of y'all?" Laurence asked grumpily from the doorway.

"If you guys don't shut up and get back to work, I'm putting all of you on double duty for the next two weeks," Chief Borton snarled from somewhere in the depths of his office.

I sighed. And to think this was the closest thing to a family I had.

God save me. I did love them, though.

JULIAN

"You *are* getting along alright there, aren't you?" my mom asked, and even the densest of people could've heard the heavy anxiety in her voice.

"I'm getting along just fine, Ma," I told her as I looked over the circuit board in my hand. Nudging my phone over, I set it down with the other electronics and picked up the soldering iron.

"Well, you just don't talk much about what's going on, is all," she said, and I could practically hear her wringing her hands.

Probably because telling her much of anything would send her into another spiral. Worry and fear had been pretty much my mother's entire life for as long as I could remember. There was no way in hell I'd do anything that added to her already long list of worries.

"I don't talk about much of anything," I reminded her for the millionth time as I carefully applied the iron to the connecting point.

"So much like your father," she said, causing my attention to waver at her wistful tone.

"Ma," I warned, pulling the iron away to look over the work.

"He was a good man," she said. "I always hoped you and your brother would be like him."

"Well, we're both still here, with you, so we're already doing one better than him," I grumbled, turning the iron off and setting it aside. The topic had already shifted, and I could sense my mother drifting away from reality.

Just like she'd done since my father left two decades before. I don't know what it was about him, but his sudden absence in our lives shattered my mother. Tristan had only been four, while I had been old enough at eight to feel the ache of his absence. For my mother, however, it had been world-ending, and she hadn't been the same since.

My mother had always cared, but she'd never quite been able to *be* there. She was like fog, sometimes there, thick and holding close, and yet disappeared at the first hint of heat. She barely managed to keep things together, and even then, I still had to find ways to help her.

And without me, Tristan wouldn't—

"I wish you wouldn't talk about him like that," she said, and I felt a stab of guilt deep in my gut. I hated talking to her most of the time, especially when she was like this. But when I avoided it, I felt just as bad. I couldn't free her. I couldn't save her. I couldn't—

"I know, Ma," I said, leaning back and looking around the small apartment. It was cluttered and disastrous looking, but at least I was alone. "How's Tristan?"

It was an easy topic shift, and she almost immediately sighed in relief. "Oh! Well, you know how he is. He's always done well—"

Which was when I tuned her out now that I knew she was no longer wavering on the edge of her own version of sanity.

So long as she had my younger brother to talk about, she would be perfectly fine.

Oh, how wonderful it was that Tristan was almost done with school.

Oh, how wonderful that his grades were so perfect and his girl-friend was perfect.

Oh, how wonderful that he's never been in any trouble in his life.

Never mind that Tristan was only where he was because I—

"Oh?" I finally broke in, shoving my bitter thoughts away for the moment.

"Well, you know," she said, and I could practically picture her scuttling backward to make excuses. "You know how it goes. Tristan is so busy between school and those intern-ships. He doesn't have time for much else, and Elise couldn't really handle that."

Whether that was the truth or simply what my younger brother had told her was up for debate. Not a debate I was going to have with my mother. Any question about Tristan's believability was an attack on her worldview, something I had learned a long time ago.

"Of course," I said, looping the power cord around and plugging it into the base of the computer I'd been fiddling with for the past couple of hours. My brow rose as I watched the lights flicker to life and heard the hum of the fan. "He has his own things to worry about, and so does she."

"Exactly," she said with a sigh of obvious relief. "And I do wish you were here sometimes," she said as I pushed away from the computer, pleased everything was working right.

"Yeah?" I asked, locking back into the conversation as I glanced at the clock on the wall. As handy as digital was, I still kept an analog clock in every room. Maybe it was the ticking or the certainty of its mechanical process, but I liked it all the same.

And it was time to get ready for my shift.

"Well, you know, sometimes things get hard around here," she explained, lapsing back into her worry. "And Tristan might be coming this summer. I just wish you were here to help with things instead of all the way out there."

"I know," I said because, of course, she needed me to help her. Not just because my brother 'might' visit over the summer but because life had never been kind or come easy to her. "Well, if you know when he's coming, I can take time off. Chief Borton is pretty understanding."

"No, no, no, I don't want you to get in trouble again," she said frantically, as though the words didn't shove a sliver deeper into my chest.

Again.

"It's not a problem, Ma," I told her as I stepped into the bathroom to look myself over before getting ready for the day.

Not much had changed or mattered to everyone else. Still so tall, I had to hunch to see myself in the mirror. Still the same bright red hair that drew everyone's attention even when I wished it wouldn't. The same ugly scar under my bottom lip and the one through my right brow. Still the same squat, mean features that thankfully meant people left me alone.

"Chief Borton is a family man," I told her as I turned to enter my bedroom. It was mostly empty except for a bedside table made from a cinderblock and the double bed that barely managed to fit me. "He's not going to give me shit if I need to help you."

"Well," she said slowly, and I could hear her coming around. "I suppose I could use some help. Especially if Tristan is going to come around."

"Which he will," I lied, knowing damn well my brother had left our tiny town of Fovel and never looked back. In fact, he had seen her precisely once in the past eight years, and that had been his second year at college when he needed money. Not that we'd ever had real money, but if I had to help her out, that was how it went sometimes with family. "Which means you need to call me when ya need me."

"Of course," she said, sounding relieved. "I just know how things have…have been."

"Don't worry about that," I told her, grabbing my keys from the bowl on the cinderblock and heading toward the door. It wasn't a bad apartment building, hell, probably a lot better than the one I'd grown up in Fovel, but I still locked the door behind me. "Chief Borton—"

Well, how did I explain it to my mother?

"He's…alright, he's understanding," I finally said, feeling lackluster and lame, like I usually did with her. "He's not going to give me shit if I have to take a couple of days."

"Well," she drew out as I jogged down the stairs, and I could hear her coming around to the idea once again. "Okay. I just—"

"I know," I told her, not glancing around as I swore one of the other people outside waved in my direction. It wasn't that I didn't want to deal with people because I didn't, but what the hell was I supposed to say to them?

Hi?

How's the weather?

How's life?

How're the screaming matches between you and your partner going?

Nah, not my thing. Not the way things went. You minded your own business and went about things without worrying about other people helping you, and the same was expected back. The more people that came into your life, the more

21

potential trouble there was. Putting your head down and going about life was the best way.

Interfering or getting involved was how you got into trouble that wasn't yours.

"Well," my mother said, her voice reaching an almost indignant pitch. "I don't want to keep you."

I was tempted to let the pause become uncomfortable for a moment before I grunted, starting my car with a shaking roar. "I'm just heading to work, is all."

"Oh! Well, I wasn't sure how often you were working lately."

"I'm working."

"Yes, well, that's good."

Gritting my teeth, I backed out of my parking spot. "It is."

"Well, I wouldn't want to keep you, honey," she said, and I could hear her attention was already diverting. Whether that was toward the TV in the background or perhaps toward the bottle of vodka she pretended wasn't always in her freezer, I didn't know.

"I'd have to let you go soon anyway," I reassured her, knowing she was trying to get rid of me. "So, now's a good time."

"Works out well for us both, then," she said cheerily. "Love you, sweetheart."

"And you," I said.

The phone beeped in my ear, and for a moment, I considered throwing it through the passenger side window that hadn't fully closed since January. It would make the draft in my car more unbearable when it was cold again, but maybe it would make me feel better.

I didn't do it, but I thought about it.

* * *

MY CAR RUMBLED and popped as I pulled into the small parking lot behind the fire station. I felt it vibrate almost dangerously beneath me before slamming it into park and killing the engine. It had sounded like it was going to kill me for a few months now but had yet to do so. So I wasn't going to worry too much. Fairlake was smaller than Fovel, and if I had to, I could walk to work if my car decided to die permanently on me.

Grabbing the handle, I shoved the door open and stepped out. It felt like several clowns emerging from a car, as it always did, and I slammed the door shut to ensure it stayed closed.

"Nice acoustics, Maccomb!" a familiar voice echoed across the parking lot.

I turned to stare at the twin I knew was Terry. As much as people liked to pretend that twins were hard to differentiate, all I had to do was wait for one of them to open their mouth. Terry thought he was the jokester of the two, while Larry liked to watch with what I was sure he thought were knowing eyes.

"Didn't your parents buy you your first car, Terry?" another voice called from the lot, and I felt my nerves settle when I caught Isaiah's familiar lighthearted if slightly catty tone.

He always sounded serious and teasing at the same time. I honestly hadn't known what he was doing when I'd first met him, even when he smiled, because even then he seemed to be mocking me. A few months later, I still wondered, especially when he turned to catch my eye from across the parking lot and gave me a lopsided smile.

"So did your parents," Terry shot back because, as I'd learned, both the twins and Isaiah came from rich stock, especially by small-town standards.

"Yeah, and I didn't have to share it with my parents *or* give someone else shit over it," Isaiah shot back.

I might not always be sure about Isaiah, but I could appreciate he wasn't one to back down easily. Early on, I thought that he, like a lot of well-to-do, rich kids, was just cocky. That was until I had been pulled aside by Chief Borton on my second day and told Isaiah was gay and that no discrimination would be tolerated.

Which wasn't a problem for me. Like I gave a shit what someone did in their spare time. But what mattered was that I'd noticed over the past few months that Isaiah didn't speak about any family, only a couple of friends he had. Or when I learned he lived by himself and tended to do holidays in a very vague way.

He was alone.

So yeah, former rich and spoiled kid, I got the feeling he was alone, even if he never said it, and I would never ask. But he had a toughness I could respect, even if he was absurdly perky much of the time. Unlike the others at the station, he didn't ask questions, and I didn't feel I had to explain myself.

Grunting, I twirled my keys around my finger and headed into the building, ignoring what clearly looked like an argument ready to happen. I felt Isaiah's eyes on me but barely gave him a look as I entered. I didn't like meeting his eyes because despite how little he demanded of me, there was still *something* about him that seemed to ask questions I wasn't willing to answer. He may not give it words, but the words always seemed on the tip of his tongue.

"Maccomb!" a shout echoed down the hallway as I stepped in.

"Yes, Chief," I called back immediately, habit taking over before I could even wonder what the hell I had done.

"My office," Chief Borton told me behind his thick, bushy brows. Then, he turned on his heel and left me alone.

"Yes, sir," I muttered, more out of habit than anything else. Chief Borton was a man who appreciated action more than words, and he wouldn't care what I said to him, just so long as I did as he ordered.

I entered the office behind him, Borton gesturing toward one of the hard plastic chairs he kept in front of his desk. A few filing cabinets were shoved into one corner with stacks of folders atop each. A small glass cabinet in the other corner held pictures, three of which were of the firehouse and its team from the past decade. There was also one of Borton with the police chief and the mayor. Finally, the picture of Borton with his wife and kids took residence on his clean but slightly cluttered desk next to his computer.

"Pulling you in early," he explained as he dropped into his rolling chair. The chair looked barely more comfortable than the one I sat in. Clearly, he didn't think he should have more comfort than anyone talking to him. It seemed a little unnecessary, but at least it was consistent with his hardass persona.

"I know I'm not supposed to do this for another few days, but I'm not going to be here this weekend, so we're doing it now," Borton said, pulling himself up to his desk and tapping away at the computer.

"Sure," I said with a shrug.

Borton eyed me. "Problem?"

"No," I said. "I know how it works."

Do the crime, do the time after all.

"Good," he said, clicking his mouse before leaning back to eye me. "Haven't heard any complaints, but gotta check. Still seeing that shrink?"

"Counselor," I corrected without thinking, then shrugged. "Yeah. Once a week, just like I'm supposed to."

Anger management classes, what a ridiculous concept. I didn't *have* anger problems. I had people problems. Trying to explain that was pointless, however, and I knew better than to make the point to Borton. I suspected he probably had similar issues, considering how little I'd seen him talk with other people. Even if he didn't, he wasn't the type to care about my 'excuses,' just so long as I was doing what I was supposed to.

"Good," Borton grunted, steepling his fingers over his stomach. "Any progress?"

"You'd have to ask the doc."

"I'm asking *you*."

I shrugged again. "I guess."

"I want something better than a guess."

"We talk. Well, he talks, I listen. Haven't had any issues since, so I guess it's working."

Borton sighed, brow stitching together as he leaned forward to rest his arms on the desk. "Look, when I agreed to transfer you here, it was a favor for Chief Bones."

I returned his frown, confused by his irritation. "A favor for him?"

"He asked me if I would take you on since he knew we had a vacancy and thought you'd do well here. He didn't want to let you go."

That was news to me. Chief Bones had barely paid attention to me for the few years I'd worked under him, which suited me just fine. I wasn't keen on being the focus of anyone's attention. Thing was, I had been almost completely sure he'd been glad to see the back of me after I'd broken Donovan's jaw.

"I didn't know that," I admitted quietly, dragging my eyes down to the desk.

"Said you were a good kid, and he didn't want to see you thrown out on your ass if there was a chance you could do something with yourself," Chief Borton told me.

"Oh."

"Just 'oh'?"

I shrugged. "Oh."

Borton sighed, and I could see him shake his head. "I've been doing this job for almost thirty years. Started where the rest of you are and somehow found myself in charge of the knuckleheads that come to work here. In three decades, only one other man spent time here that you remind me of."

"Okay," I said, finally looking up to find the chief examining me.

"He didn't like talking much either," he said, tilting his head as he watched me. "Got drunk with him one time, and he told me talking wasn't his thing and that most of the time, words don't mean shit. Said most people talk out of their ass and don't listen to shit."

I had to admit, whoever this man was, I could see myself liking them. In my experience, people said one thing and then did whatever the hell they wanted when they thought they could get away with it. Sure, there were people in the world who *tried* to mean what they said, but if life had taught me anything, it was that people were generally weak, indecisive, and difficult creatures. And that included me.

Hell, it went double for me.

Chief Borton extended a finger, waving it slowly at my face. "If I've learned anything from you being around here, I just saw approval on your face."

"He a troublemaker too?" I asked, not bothering to hide the bitter sarcasm in my voice. Borton could say that Bones had asked for me to be transferred here all he wanted, but I didn't see the point in ignoring the fact that I was considered trouble. A felony charge followed me when I came under Chief Bones' leadership, and the incident with Donovan propelled me to reside under Borton.

Like my mother's worry was fond of reminding me, trouble was sure to follow wherever I went.

"Kept to himself, much like you do," Borton said, missing or ignoring my tone. "Big like you too. Real big."

"What's your point?" I asked because despite how long-winded he was being, Chief Borton had never been an idle chatterer before.

"My point is that he was a damn fine addition to the station, worked hard for over ten years, didn't cause any trouble, didn't make the station look bad," Borton said, and I watched him twist his wedding ring. I'd only seen him do it a few times before, generally when he was agitated...and he didn't look all that agitated at the moment.

"Okay," I said, unsure if that was the point or if he was waiting for me to say something specific.

"Didn't have any friends either. Don't think he had family to speak of, not that he spoke much."

"Right."

"Seemed pretty stable. Pretty much in control."

"You have a point?"

I almost swore the corner of Borton's mouth tried to twitch. "Then one day, he stops showing up for work. Didn't answer his phone and wouldn't answer the door when we went to his house to find out what happened. Took almost a week before his neighbor noticed a funky smell coming from his side window, peered in, and well, seems ol' Cash had a few more demons than we thought. Trevor said there wasn't any question what—"

"Who?" I asked, then immediately regretted the interruption and looked down at the floor.

"Chief Price," Borton corrected the police chief's proper title. "Trevor wasn't chief at the time. Barely been on the force a few years. Good kid, though there was always something about him that seemed distant. Doesn't matter, though, he believed in what he did, and he wasn't one to make a decision without a good reason. And he was real sure poor Cash did the deed himself."

"How could he be sure?" I asked because I knew full well that while things could look one way, they could be another altogether.

"No evidence of a break-in. Everything was locked up tight. The gun was Cash's, and there were powder burns. Plus, if you're going to use a weapon to murder someone and make it look like a suicide, you don't use a shotgun."

My lips thinned at the thought. "Hemingway."

"What's that?"

"Doesn't matter. I guess he, uh, was done."

Borton's brow rose slightly, and I had a moment to realize it was probably the wrong thing to say. Bluntness didn't just come easy to me. It was pretty much the only way I knew how to speak to other people.

One of my earliest memories was finding my father passed out on the couch as my mother tried to wake him from his drunken stupor.

"Help me wake him up," she asked me, and I stared at her in confusion, my eight-year-old brain trying to understand her reasons.

"Why?" I'd asked. "Things are better when he's not around."

It had been the truth, but it was a truth that had reduced my mother to tears. As she fled the room, asking how I could be so thoughtless, I realized that even when the truth didn't hold any malice, it could still hurt. It was the first time I thought it was better to keep my mouth shut.

"Yeah," Borton said softly. "I guess he was. I suppose you'd have to be pretty done to figure out a way to take a shotgun to the skull."

"Why?"

"Why'd he do it? Don't know. There wasn't a note. No

one had any warning. He didn't drink or do drugs, far as we knew, which wasn't very far at all. We didn't hear anything about debt or a bad breakup. I think, well, like you rightly put it, he was just done."

"Oh."

"Sometimes shit in this life doesn't make any sense, especially the shit people do," Borton said, shrugging one shoulder. "But you ask me, I think he just didn't have anything to live for. Sometimes that can be enough. People aren't meant to be alone, even when they think it's better."

I wasn't the quickest learner, but I wasn't stupid either. "That's your point?"

"Look. You're doing everything you're supposed to be doing. You're going to your shrink, you don't miss a day here, and you haven't started any trouble," Borton said, finally leaning back in his seat. "But I pay attention to all of you. I see the shit that goes on around here."

"You care for them," I said with a shrug.

Borton was a hardass a lot of the time, but even as dense as I could be, I could see how much he cared for the other guys. It was precisely why he'd dragged me into the office on my first day to give me the lowdown about everyone and how I needed to watch myself. Not that it mattered that Maurice was going through personal troubles. It didn't matter that Isaiah was gay, and Borton didn't want him getting any shit for it because Isaiah's sexuality didn't matter to me.

"I care for all you idiots," he said, frowning at me. "Even if I can't figure you out most of the time."

I said nothing simply because nothing I could say would've helped the conversation. Sure, Borton clearly cared about the guys at the station, but as far as I went, he didn't know me. He'd had plenty of time to get to know the rest, and he'd been watching over them for ages. I was the one person who'd come here offering nothing but a favor asked by another fire chief and a whole history of trouble in my wake.

"I'm not going to make you do anything you don't want to, not unless it's part of the original deal letting you work here, that is," Borton said, glancing at the computer screen. "So I'm not going to order you to make friends or try to be friendlier. What I will say, though, is you'd be doing yourself a favor if you tried."

"I'm okay."

"So was Cash…until he wasn't."

"I'm not suicidal."

Borton snorted. "Nor was Cash, until—"

I frowned at the implication but, once again, chose to say nothing. Chief Borton had made his point, which was all that mattered. It wouldn't matter what I said or did. His mind was made up.

To my surprise, he chuckled. "I don't know if you know this, but you kind of give yourself away at times with that face of yours."

"Sure," I said, agreeing because it seemed the only sensible thing to do.

"You're going to be stubborn about this, and as a stubborn man myself, I'm not going to fault you," he said with another low chuckle. "But can you at least do me one favor?"

"Sure," I repeated, because what the hell else was I going to say to the man who, no matter his reasons, had given me a chance to continue my job?

"Just think about what I said and that little piece of advice. Someone once said, no man is an island and—"

"John Donne."

"Hm?"

"Doesn't matter."

He watched me for several heartbeats before clearing his

throat. "Point is, you're here, and you're working with the rest of us. You're in Fairlake, and while the people here can be busybodies, they're mostly good folk, especially at this station. So if you ever get sick of being on your own, maybe give them a chance. Think on it."

"I'll think on it," I told him. It was what he needed to hear, after all. He didn't need to hear that I didn't do people, and they didn't do me in return. It wasn't like I was lonely, I knew how to do things by myself, and I was okay with that.

"I hope so," he said, and even I could tell he didn't believe me. "That said, I've got no issue with how you're doing things around here. You work hard, and hell, you fuck around a lot less than half the assholes here, so I can't complain. You're doing what you agreed to do, so I can't say shit."

"Okay," I said, staring at him to see if there was anything else.

"So, go," he said with a brisk wave of his hand. "Schedule got shifted around a bit, so you might wanna take a look. You got any issues with it, let me know, and maybe I can work with it. Isaiah can take anything you can't. He's earned it."

That caught me by surprise, considering out of everyone working there, Isaiah would have made it to the top of my list of 'people least likely to get in trouble' at the station. "He has?"

"He can play innocent all he wants, but I wasn't born yesterday," Borton grumbled in a flash of annoyance he hadn't shown once during our conversation. "If he wants to throw all safety and sense out the window, he can do it off hours."

I blinked and then realized what he meant. "Oh."

"Yes, oh."

"Where'd he climb this time?"

"The steeple. His usual perching spot. Man would get

away with it if he wasn't a smart idiot. Lost his damn keys up there this time."

I couldn't help the small smile at the thought, pushing myself up out of my chair. I wouldn't say it to Borton, but the situation was oddly comforting. Isaiah was probably the closest thing to a poster child for the station, and I'd yet to see anyone who didn't like him. Not that I necessarily blamed them, I could see the man was personable and friendly, and I'd yet to hear him have a bad word to say about anyone. That he could pull off a look that would make even cartoon animals envious of its sweetness probably didn't hurt.

Yet he was still capable of getting on Chief Borton's nerves. Despite that, it seemed Isaiah wasn't one to be disheartened and kept doing what he wanted. It didn't get anyone else in trouble and didn't endanger anyone else, so I didn't see the problem. Then again, I wasn't technically in charge of his well-being either, so I wouldn't fault Borton for being annoyed.

"Just remember what I said," he grunted at me as I left.

I said nothing as I stepped out of his office, frowning at his parting shot. Turning the next corner, I grunted in surprise as I collided with something solid. The figure gave a soft 'oof' and stumbled backward, threatening to teeter off their feet. My hand snapped out, catching him by the shoulder and yanking him closer.

Isaiah let out a breathless laugh, bringing his hands up to my chest to steady himself. "Sorry about that! I ran right into you."

"It's fine," I grunted, almost immediately taking my hand off his shoulder now he was on his own two feet.

"It was my fault," he added, pulling his hands away quickly, and though I didn't know why, I could swear I saw a flash of hurt on his face. "Coming back from getting chewed out by the chief?"

"No," I grunted, shoving my hands in my pockets so I had somewhere to put them.

"Oh, okay," he said, stepping away to look me over in confusion. "You working today?"

"Dunno," I said, glancing at the bulletin board on the far wall of the garage bay.

"I always forget to check who's working and who isn't," he said with a small, almost shy smile. "If we end up on a night together, I'll bring cards or something to keep us occupied."

"Sure," I said, my feet itching to get moving. I never knew what to say around Isaiah, a common problem, but it often felt worse whenever he talked to me. To be fair, he did genuinely seem to want to try to talk, but all he had to do was look at me, and I wondered what I was supposed to do. It was generally easier to get away from him than to try stumbling through conversation.

"Sounds…good," he said, and his smile faltered. "You, uh, take it easy, Julian. Don't let the chief get to you too much, he's a grumpy hardass who likes to threaten people, but he's a softy."

"You are literally five feet away from my office," Chief Borton's irritated voice rumbled from the nearby hallway. "I can *hear* you."

Isaiah winked at me. "He says as if I didn't know that."

"Aren't you supposed to be cleaning out the supply room instead of flirting with our newest addition?" Borton barked out.

To my surprise, Isaiah's face colored heavily as he made a choking noise. "I'll see you later, Julian."

I watched him go, though he never glanced over his shoulder before disappearing. I didn't think I'd ever seen

Isaiah so taken aback by something someone said, and I found myself frowning at the office doorway.

Was that flirting on Isaiah's part?

The thought made my feet itch even more, and I continued walking to look over the schedule. Finally, after a few steps, I managed to shove the question aside before it found a way to entrench itself.

The last thing I needed was some stupid thought to obsess over.

ISAIAH

I'm telling you. I texted Bennett. *The guy hates me.*

Guiltily, I glanced across the break room to find Julian staring at his phone, legs curled up on the ratty couch. He clearly wasn't paying me the slightest attention as he ran his thumb over the screen. It didn't change the fact that I wondered if somehow he knew I was talking about him.

I don't think I know anyone who hates you, Bennett's returning message told me.

The guy glares at me if I so much as say hi to him, I shot back.

Sighing, I took the next card off the deck, looking at the seven rows of cards I'd laid out. I slapped the six of spades onto the seven of hearts but knew that wasn't going to help me much. That might not have been a problem if Julian had actually agreed to play a game of *something* with me rather than shrugging when I asked him.

So instead, it looked like it was going to be me and a pack of cards for the rest of the night shift. Laurence was somewhere in the building, but he'd agreed to take radio duty for the next few hours. Which meant that until it was my turn, it was me, the cards, and Bennett, for however long he stuck around to keep me company.

You sure that's not a smolder? Bennett asked.

I rolled my eyes. *I might not be getting laid like you are lately, but I know what a smolder looks like.*

I'm not getting laid.

Right, so is Adam hung or not?

I felt appropriately smug about being slightly sly at calling out what I *knew* he was doing with his supposedly straight best friend. Bennett could try to hide it all he wanted, but I wasn't stupid. The man spent a lot of time around Adam, to the point that I was pretty sure if they weren't working, they were together. Which might not be a big deal, but I'd seen a couple of marks on Bennett that, if they weren't hickeys, he needed to get to the hospital to report some strange bruising disease he'd contracted.

I should have known Bennett's response would ruin my smugness.

Julian's the big dude with the red hair, right? Pretty sure it's his dick you're wondering about most.

"Goddammit," I muttered, slapping the phone on the table so I didn't have to look at his message.

To make matters worse, Julian looked up and frowned at me. Whether out of annoyance or curiosity, I couldn't tell, but I could feel the heat rising in my cheeks as I quickly glanced back down at the game I just lost.

Damn it, I hadn't said one word to Bennett about Julian other than to mention he was around. How the hell did he know? Then again, even if Bennett was caught up with Adam like he was, the guy wasn't blind. It wasn't exactly hard to look at Julian and see sex on legs. I wished I could say his dour, scowling demeanor was a turnoff, but if anything, it only added to his allure.

I winced when my phone buzzed, signaling another message, and I picked it up to read, *Btw, he's hung just right.*

"I knew it!" I screeched without thinking, pumping my fist in the air out of sheer triumph.

I froze when Julian jerked, dragging his legs out from under him to slam his feet onto the floor and look around with sharp jerks of his head. He met my eyes, brow furrowing, and I stared back in surprise.

"Uh, sorry," I said slowly, suddenly realizing I'd scared him. "Got some, uh, well, confirmation on something I knew about a friend of mine."

Julian's face fell into a deeper frown, and I winced in apology. I hadn't meant to startle him, but his reaction had been sharper than I would have anticipated for mere surprise. For a moment, I wondered what sort of thing had run through his mind when he heard me yell, but I swallowed it down.

To my mingled relief and discomfort, Julian only grunted, leaning back onto the couch. I noticed he didn't draw his feet up again, as though he was still prepared to leap up. There was a tension in him I wasn't used to seeing, and I felt guilt pool in my gut as I set my phone aside, my triumph forgotten.

A shrill alarm rang through the air, jerking me back to reality. Absurdly, Julian only glanced up, his shoulders going tense as the alarm blared through the room. I stood up, eyes wide, glancing toward the speaker in the corner of the break room, waiting for the inevitable.

"Got a good one out on Outer Ridge Drive," Laurence's voice piped out through the speakers. "Suit up, you two. I'm dialing the twins to meet you out there."

"Got it," I said, even though the speakers only worked one way.

Julian said nothing as he followed me into the hallway. His long legs should have overtaken me, but he kept behind me as we marched to the bay and began yanking on our equipment. Without thinking, I reached out and adjusted the strap of his pants, ensuring it was flush with his shoulder. Smiling a little, I shoved his thick coat at him before pulling mine off the hook and putting it on. Outer Ridge Drive was on the outskirts of Fairlake, which meant we needed to move as quickly as possible.

"You or me?" I asked like I always did when it came to driving one of the trucks.

Julian said nothing, grabbing the thick key ring off the nearby hook and tossing it to me. I snatched it out of the air without question and headed for the driver's side as he opened the bay doors. I yanked myself into the driver's seat and got the truck rumbling. The passenger side door opened, and Julian pulled himself in with the grace of a man who'd done this plenty of times and was more in control of his body than most people his size.

As I backed the truck out, Julian grabbed the radio from its cradle. "Address?"

"It's the Putter place," I muttered, shoving my palm against the steering wheel to swing the truck around.

"1180 Outer Ridge Drive," Laurence fired back over the radio with barely any hesitation. "The old Putter place. There's no real water flow out that way."

I glanced at Julian, whose brow furrowed, and I grunted as I gunned the truck out onto the road. There would be next to no traffic in Fairlake at this time of night, so I flipped the lights on and left the siren off. Whoever was out at this hour would see the lights in the dimly lit town, and I wouldn't have to wake everyone up.

"Save people and minimize the damage to everything else," I said in understanding.

Julian grunted, hitting the button on the radio. "Understood."

Thankfully Chief Borton had enough sense to know just what kind of town we were working in. Our trucks had their own water supply that could be pressurized if it came down to it. It wasn't a lot, but it could be enough to make the difference between a barn fire spreading to a house or being contained. Whatever was burning out on Outer Ridge would be left to burn while we worked to prevent damage to everything else.

"When are the twins coming in?" I shot to Julian as we barreled down a street as fast as I dared.

"Back up?" Julian asked the radio.

"The Shining responded. They're going to grab the other truck and make their way out to you," Laurence fired back quickly. "You'll be first responding. Got a squad car out there and a couple of ambulances on the way."

"Not good," Julian muttered to the air rather than Laurence.

"Yeah," I grunted, turning the wheel as I braked as much as I dared toward the next intersection. Despite the sheer size of the trucks, I had never felt anything but comfortable driving them, even at high speeds. "There's a whole family living there."

"Yeah?" Julian asked, as expressive as ever.

"Putters have lived out there for almost as long as Fairlake has existed," I explained, letting my words drown out the worry bubbling in my chest. There were far too many factors involved for this night not to go wrong potentially. "They've tried to do all sorts of things to keep afloat. An old family, trying to keep relevant."

"Like yours?" Julian asked.

I snorted, though whether it was out of annoyance or surprise that Julian was asking something personal was up for debate. "Don't know who you've been listening to, but my family stopped being relevant over a century ago when mining disappeared from Fairlake. Took them a few decades to figure it out, but the Bentlys gave up on Fairlake and are long gone."

"You're not."

"No, because unlike my parents, who were the last Bentlys to stay here for business, I give a shit about this town. It was about business and money for them."

"Not you?"

"Nope," I grunted, trying to turn the truck into the next intersection without losing too much speed. "Blood isn't my priority, and their ideas about what's important aren't shit."

My family had bailed shortly after I'd turned eighteen and were *still* furious I hadn't followed them north, where mining was still viable and prosperous. Times might have changed and modernized, but mining was mining, and it was what my family had always known. Personally, the idea was the last thing I wanted. I might risk being buried alive by a burning house in my current line of work, but at least that wasn't several tons of rock and dirt.

"Plus, my dad and I haven't spoken since he realized I'm a giant homo," I said with a laugh as we barreled down the long stretch of Outer Ridge, where only a few houses existed. Even from a few miles away, I could see the fire blazing.

"Yeah?"

"Yeah. Though, I'm pretty sure he would have been alright with it if I just pretended. You know, got a wife, had a few kids, buried any 'scandal' over liking dick, that sort of thing."

"Oh."

"Don't worry," I assured him with a smirk and a glance. My heart was racing, and my nerves were tight, but the adrenaline and sheer madness that came with every call was starting to affect me. At this point, I didn't care what I said or did because when everything collapsed into chaos, who really gave a shit if you were following 'normal' rules? "I'm not going to come onto you."

"Okay," Julian said, but even in the dark of the truck's cab, I could feel his eyes burrowing into the side of my head.

"Even if you *are* pretty fine to look at."

"Uh…oh."

I couldn't help my snort of amusement. It was probably the first time I'd heard him sound surprised and maybe even a little awkward. That was until I realized what I was seeing and hissed, "Shit, it's the house."

"How many people?" Julian asked, and despite my dismay, I had to appreciate how minimalist he was.

"Last I knew, two grandparents, two parents, eight kids," I told him as I forced myself to slow down at the driveway. The last thing I wanted to do was run over a family member we were trying to save while getting to the house. "The Putters are pretty isolationist, though. Don't like relying on anyone."

"Still called 911," he grunted as we slowed to a stop.

Any appreciation for his irony died as I stopped the truck and stared at what we were dealing with. The house was nearly as old as Fairlake and was completely engulfed in flames. Fire licked up into the sky as inky black smoke rolled out the windows, blotting out the stars and even the moon. Only the large wrap-around porch at the front looked untouched as flames flickered from the windows and even the front door.

"Headcount," I told Julian as I jerked the door open.

"You do the talking," he grunted, and I almost laughed at the idea. Well, maybe he really was just bad with people in general.

We had barely stepped out of the truck before a woman came running toward us. I tried to step forward, but she barreled straight into Julian, gripping his arms. I honestly didn't know who was more surprised at this turn of events, me or Julian. Yet I had to give him credit. He didn't hesitate to hold her up as she almost collapsed against him.

"Tell me," he said in a low voice that somehow managed to carry over the ferocious crackle of the fire.

"Reg and Tori are still in there!" she called over the roar of the flames.

I stood by, waiting as Julian caught her eye. "Where?"

Dahlia Putter took a deep, shuddering breath, jerking her finger toward the house. "There."

We both looked to where she pointed, right above the porch and slightly to the right. I sucked in a breath. "Julian—"

"I know," he said, and I couldn't help but notice how he squeezed Dahlia's shoulder before drawing away. "We've got this."

I couldn't help my small smile. "Yeah we do."

Dahlia looked at me, blinking rapidly before speaking. "You're Thomas' boy."

"Don't tell him that," I snorted.

"Please," she pleaded, reaching for me. "My children—"

"Dahlia," I told her, remembering her from when I was a boy. I'd barely been seven years old and exploring the town. I'd found the Putter's property and wandered onto it when I'd seen her eldest children playing in the yard. My last name had made them recoil, and she'd appeared quickly on the front porch to chase me off, threatening me. "We're going to do everything we can. Now get back to your family while we do what we need to."

If she remembered the scared seven-year-old she had threatened, she showed no sign of it as she gulped and stepped back. I turned to Julian. "Masks and tanks. The twins can help us contain it when the other truck arrives, but the kids are our priority."

"Yep," Julian grunted as we headed toward the truck. It was the first time I'd ever been on a call alone with him, and I was a little surprised at how easily he rolled with things. Gone was the sullen man who refused to join the rest of us during breaks, and so too was gone the man who had almost panicked just because I yelled in a quiet room.

We helped each other with tanks of clean air, and I wrestled a mask over my face, checking the seals. "You hear me?"

The short-range radio crackled to life in my ear, Julian's voice piping up. "Yeah."

"Good," I said, marching toward the house. "I'm going up. Taking the porch."

There was a moment of hesitation even though I could sense Julian was behind me. "You sure?"

"No offense, big guy, but you're a big guy," I told him as we drew closer. "You'll bring the porch down faster than I will. Plus, I'm a pretty good climber. I can get up there faster than if we get a ladder out."

"The others?"

"Probably won't be here in time."

There was a long enough pause that we managed to reach the edge of the porch. Even with the protective layers around me, I could feel the overwhelming heat of the fire as it tried to bring the house down to its foundations. Most of it was focused on the main floor, but it wouldn't be long before the second floor was engulfed. If those kids were still alive, they wouldn't have much longer.

"You sure?" Julian asked as I peered at the thin lattice on the far edge of the porch.

I glanced back at him, seeing only his eyes peering out at me from behind his mask. "I've got you backing me up, right?"

"Yes."

The almost immediacy of the answer made me smile.

Maybe the guy didn't like me much, but I believed him without hesitation. "Then yeah, I'm sure."

"Okay."

Again I found myself comforted by his minimalism and stepped toward the lattice. It was made of stronger stuff than you'd find at Greene's Market. I wasn't as sure of my plan as I'd made out, but I knew few other options would work as quickly.

With a deep breath, I hooked my fingers through the holes and clambered up. I couldn't move as quickly as I wanted, my gloves were thick, and my heavy boots could barely find purchase. Only by my lifelong habit of climbing and the friction from barely growing plants could I find a way up.

"Isaiah," Julian hissed through the radio as I heard a crack when reaching the porch roof.

I didn't need to be told twice, hooking my fingers into the more solid roof and yanking myself over the edge. The lattice gave way with a sharp crack as I shoved myself upward, hooking my foot on the top. My heel dug into the tiles as I fought to steady myself, knowing from years of experience that at a moment like this, balance and control were more important than strength and momentum.

"Isaiah?" Julian's voice inquired through the mask, but I ignored him as I took a deep breath. I pushed calmness through my thoughts as I hung there for a moment, using my hanging foot to press against one of the support pillars. From there, I gave a good shove, rolling with the momentum. I awkwardly landed on my back, but I was on the roof, which was all that mattered.

"I'm good," I finally piped back, taking another deep breath and rolling over to get to my feet. I could hear the porch creak in complaint, but I knew better than to assume it was because of the fire. The damn thing probably hadn't held anything heavier than snowfall in years, and while I wasn't the giant Julian was, I was still pretty big. "I'm going toward the bedroom."

"Got it," he quipped back, earning a small smile.

I stumbled forward, peering through the window Dahlia had pointed at. The glass was smudged and darkened by smoke, but I could see twin beds. The color scheme was plain, but I could make out the toys littering a handwoven rug in the center of the room. The bedroom door was closed, and while the room was filled with smoke, it didn't look touched by the flames.

"Fuck," I hissed, jamming my fingers into the bottom of the window frame and yanking it upward. It fought my efforts, but paint and wood squealed as I shoved it free. "Reg and Tori?"

I couldn't hear anything over the roar of the fire that intensified the moment I opened the window, but I saw a flash of movement from the closet. It was quick, but I swore I saw a small, bare foot retreating into the darkness. Grunting, I squeezed through the window with my thick outfit and an oxygen tank on my back.

"I'm a fireman!" I called out once I hit the floor with an awkward and graceless thud.

Despite the roar of the flames, I could hear a sniffle followed by a low, restrained cough. Pushing myself up, I shuffled toward the closet. Pushing the doors open, I found two girls huddled on the floor. One shrank into the nearest corner while the other held her arms out as if to warn me off.

"Get back!" she shrieked, and I blinked as she threw a shoe at me.

"I'm a fireman," I repeated gently, crouching to make myself appear as small as possible. A feat considering my equipment and probably the alarming sight of my mask. "I'm here to get you to your mom and dad."

"We're not under arrest?" the girl asked.

"I'm not a cop," I told her with a smile she couldn't see. "Just here to get you out."

With a strength that didn't befit a seven-year-old, she reached out with the faith that did. I took her hand in my glove. "Okay."

"I need you and your sister to stay low," I told her. I might have a mask that made it easy for me to move through the smoke, but they didn't, "and follow me to the window. Do you think you can do that?"

I was probably more patient than the situation allowed, but she nodded and whispered something to her sister. They dropped to all fours, and I wondered if they had already been taught how to handle a fire. As we reached the window ledge, a low groan echoed through the house, and I felt my chest tighten.

"One then the other," I told them. "There's another fireman down below who will help you."

"You first, Tori," the girl said, picking her sister up and pushing.

"Victoria, huh?" I guessed at the meeker girl, who offered me a small smile. "Through the window you go then, Victoria. Walk to the edge, and you'll see someone who looks a lot like me waiting for you."

"Hurry," I heard Julian hiss in my ear, reminding me he could hear everything.

I helped Victoria through, letting the little girl get to her feet before turning to her sister. "Which probably makes you, Regina?"

She turned her chin up toward me. "Yes, sir."

"Aren't you polite?" I chuckled before reaching for her. "Do the same thing as your sister. My friend will get you down safe, okay?"

"Sure," she said, watching me warily but still allowing me to pick her up and get her through the window.

"Got one," Julian grunted in my ear, and I wondered if the girl had been bold or hesitant before she jumped down.

"Your sister's waiting for you," I said, giving her a push. "Go."

She hesitated, and I wondered if her courage was breaking in the face of a simple one-story jump. And then I heard it. It started as a rumble that worked its way up through my boots, followed by the cracking and almost scream of splintering wood.

I whirled around on the girl. "Go!"

I watched as she darted toward the edge of the porch and heard the screaming grow louder. I reached out toward the window once more to grip it...and felt the floor give out under me.

"Isaiah!" I heard a shout in my ear.

I barely heard it as I held onto the window, my legs dangled over a burning abyss. The muscles in my arms strained as I fought to hold on tight, knowing I needed only to pull myself up and out the window, and I'd be safe. My whole body felt slick with sweat as I held on, but I felt my grip slip and slip some more before I finally tumbled backward toward the flames.

I only knew I'd hit the ground when the air was knocked from my lungs and agony shot through my back. Staring up at the hole in the ceiling above me, I could barely hear the frantic chatter of voices in my ear. Dimly I was aware that the twins had shown up, but I couldn't make out their words or Julian's.

Groaning, I tried to move my leg, but it stayed put. Lifting my head to squint through my swimming vision, I saw something pinning my leg to the ground. Reaching out, I tried to give the object a shove but only succeeded in making my already aching arm hurt even more.

"Don't!" I heard one of the twins bark.

"Fuck off," Julian snarled, and I heard glass shattering. Turning my head, I could just see a large shape squeezing through the window at what I thought was the front of the house.

"No," I muttered, trying to get my thoughts back in order. The room was rapidly filling with smoke. It wouldn't be long before the entire place was ablaze, and someone was risking themselves to pull my unlucky ass out of the fire.

"You shut up too," I heard Julian growl as he stomped over to me. "We're getting you out of here."

"The kids?"

"With their parents," he grunted, bending down and hooking his fingers around what I now recognized was one of the beams from the ceiling. "This is going to hurt."

"Julian, don't—" My words were cut off as he hefted the heavy beam with no problem. He hadn't been kidding about the pain, and I was forced to hiss as my legs began throbbing. "Fuck me, that hurts."

"C'mon," he grunted, grabbing me by the upper arm and dragging me toward him.

"They're not broken," I said, getting to my feet and trying to stop him from picking me up. "They're gonna be all bruises later but not broken."

"Lucky," he grunted, giving me a push. "Front door, you aren't climbing out windows."

Despite the push, he kept a hand on me as we stumbled into the front hallway. Even with masks to protect our eyes, it was nearly impossible to see. Using the wall to guide us, Julian's hand on my back pushed me down the hall as we both stumbled over our own feet and what I suspected had once been a small table that lay in pieces in the middle of the hallway.

The front door, which must have been opened when the family fled, was a rectangle of flashing lights from the trucks. My feet stumbled when a hellacious cracking sound filled the air. Dust and pieces of drywall clattered to the ground, bouncing off us as we tried to get to safety. I could have sworn the air itself vibrated, and I felt the floor shake. It seemed our time to get to freedom was shorter than I initially thought as I felt the house begin to collapse around us.

"We have to—" The hand at my back drove into the middle of my spine. The blow took the wind out of me almost as much as the fall through the floor, and I was launched forward.

Unbelievably, I flew far enough through the door that I landed in the middle of the porch, sliding another couple of feet toward the steps. My vision was still spinning, and I grunted as I tried to push myself upright, seeing a large figure coming toward the doorway as two pairs of hands grabbed me and yanked me back.

"Wait!" I cried out as I watched the front of the house buckle and fall inward. "Julian!"

"Stop, Isaiah, stop!" I heard one of the twins bark at me, but I struggled as I watched timber and flames cascade down, sending an acrid plume of soot and foul smoke into the sky.

"Julian!" I bellowed, managing to get one arm free and trying to lurch back toward the house. Either I got into that house, or I sure as shit just got Julian killed. "I can see him! Let me go!"

The other pair of hands loosened on my arm, and I stumbled forward, collapsing on the front lawn. One of the twins grunted. "Shit, he's right."

"Stupid," the other said.

"Yep," the first agreed.

As I tried to push myself up, finding my body simply didn't want to cooperate, I watched two pairs of legs stomp past me and into the ruined front of the house. The rest of the house was still standing, but it was only a matter of time before it too collapsed.

Groaning, I watched as the twins became foggy and hazy as they climbed onto the porch. Even with the obscuring smoke and ash, I could still see the large shadow that surely marked where Julian lay, sprawled just inside the doorway. To my greatest frustration, however, I could barely move without feeling like I would collapse.

Even worse, I was once more grabbed by a couple of people and pulled back from the house. I only managed a groan as I was dragged away and carefully eased onto my back, my mask pulled off. The brightest stars twinkled against the sky overhead, the rest blocked by the sheer intensity of the flames.

"Hey there, Isaiah," a warm voice said, bending forward so I could see the owner.

"Brendan?" I muttered to the paramedic, trying to bring his face into focus.

"Wrong brother," he chuckled, and I could feel his hands on me.

"Right, right, Brendan left. Sorry, Kyle." I tried to push myself upright. It'd been a few years since I'd last seen Brendan, who had moved down to Denver to continue his career as a paramedic while Kyle had stayed behind. They were three years apart, but even if I could think clearly, it was insanely easy to get them mixed up.

"Don't even think about it," Kyle told me lightly, pushing me back down. "You're not going *anywhere*. There's a nasty split on the back of your head."

"No, I'm fine," I grunted and hissed as he reached behind and tapped the back of my head.

He raised a gloved hand to show blood smeared across the latex. "You're not."

"Julian," I muttered, wondering why the sky was getting darker. There was no way the fire was dying down, not while there was still plenty for it to devour.

"The twins have him, and my partner's checking him out."

"Okay. Okay, good."

"Uh, Isaiah?"

"M'okay," I said, sensing his worry and trying to reassure him. I was just relieved things were getting quieter, which meant I'd been wrong, the fire must be dying down, and people weren't panicking anymore. That went a long way to explaining why things were getting darker too.

"Fuck," I heard Kyle mutter, only to raise his voice. "I need someone else over here. He's fading!"

I had no idea what he was talking about, but at least the panic tearing at my chest only minutes before was a lot quieter now. If the twins had Julian, and Kyle's partner was fighting hard to keep him alive, then there wasn't much more I could do right now. The best I could do was lay there, wishing I could feel the coolness of the grass on more than just the back of my neck, and let myself...relax.

JULIAN

I fucking hated hospitals.

They were hands down the most miserable places in existence, and I'd always avoided them whenever I had the choice. Of course, there weren't a whole lot of decisions I could make while unconscious and being loaded into an ambulance. By the time I woke up, I was being lifted into a large bed in the ER so they could work on me.

Now I was sitting in a small room, glaring at the nervous doctor, glancing down at my arms. "You've got to be kidding me."

The doctor gave me a pained look. "Look, Mr. Maccomb, I understand this is frustrating and painful—"

"I don't give a shit about the pain," I grunted, even if the stabbing pain in my arms did border on agony depending on how I moved. It was the casts, one on my right wrist and part of the hand, and the other covering almost my entire left arm. "How fucking long am I going to be in these?"

"At best, you'll have use of your arms in about eight weeks, possibly up to twelve. The healing process can be different for everyone."

"Eight weeks?" I asked in obvious horror and shock.

"And even then, you'll be advised to refrain from straining yourself too much for several weeks," he continued, still looking nervous. I wasn't sure what he had to be nervous about. The worst I could do was kick at him limply since one of my ankles was wrapped in gauze. "Otherwise, you risk breaking the healed bones."

"Even more?" I asked, now growing beyond horror into anger. "That's fucking ridiculous."

"Julian," a growl from the nearby doorway cut me off before I could add more of my opinion to the discussion. We both turned, and I found Chief Borton standing in the doorway, arms over his chest. "Quit yelling at the man, he's just doing his job."

I frowned, not used to seeing him in blue jeans and a simple shirt. "What're you doing here?"

"Boy, I get a call in the middle of the night that two of my guys are seriously injured. I wonder why I might be here," Borton told me in the driest tone imaginable.

"I'm fine," I said, feeling slightly uncomfortable at his words.

"Yeah, you look it."

I blinked, fully absorbing his words. "Wait."

"Yeah?"

"Isaiah?"

"Yep, he's here too."

"Is he—?"

Borton's brow stitched together. "Pretty sure that's the first time I've seen you care about anything...except those arms of yours."

I jerked my eyes away from him to glare at his boots. "Is he okay?"

"He took a good knock to his head. I'd say I hope it knocked some sense into him, but knowing my luck, it knocked a few more screws loose," he said, sounding annoyed. "They're keeping him here for the rest of the day and probably the night too. They wanna make sure his concussion isn't too bad."

That was something, at least. His fall through the floor had been pretty nasty. I was almost certain he'd been dead when I heard the crash and watched him disappear. Taking just enough time to get the girls to safety, I'd hoofed it back to the house as fast as my gear would allow. It had probably been stupid to go through another window, but I had seen him lying in the middle of the living room, barely moving, and reacted.

Borton turned to the doctor. "Is there anything else he needs to know?"

"We've gone over most everything. If he has any questions, we'll send him home with paperwork that'll give him answers, and he can always call," the doctor said, clearly relieved there was someone else in the room. "I'll have someone get your exit paperwork together."

I glared at him as he practically fled from the room, holding his clipboard close to his chest. I knew there was nothing the guy could do to help me, but that didn't make this situation any less frustrating. There was *nothing* I could do, and for what, the next eight weeks? Maybe twelve? I was essentially useless to anyone for just about everything, and I was what, just supposed to grin and bear it?

"Seems like I probably should have come to see you first," Borton grunted, stepping into the room and looking me over. "They told me you got banged up, but I didn't realize you'd decided to go and break just about every bone you had."

"I didn't," I scowled.

"Mean to do it or break every bone?"

"Yeah."

Borton sighed. "You know, there's a fine line between being a man of few words and being a pain in the ass."

I shrugged or tried to, aborting halfway through when my left arm felt like I'd dragged it through glass. Closing my eyes, I cut off my hiss of pain and swallowed it down. The last thing I needed was to make my situation worse by showing more weakness.

Borton snorted. "Seems like you'll have to find a different way to communicate. Maybe this will be a good way to expand your horizons."

I scowled at him as he dropped into the only other seat in the room. "No brain damage?"

"They told me your head was one of the few things that didn't take a beating."

"Chief."

Clasping his hands together, he rested them in his lap and watched me for a few heartbeats. I found it uncomfortable to meet his eyes as he remained quiet. I felt…evaluated, like he was looking for something or making a judgment about something he'd already spotted. I really didn't like it when people tried to pick apart my brain or think they understood something.

"He took a pretty good crack on the head, and his brain is swollen," Borton finally said, tapping his fingers against the back of his other hand. "He's been awake, and they say he was lucid and clear, so they don't think it's going to be anything more than a good headache for a few days and maybe some confusion. All in all, you came out the worst by the looks of things."

That was putting it mildly, but at least Isaiah wasn't in the same boat. The last thing our station needed was to have two more people out of commission. I was sure Isaiah would probably be back at work within a week, which I knew would make everyone at the station happy. As much as they liked to give him a hard time, they were all incredibly protective of him.

Not that they let him know that, and even I couldn't miss the independent streak in him that went for miles. Considering his comments about his family in the truck, I wondered if that was a big part of his reasons. If he was like any of the other rich kids I'd known growing up, he had probably been coddled for a good chunk of his childhood. To lose that, along with his family, had to have been rough. So either that had spun him into a desperate need to be independent, or he'd always been one to stand on his own. I couldn't say one way or the other.

"Of course, he was asleep when I went to see him," Borton continued wryly. "Whether he was actually asleep or pretending so he wouldn't have to get an earful is a mystery I'll solve some other time."

"Why would he pretend?" I asked.

"You mean other than the fact that he ran in there without Terry and Larry to back you guys up? That he put you in danger to try to save his ass?" Borton asked with a snort. "I can only imagine why I might want to have a word with him."

"If he hadn't, it would've been those two little girls who fell through the floor," I pointed out. "He did his job."

"Part of the job is following protocol. You two were the only ones—"

"We wouldn't have been fast enough if we waited."

"So what, he just decided on his own?"

"No. I backed him up. The house was full of smoke, fire everywhere. Quickest way up was that porch roof, and he weighs less than me. If we were gonna do it, it made sense he was the one. He went as fast as he could, couldn't predict the floor would give out."

There had been no warning, and what little there was

didn't come soon enough. The little girl had scrambled into my arms just as I heard the horrible sound of the floor giving way. Isaiah had barely managed a sound before he disappeared from the window he'd meant to climb out. I hadn't needed to look through the front window to know where he landed, but as I hustled the girl to safety before returning, I needed to see if he was still in one piece.

"Right," Borton said slowly. "And you rushed in even though you were told to wait?"

I tried to shrug, thought better about it, and used my right arm only instead. "He was still alive. So I did my job."

"Okay, well, him going through a window, I get. There weren't safer avenues for him to get through, and even with equipment on, sounds like he could fit through. But your big ass?"

"Seemed fastest to me. I fit."

"They told me they think you pushed him."

"I did. Got him out, didn't I?"

"You did," Borton said, and I was struck by the feeling that he was trying to read my thoughts. "And against my better judgment, I should point out that's the most I think I've ever heard you say in one sitting."

"You asked."

"Not what I meant."

"Then what?"

"I ask about you? You barely offer any explanation, just your normal quick bullshit. I ask about Isaiah, and you got a whole report ready to list off."

Annoyance flashed through me. "You asked."

"I did," he said simply, still watching me.

My discomfort at the conversation only fed my irritation. "What?"

It took him longer than I would have liked to reply. "Nothing."

I didn't believe him for a second, but I wasn't stupid enough to prompt him for more. Knowing my luck, the chief was in the mood to give me more of an explanation, and I sure didn't want to hear anything else. I didn't know what he was driving at, and all I wanted was to be back in my shitty apartment, feeling annoyed with my life.

"Which," he said, clearing his throat. "Means we should probably talk about what to do with you."

"I can get my shit soon," I said, wondering how I would manage that. I clearly couldn't drive. I could barely bend one ankle at the moment, though I was told in another week or two, I should be able to walk around a bit. Still didn't mean I'd be able to drive for several weeks after that, not with the absurd casts on my arms.

One of them was pink for some reason.

Borton frowned at me. "We can get your car, but I'm keeping your keys in case you get any bright ideas."

"I don't—"

"And I sure as shit don't like the idea that you're thinking you're getting the boot. You do know what medical leave is, right?"

"I—"

"Because last I checked, we worked for the city, doing a dangerous job. Which means we're covered when it comes to shit happening. Matter of fact, if you didn't glare at everything and tried reading once in a while, you might have seen that in all that paperwork you filled out months ago with Bones and then again with me."

"I read," I said with a scowl.

"Good, then you got no excuse for not knowing you're covered. You're not fired, you'll get paid, and you're going to rest while your bones heal," he told me, standing up. "Now, you don't have anyone listed as your emergency contact. I *told* you to list someone."

"I don't," I said.

"Chief Bones told me you had family."

Panic whipped through me, and I straightened, eyes going wide. "Don't. Leave...just don't."

Christ, the idea of my mother hearing about what happened filled me with absolute dread. She had *never* been keen on me becoming a fireman, nearly hysterical about the idea. She'd repeatedly pleaded for me to consider something safer like my brother, something that wouldn't put me in danger but could still provide stability and a steady income for me...and partially for her.

If she heard I'd been badly injured on the job, she would lose her mind. It had been years since I'd seen her have a meltdown, and I was *not* going to be the reason she had another one. The only reason she had managed to hang on this long was my brother's apparent success at school, the income I helped to supplement so she could live comfortably, and the fact that no significant changes had been made to her life.

No, I had managed some vague semblance of stability and being reliable in her eyes, allowing her to remain relatively calm. I wasn't going to tip that balance.

Borton watched me for several seconds before grunting. "Alright, if that's the way you wanna play it, what's your plan?"

"What?"

"In case you haven't noticed, you aren't exactly in any state to take care of yourself."

"I'm—"

"Shut up," Borton grunted. "I'd be surprised if you could take a piss without needing both hands and five minutes to pull it off."

My face warmed as I immediately wondered what I was going to do when I needed to piss. I still had the fingers on my left hand, but I was right-handed, so it would be awkward and slow. I had less use of my right hand but more use of the whole arm, so I could probably use that to—

"You're gonna need help doing more than that."

"I can—"

"Stop. Fine, you can probably manage that, but you get my point. You're gonna need help."

"Bor—"

"I'm sure we can come up with something, whether or not you want the help."

"I don't—"

"Have a choice, correct. Glad you recognize that. I'll see what I can figure out, but unless you think you can somehow take care of yourself without making it worse, you're going to shut up and put up with whatever I say. If you don't, you're gonna find yourself on my shit list and trust me, you don't want that."

I was clearly not going to be given the chance to say a word despite how little I talked as it was. Chief Borton wasn't in the mood to hear anything I had to say, and I swallowed my frustration. I hadn't even had the chance to find out what I could do, and already I was being treated like a helpless victim. It was a bitter thought, but I kept it to myself as Borton crossed the room toward the door.

"Get some rest while you wait for your paperwork. Once you're released, we'll figure out a way to get you home and deal with things after that," he told me, shooting me a frown.

Right, as if I was going to find a way to sleep.

* * *

I woke groggily in the hospital bed, peering around in confusion. It took a few seconds to recognize I was still in a hospital. Blearily, I looked at the clock on the wall, frowned when I did the calculations and realized it had been nearly six hours since Chief Borton had left.

"The hell?" I muttered, rubbing at my face.

"I'll call this good timing," a female voice announced, and I frowned as a nurse entered the room, waving a paper cup. "Caught you just in time for your meds."

"No more meds," I told her gruffly, sticking the responsibility for my grogginess on the back of those pills. "I'm supposed to be leaving."

"Good thing these things are just strong Ibuprofen then, isn't it?" she asked, setting it down on the tray next to my bed, along with a glass of water.

I picked the paper cup up warily and looked, finding the pills *were* different than what they'd given me earlier. The pills they'd given me earlier had helped with the pain, but I disliked how foggy they left me. I suspected part of why I'd been so...weird around Chief Borton had been the meds. I really didn't like anything that made me feel different than I usually did.

"Believe it or not, but there's this whole rule about lying to patients," she told me, nudging the water glass closer. "That and we don't want patients having too many painkillers if it can be helped. Can't have them getting attached to them."

"Addicted," I grunted, tilting the cup back and swallowing them down with the glass of water. What she said made sense, and even if they *were* some other painkillers, I could at least rely on the fact that I was leaving soon. In the comfort of my own home, they wouldn't be able to force me to take anything I didn't want to.

"Pretty much," she said, taking the paper cup from me and throwing it in a nearby bin. "And I've been told to tell you that your exit paperwork might not be done until tomorrow morning."

"What?" I barked, sitting upright and hissing when it sent waves of agony through my arms.

"Right, and I was told you were a difficult one," she said with a chuckle, laying a gentle hand on my chest. "Welcome to bureaucracy and paperwork. Don't worry. You'll find your way out of here."

"Sure, but when?" I huffed, allowing her to push me back despite the fact that even in my state, it would have been absurdly easy to overpower her. Something about her drew me enough to trust what she was saying, and I didn't see the point in fighting her.

"When the people wielding the pen decide to let you go, which should be soon," she told me.

"Give me a sword any day," I muttered.

She laughed. "That doesn't surprise me, now lay down and relax, handsome. We'll get you home soon, alright?"

"Yeah," I said, frowning at the unexpected term of affection. It wasn't like I didn't know women found me attractive, but I wasn't very good at knowing what to do with that fact. Not that I *hadn't* done anything about it before, I understood sex a lot better than I did a lot of other things about people, but there was a difference between a compliment meant to attract me sexually and one that just...wasn't.

She smiled before leaving me to my thoughts, and I settled back into bed, trying to get more comfortable. As much as I didn't want to remain there, I knew there was no point in fighting it. At best, I would bully my way into earlier freedom and earn myself the growing irritation of my boss. At worst, I would end up fired without the benefits I was supposed to have.

"Uh, hey, Julian," a new voice piped up, and I jerked in surprise only to frown when I saw the pale, bandaged owner of the voice.

"What are you doing?" I demanded of Isaiah, eyes

narrowing when I saw he still had IV tape on his arm and a hospital gown wrapped around him.

He shuffled through the doorway with a glance over his shoulder. "Uh, hi?"

"You're supposed to be resting," I reminded him with a scowl.

"Well," he said, glancing over his shoulder again before shuffling out of sight of the doorway.

"You're not supposed to be here," I realized with a sigh.

"No," he said, looking around the room. "I, uh, heard, well—"

He grew silent, and I looked him over. There were bandages on the back of his head, and I wondered if they were even necessary. If he'd taken that bad a blow to the head, he would have been watched more closely. If he hadn't, then it meant he'd probably already been stapled and was sneaking out between nurse rounds.

"What?" I asked him, realizing he was here for a specific reason.

"I'm really sorry," he began, and before I could work with that, he continued. "You're only in here because of me right now. I asked you to trust me and look at both of us."

I frowned at him. "We were doing our job. What we were supposed to do."

"I...maybe if I'd waited," Isaiah said with a grimace, "for Larry and Terry to show up, we might have been able to get those girls out without, well, requiring you to save my dumbass."

"Are you sorry you saved them?"

"What? Of course not!"

"Then stop."

I didn't see the point of obsessing over what had happened. It was just like I'd told Chief Borton, we had done the best we could with what we had. Anything else was just pointless obsessing, the sort of thing politicians and people in charge had to do. Our job was to…well, do our job. Maybe we had broken protocol, but our job meant not just fighting fires and obeying every rule to the letter. Saving people's lives should take priority.

"Yeah, alright," Isaiah said quietly, and I almost groaned at the 'kicked puppy' tone of his voice.

"Look," I said, clearing my throat roughly. "I know Borton is going to give you shit, but fuck him."

"I'd rather not," Isaiah said with a small smile.

I frowned. "He's just doing his job. Just like we were doing."

"So, it's his job to yell at us, and it's our job to make him yell at us?"

"That's…not what I said."

Isaiah smiled, reaching out to gently pat my stomach. "I know. I make jokes when I'm nervous."

I frowned at the strange flutter in my stomach from his innocent touch and his comment. Just what did he have to be nervous about? It wasn't like, even if I was pissed about the whole thing, there was a lot I could do about it in my current state.

Isaiah sighed, shaking his head. "I know we did the right thing, and I'll take the chief's chew out later too. It's not like it's the first time he's given me an earful."

"Climbing?"

Isaiah smiled crookedly. "Probably shouldn't do that for another week or two, just in case. Last thing I need is to get dizzy, fall, and prove the chief right. He's right about too much as it is. I don't want to add to the list."

I frowned, trying to figure out just how the logic of Isaiah's brain worked. The man seemed terrified of what I might have said about our decisions and was avoiding the chief, yet he didn't flinch about getting in trouble for other reasons. There was bound to be a story behind it, but it wasn't my place to start digging into his past.

"I know everyone wonders why the hell I keep doing it when Chief always looks like he's going to have an aneurysm over it when it's brought up," Isaiah said with a half-smile. "But it's just...I don't know. I like doing it. Even as a kid, I gave my mom conniptions because I liked climbing. First, it was furniture, then trees, and then buildings. Then it was anything I could figure out how."

"You're gonna end up looking like me one day," I told him.

Isaiah laughed suddenly, the sound surprising me in the quiet of the hospital room. "That's what people keep telling me, and it hasn't happened yet. Maybe one day I'll learn that I need to stop doing it. Maybe I'll break something and keep doing it anyway, or maybe I won't break anything at all."

"We can trade if you're that interested," I grunted.

Isaiah leaned back, blinking rapidly. "Did...did you just make a joke?"

I shrugged, once more remembering why that was a terrible idea. This time the hiss did escape me, and I winced, mentally chiding myself. I supposed this was something I'd have to remember from here on out. There were bound to be more things I'd have to get used to not being able to do, not without hurting myself in the process.

"Geez," Isaiah said, his hands reaching toward me before he stopped. "You okay?"

"I think you can look at me and answer that," I grumbled, then caught his strained expression and sighed. "Just keep forgetting I can't shrug, is all."

Isaiah's hands hovered over me hesitantly, as though he couldn't decide whether to draw them back or touch me. I watched, curious about what he would do. I wasn't all that big on people touching me unless I was having sex, but I couldn't see an issue if it was Isaiah. There was an innocence to his touches that even I could see came from a place of worry more than anything...else.

"I ain't havin' no sissy for a son!"

The memory of my father's voice popped into my head with all the subtlety of the house that fell on me. I flinched, shoving it away before everything else attached to it followed suit. I was already miserable enough and didn't need to add memories of my dear old dad—especially *that* memory.

Isaiah drew his hands back sharply. "Well, look, I just came up here—"

"Snuck," I said, watching his hands for a moment before looking at his face.

"What? Oh," he chuckled. "Yeah, okay, I just snuck up here to tell you I'm sorry you had half a house fall on you to save my ass. And that I'm sorry you're...like this now because of it. I can't even imagine what must be going through your head."

"Nothing good," I admitted, looking over my cast-covered arms with dread. My whole life was about to be tipped on its head, and I had barely even started.

"What, uh, what are they going to do?"

"They?"

"Well, Chief Borton, I guess."

"Says I have leave. So I'll be covered."

"What, uh, what are you going to do?"

"Do?"

Isaiah gestured to my arms. "It's not like you're in a good place to deal with...well, a lot of things. Do you have family?"

"Not...really," I admitted slowly, simply because the explanation was too long and detailed to launch into.

He smiled a little at that. "Fair enough. Friends?"

"No."

"Girlfriend?"

"No."

"Oh."

I expected pity or annoyance on his part, two reactions I commonly got from anyone who got a brief glimpse into my life. To my surprise, I saw only a thoughtful expression as he looked down at his feet.

"You can't exactly..." he began, then looked up, eyes widening. "You're probably used to doing things on your own, but—"

He gestured toward my arms, and I grunted in response. I had already gone through this entire conversation with Borton, and I didn't look forward to repeating it. The last thing I needed was to go over the fact that I was going to end up practically helpless. With Borton, it had been frustrating, but the idea of doing it with Isaiah just felt embarrassing.

"Is this where you tell me I can't wipe my own ass?" I asked him with a huff.

Isaiah's face flushed, and I could see the way my words hit him just right, and I felt a stab of guilt. "No, I'm pretty sure you could manage that much with one hand. It's just, you know, it's going to get exhausting, and—"

I waited, unsure I'd ever seen Isaiah struggle with words. It was oddly interesting, seeing this normally chatty man reduced to sputtering and stumbling. After a few seconds, however, I began to feel bad and figured I should take pity on him.

"Look," I said. "I'll figure it out."

"I could help," Isaiah finally said.

I blinked. "What? No."

A grimace flashed and disappeared on his face. "Right, yeah, of course."

"I'm okay," I said, suddenly confused about what was happening. When I saw how Isaiah's eyes drifted over my arms, I frowned again. "I will be."

Isaiah chewed his bottom lip, looking more vulnerable

and helpless than I'd ever seen. I felt anxiety bubble in my chest, tightening as I wondered what I was supposed to do. No part of this was his fault, but it seemed that no matter what I said, Isaiah would still blame himself. I almost wanted to reach out and shake him a little, remind him we were doing our jobs, and even if I had the chance to go back and change what we did, I wouldn't.

"I get it," he said slowly, brushing at his gown as he stood up straight.

"Excuse me," a voice piped up, and I saw the nurse from earlier standing in the doorway. Her brow was raised, and I couldn't tell if she was amused or annoyed as she stared at Isaiah.

"Shit," Isaiah hissed, whirling around to face her. Absurdly, I realized he was only wearing underwear under the gown. They were short trunks, bright green, and hugged the upper part of his thighs. My face warmed as the image stood out before the gown settled and covered Isaiah again. "Uh, hi."

"Something tells me you're probably not supposed to be up here," she said, stepping closer to Isaiah. "You're the other firefighter they brought in, aren't you?"

"Geez, word spreads fast, doesn't it?" Isaiah asked with a nervous laugh.

"We don't usually get too many people from Fairlake out here," she said, reminding me that we were probably at the hospital in Fovel. It was bigger, and most towns used Fovel's hospital in emergencies. "And we were warned you might wander out of bed...and end up here."

"What?" Isaiah asked, frowning at her in what I thought was confusion.

"Borton," I grunted, knowing only one person would try to warn the staff about 'escape' attempts.

"No idea," she said with a smirk. "Just that you'd wander and 'mother hen' your way up here."

"I wasn't—" Isaiah began with a scowl.

"You were," I told him, finding the expression endearing on his ordinarily happy face.

"You shut it," he told me sharply.

I couldn't help but smile, holding up the arm that wasn't entirely in a cast as a show of surrender. Isaiah's expression softened almost immediately, and he watched me curiously for a few heartbeats before turning back to the nurse.

"What are the chances I could get back to my bed without getting into trouble for this?" he asked her.

"I might be willing to call Julie in your block, so she knows you're coming back, and we can forget all about this if you get back there right now," the nurse said with a chuckle.

Isaiah immediately brightened at the knowledge he was again getting off scot-free. "Now that's a deal I can agree to."

"Good, get moving. You both need to rest," she said.

"I'm supposed to be leaving," I growled at her.

"Is he always like this?" she asked Isaiah.

I was startled to see Isaiah smile. "Yeah, he's the quiet type. I don't think he's as angry as he sounds. Pretty sure that's just how his voice works."

My surprise at his opinion of me kept my mouth shut as the nurse led Isaiah into the hallway. He glanced at me thoughtfully before disappearing out of sight, the nurse lingering in the doorway before coming back into the room.

"Thanks," I muttered.

"Is that sarcasm or genuine?"

"For making him go."

"Oh, not a big fan of him, huh?"

I scowled at her. "He needs to rest."

She smiled, taking my water glass from the bedside table. "Ah, I see. That makes sense."

I looked at her in confusion, but she smiled benignly as she left the room, promising to bring back juice this time. Apparently, I wasn't going to get any more answers out of her and settled back on the bed to stare up at the ceiling. I thought Isaiah overdoing it to come up here and apologize for nothing had been stupid on his part. It was for the best that someone had come along and chased him off because I hadn't been doing a very good job of it.

He was such a strange guy, and I wasn't sure what to make of him. Isaiah had always been friendly toward me, though he'd never tried to hold a conversation, which I appreciated. This was the first time I could remember conversing with him, and despite how uncomfortable it had been to see him so stressed, I hadn't minded too much.

Maybe over the next few weeks, I could think of *something* to make Isaiah realize he hadn't done anything wrong. Comforting wasn't something I was good at, but maybe I could find something indisputable to convince him. He was a decent guy and didn't deserve to feel like shit over something stupid.

In the meantime, I had a lot of other problems to worry about solving.

ISAIAH

"Are you sure about this?" Chief Borton asked from the driver's seat.

I sighed, trying not to get *too* irritated. "You've asked me that almost a dozen times now, Chief, c'mon."

The older man gripped the wheel a little tighter. "Julian hasn't let anyone come over in the past few days. What makes you think you're going to be any different?"

"I never said *that*," I said with a snort, leaning my head against the passenger window, only to wince when the jostling from the truck sent a wave of pain through my skull. I'd only been out of the hospital a few days, and my head was still pretty tender.

I was cleared for 'light duty' back at the station, which basically meant I was allowed to clean so long as I agreed to take frequent rests. I didn't care how often I had to sit down and drink water, just so long as I could do something besides sit around on my ass, bored out of my mind. It wasn't like I was so stubborn about how 'tough' I was that I refused to take care of myself.

"All you said is you wanted to go over there," the chief continued, stopping at a sign. "Literally. All you said. Doesn't matter what someone tells you, that's all you say."

"Because I want to go over there," I said, refusing to look at him.

It had been almost four days since Julian had been released from the hospital, and he point-blank refused to let anyone into his apartment. Chief Borton had been over there half a dozen times to check up on him and was stonewalled for his attempts. Julian was apparently "grumpy," which was saying something for him, and kept people at the door.

Laurence and Larry were content to let Julian do whatever he wanted, though I suspected it was because neither of them was all that fond of him. Chief Borton was frustrated because, just like I did, he knew Julian would need help but was refusing it out of, well, stubbornness or pride. I couldn't decide which.

"Is this a guilt thing?" he asked. "Please tell me it's not a guilt thing."

"It's not a guilt thing."

"You telling me the truth?"

"You asked me to tell you that, so I did."

"Oh, so suddenly you're willing to do what you're told?"

I turned to glare at him. "Is this where you try to make me feel bad about what happened? Again?"

The chief scowled at me. "I'm not—"

"You were."

"Of course I was. You broke protocol. You should have waited for Terry and Larry to show—"

"So Julian and I could have gone in as a team to back each other up, I know," I finished with a sigh, turning back toward the window. "You keep reminding me, and I keep reminding you that I know. Trust me, I'm aware."

Whether or not I'd do it differently? Well, that was a question I hadn't been able to answer yet. I'd been injured and was insanely lucky that all I'd received for my trouble was a bump on my head. Yet Julian not only had to put himself in danger to save me but he'd been injured worse than I was. If we *had* waited, those girls would have been stuck in that closet, and the chance to save them would have dwindled to nothing, considering how quickly the house fell apart shortly afterward.

"And what makes you think it'll go any differently?" he asked, apparently deciding he'd twisted my guilt enough. "For a guy, you think doesn't even like you."

I looked up, startled. "I never said that."

"Not to me, but you've said it."

"I'm going to kill—"

"No one said anything. I've got ears that still work, Isaiah. I know what goes on around my station. And I've got a brain."

I sighed, leaning back in my seat. "I don't think he likes *anyone*."

"Not liking someone isn't the same as disliking someone."

"I…" hesitating, I glanced at him. "What?"

"Not liking someone just means you don't have any positive feelings about 'em," he said, turning at the next intersection and slowing down as the speed limit dropped. "Disliking someone means you have negative feelings. There's a big difference."

"Oh," I said, seeing sense in his words. "Yeah, that makes sense. But what's your point?"

"I just mean I don't think that man likes much of anything, at least not when it comes to people. I also don't think he dislikes most people."

I frowned. "That sounds lonelier than if he just disliked people all the time."

"Probably," Chief Borton said as he slowed to turn into the parking lot of the Mountain Crest apartment complex. There were only two in Fairlake, and this one was by far the shabbiest. The faux brick exterior was chipped, revealing walls plastered over in several places. The 'porches' of the apartments in the single-story building were simple gray slabs, cracked in places. "But that doesn't mean you're gonna suddenly make him like you."

"I'm not trying to make him like me," I protested, pulling my eyes away from the window.

He gave me a doubtful look. "Isaiah, you always want people to like you."

"I do not!" Sure, I liked it when people liked me. I was sure most people liked to be liked.

"Right, his not liking you doesn't drive you nuts?"

"No, well, I mean a little. It's just kinda…it doesn't make sense. I didn't do anything to make him that way toward me, and it bugs me. If I *did* something, then I'd get it."

"You do remember what I said a second ago, right?"

"Yes," I groaned. It certainly made a little more sense. Deep down, I'd always suspected Julian simply…didn't like people, and it was nothing personal. The fact was, sometimes, I wondered if it was a little more personal with me. "But that doesn't mean I'm trying to get him to like me."

"Trying to understand why he might not like you ain't gonna help either," he said, frowning.

"What is this? What are you doing? Are you pulling the Dad card on me right now? Is that what's happening?" I asked, swatting the air in front of his face. "I'm not your daughter. Quit it."

"If you were my kid, I wouldn't have driven you out here."

"Yes you would," I told him with a snort.

"Oh, you think?"

"I know. Because if you didn't give me a ride, I would

have found someone else to do it. And since Bennett is…" I wasn't actually sure *what* was going on with Bennett. After my stay at the hospital, he'd all but dropped off the map. I hadn't seen him on his routine run, which was unsettling, but he wasn't responding to my texts either, "busy, I might not have found anyone. So I'd have had to walk. And were you really going to let me walk all that way?"

That kind of distance definitely went against the medical advice I'd been given. I was also forbidden from driving, though that came from the crew rather than any medical advice. So if I wanted to get around quickly, I had to rely on the crew.

"Maybe havin' to walk woulda been a good lesson. Maybe collapsin' on the way would teach you to listen."

"Then I'd be right back in the hospital, and you'd be right back up there."

"And then I could fire your ass for not listenin'!"

"What, so you couldn't pester me anymore? Pfft, as if."

He glared at me. "You wanna know what woke me up that night when you dumbasses went and got yourselves hurt?"

"Pretty sure Laurence was on the phone faster than me falling through that floor," I told him, taking pleasure in his annoyed scowl.

"When were you gonna tell me you put me as your medical emergency contact?" he asked.

"I…"

"Yeah, because the hospital woke me up, not Laurence. Don't worry. He already got an earful for forgetting to call me when two of our own were hurt. Not the point."

"Oh, um," I said, finding the hem on my jeans extremely interesting and tugging at it. "I meant to tell you at, uh, some point."

"Still ain't heard from your folks?" he asked softly.

"I don't have any 'folks,' remember?" I asked him in a stiff voice that still carried bitter undertones. My family was perfectly happy to pretend my younger brother was an only child, ignoring that their firstborn was still living where our family had first sprouted and then flourished. I was their secret shame, the one they worked hard never to have associated with them.

"So, why me?" he asked, and I wished he was growling at me again instead of using that soft voice that sounded too much like pity.

"It would've been Bennett, but he's busy being a cop, and I didn't wanna risk him being pulled off something important if I got hurt. Figured since you'd be called if one of us got hurt anyway, it made sense," I said, scraping my nail along the seam. "It just made sense, alright?"

"Fine, but next time, tell me. Left me thinkin' I was gonna have to make choices on your behalf," he grunted.

I chuckled. "That's not covered by emergency contact. You don't have to worry about all that. I know if something happened to me, I'd want you to be the one to know. You'd tell the guys, and you'd know to tell Bennett. That's all that matters."

Chief Borton sighed heavily and then pointed. "It's number three. I'll wait here."

"I can see you're really rooting for me here, Chief," I chuckled, grabbing the handle and shoving the truck door open. Honestly, the quicker I got out of that awkward conversation the better. "I've worked magic before. Who knows, maybe I'll do it again."

"I'm not holding my breath," he grumbled, but I could tell he wasn't too irritated.

I closed the door before he could add anything else and made my way toward the third apartment. A woman emerged from the second apartment, her gaze flicking to my face briefly before glancing away.

The woman didn't look at me again as I knocked on Julian's door. The paint was peeling, and there was a strange quality to the sound of my knocking that made me wonder if the door was plywood. I could hear the heavy sound of footsteps approaching and braced myself. The handle jiggled, and I could hear something hitting the other side. I could picture his fingers, partially bound by the cast, fumbling to open the door.

When it swung open, I was startled by how much he filled the doorway. It wasn't like I hadn't known he was a big guy, but either those few days not seeing him had made me forget, or the doorway was smaller than I was used to. At least the scowl on his face was familiar as he peered down at me. Before I could say a word, he leaned forward to look out at the parking lot before his expression grew even darker.

"No," he grunted, stepping back.

"Hey now," I protested as I saw him move to close the door. "At least let me talk."

"There, you talked," he said.

I rolled my eyes. *Now* he decided to get a sense of humor? "Look, let me actually talk, and then you can slam the door in my face."

"I told Borton—"

"He didn't tell me to come here."

"That's his truck."

"Yeah, well, he's the chief, so if he wants to leave the station and bring me here, he's allowed. Everyone else is working to cover our shifts, so they're stuck or sleeping," I told him, looking him over. "I can't drive."

He frowned. "I thought it wasn't bad."

"It's not," I said, rolling my eyes. "I just have to take it easy for a few more days, maybe a week, then I can return to active duty. But everyone there decided that since I'm not allowed to work too hard and took a head wound, I shouldn't be driving anywhere. So I get escorted around."

"Oh."

"Yeah, oh. So, since I had to endure him giving me shit on the drive over, the least you can do is let me talk."

I expected him to close the door in my face anyway, but I watched his shoulders sag, and he stepped back. "Fine."

To my surprise, he shambled away from the door, allowing me in. Not willing to lose the advantage, I glanced back toward the chief's truck before hurrying to enter the dark apartment.

Only one light sat on a makeshift table made from wood and two milk crates. The couch was patchy, and from the eye-watering combination of burned orange and snot green, I wondered if it was a survivor of the seventies. The carpet was threadbare, and I guessed there was just bare floor underneath it. A small TV sat on another makeshift piece of furniture, this time boards between cinder blocks. The only other thing in the room was a card table shoved into the far corner, stacked with items I couldn't make out in the dim light.

"So?" he asked, and I turned my attention away from his apartment to look him over. He wore a loose pair of sleep pants and a shirt that somehow looked big on him. There was a thick layer of red stubble on his jaw, and his short hair looked a little too shiny in the light of the one bulb.

"Have you taken a shower?" I asked him. "Since you got home."

He scowled at me. "That's what you wanted to say?"

"You haven't, have you?" I said. Although I was sure he could operate the shower just fine on his own, I wasn't quite sure how he'd be able to cover the casts. One of his hands and arms was completely useless, and his left couldn't cover itself. "You have plastic bags?"

"Isaiah," he growled in annoyance.

I crossed my arms over my chest. "Is that a no or yes? Of course you have plastic bags somewhere. Do you have tape? Like, box tape?"

"I don't need you—"

"Well?"

"I—"

"Hey, Julian?"

"What?"

"Look, I'm starting to realize maybe it doesn't matter if you don't like me," I said, thinking there were more important things to deal with right now. "But I'm not going to stand around and let you rot away because you're being stubborn, prideful, or independent. Now, I'm not here to give you shit but to try to make things a little easier. As a matter of fact, whatever I see or you do, stays here in this apartment, got it?"

Julian's frown continued to deepen the longer I spoke, and I waited patiently. Even if he wasn't the sort who didn't like people, it had been clear early on that Julian was a man of few words, and those came slowly more often than not. I could wait for him to tell me to fuck off if he needed to summon the energy and words to do so.

"I don't...not like you," he said finally, still irritated.

Now wasn't the time to show the flash of surprise that washed through me, and I unwound my arms from my chest. "Fine. Where are the plastic bags and tape then?"

"Under the sink, drawer next to the fridge," he said, as though the words brought him pain.

"Great, awesome, perfect," I said, walking around the couch and into the kitchen. I wasn't surprised that there wasn't much to the small room. There was a stack of dishes that looked like they'd sat there for almost a week. Dented pans and a single pot sat on the counter, along with a large plastic spoon with a cracked handle and a couple of spatulas.

Crouching, I opened the doors to the cabinet beneath the sink and found the plastic bags, and after taking a couple, I thought of his right arm and grabbed a thin garbage bag as well. The drawer Julian mentioned was filled with bits and bobs, a phone charger, a handful of colorful wires, zip ties, batteries, and the barely touched roll of tape.

When I returned to the living room, I found him standing in the same spot, frowning at the floor. I walked over to him, gesturing. "Arms out."

He glared at me for a moment, and again, I found myself waiting for him to tell me to fuck off. Instead, he held his arms out, and I started with the right one. It took me a few minutes to carefully wrap the limb without bumping him too hard before sealing the edges as best I could. His left forearm was easier to work with, and I made sure that when I sealed the edges, I didn't limit his finger mobility.

"There," I said, smiling. "Now go take a shower. Take as long as you'd like. I'm sure it'll feel good."

His brow still furrowed, he stared at me a moment longer before heading toward the back of the room. I listened to the sound of rummaging and a door closing before turning. First things first, I snatched up a few pieces of clothing I found scattered about and went on the hunt until I found a plastic laundry basket outside the bedroom.

Not wanting to intrude on his space, I dropped the half-filled basket inside the room before returning to the kitchen. After sincerely hoping the building's water heater was strong enough to take it, I filled one side of the sink with hot, soapy water. Then, grabbing the drying rack from under the sink, I worked through the dishes.

I was on the final pan when I turned and found a towering figure in the doorway. I yelped, jerking my hand back and sending a splash of water down my front. "Jesus!"

"What are you doing?" he grumbled at me.

"I…" Then I stopped as I realized he was wearing only a towel. "The dishes?"

It wasn't like it was the first time I'd seen him. The station did have a shower room, after all. Of course, I always kept my eyes respectfully averted with all the guys, and with someone new like Julian, I was even more diligent. However, this was someone's home.

My brain wasn't prepared, and my attention wandered over his body. I swore he had to be the biggest man I'd ever seen in my life. His chest was broad and coated in a layer of red hair that trailed down to his flat stomach, where it circled his belly button before disappearing beneath the towel. His arms were probably as big as my head, and I dimly wondered how much plaster they'd used to wrap just one arm.

"Why?" he asked, and I felt relief that he hadn't noticed the way my brain was *desperately* trying to imagine what was behind the bulge in the front of the towel.

"Because…they needed to be done," I said, scrambling for an answer while I got my brain to stop being so *goddamn horny*. "I didn't want to stand around like an idiot while you were showering, so I made myself useful."

He glanced at the dishes in the drying rack, and I followed his gaze toward his bagged arms. For a moment I could see the annoyance on his face and then frustration. I forced myself to look away, knowing full well that in his position, I would want as little pity as possible. For someone as big and strong as he was, I had no doubt his current predicament was the most frustrating and emasculating thing possible.

"Thanks," he muttered, and I wondered how much that one word cost him.

"Sure," I said with a shrug. It was probably best not to add too much to the conversation. I was clearly distracted by him, and I didn't accidentally want to say the wrong thing while my thoughts were elsewhere.

"I'm gonna get dressed," he said, lingering for a moment before leaving.

I stood at the sink for a bit longer before turning to clean the final dish. I used the remaining soapy water to wipe down the counters and stovetop. The kitchen wasn't dirty, but it was as worn as the rest of the apartment. The linoleum was cracked and curling in places, and the paint on the cabinets was peeling. Whoever ran the apartment complex wasn't all that worried about maintenance.

I found a broom in a small alcove and began sweeping. There wasn't much to clean up, which I didn't find surprising. From what I'd seen so far, Julian wasn't a slob. A little messy but not a slob. Probably didn't help that it looked like he didn't own a whole lot or did much that would cause a mess. I would have called the place spartan, but that inferred there was intent to be minimal rather than being forced to live this way. Which I thought was strange since all of us at the station made livable money.

Julian reappeared in the doorway, eyes drifting along the broom's handle before falling on my face with a frown. "Why?"

I almost laughed but managed to restrain myself save for the twitching of my lips. "Is this where I have to confess that when I'm a little nervous and don't know what to do with myself, I start cleaning?"

"You're nervous?"

"A little, yeah."

"Why?"

Other than the fact that I still wasn't completely sold on the idea that Julian didn't actively dislike me? Or that being around him always made me a little nervous, no matter how hard I tried to tell myself to be calm? It didn't help that out of everyone who tried to help Julian, I was the only one he'd let in, and that somehow felt like a responsibility I hadn't been prepared to deal with.

But I thought I should leave those things unsaid and stick with what would probably be the hardest thing to say.

"Well, I know how hard this whole thing has been," I said, sweeping the dirt into a pile. "Okay, not like...personally. Or firsthand. But I have a pretty good imagination, and I can imagine how hard this has to be. I won't rub salt in the wound, but I'm sure it's rough looking at everything you're used to doing and—"

I trailed off, looking up at his face nervously. I'd met plenty of people who were difficult to read, but in a contest, Julian would win by a landslide. It wasn't so much that he constantly looked angry, though he did. It was just that there were next to no tells. The chief was grumpy looking, but I could tell from the way he talked or how insistent he was just how bad his mood was. Julian, though, had no reference point, and as far as I could tell, there was no shift in his body language or alteration to his tone.

"Right," he grunted, and I took that as permission to continue talking.

"And I don't know if you've been pushing everyone away because of pride or stubbornness," I continued, now watching him closely. "Or you're just used to taking care of yourself." He continued to stare at me, but I thought I saw his brow shift slightly at the last sentence. "But...I genuinely want to help. Things are going to be hard enough as it is for you."

Julian's brow furrowed deeper, and he tilted his head. "Why?"

"What do you mean why? In case you haven't noticed, you're not exactly working with both of your arms right now."

"No."

"No?"

"Why do you want to help?"

"Uh? I mean, there's a few reasons. You did save my ass—"

"That's what we're supposed to do for each other."

"You're also one of us, and we take care of our own."

"That's what everyone says. That's what you're supposed to say."

This time it was my turn to frown, and I closed my mouth, cutting off the knee-jerk response before it could leave my lips. Between the wording and the way he sounded borderline desperate, I found myself hesitating.

Then it hit me, and I realized I had been right before. This wasn't a prideful man, though perhaps pride was part of it, and stubbornness most certainly was. Maybe it was because I saw something of myself, but I saw a man who had found that at some point in his life, he had to rely solely on himself and only himself. I would never make presumptions about someone's life, but somehow, I felt as though I was witnessing someone who couldn't help but doubt any hand offered to him.

"Well, maybe I just want to," I finally told him, tilting my chin up to meet his eyes. "Just because you don't want to admit you could use some help doesn't mean I'm blind. So I want to help. You can call it guilt. You can call it duty or compassion, whatever the hell you want. I still want to do it. Doesn't matter how much you question it. It's something you need."

It was not my most stellar example of compassion, and I

felt myself wither inside at the realization. I was supposed to be convincing Julian it was a good idea to accept help, not chew him out for something that probably existed for a good reason. I didn't know a thing about this man, in fact, I'd learned more about him in the past half hour in his apartment than I had in months of working alongside him. Now I was trying to navigate convincing him to agree with me, and I chose to be a stubborn dick about it.

Seconds ticked by, stretching into minutes, and I wondered how long the chief would take to come back to pick me up. This was by far the longest Julian had ever taken to respond to anything anyone said to him. It was probably a good thing he wasn't much for words, or I probably would have found myself on the receiving end of a monumental chew—

"Okay," he finally grunted.

"I get it, you…wait, what?" I asked, jerking in surprise.

He shrugged partly, only stopping to wince, and then frown. "Okay. Better you than the others."

"I don't know how to take that," I admitted, then shook myself back to reality. "But good! Good."

"No babying," he said with a scowl.

I smiled a little at that. "I'm not the babying type. But there's normal stuff people do that you'll need help with, so I can do that, right?"

There was only the barest of hesitations. "Yeah, sure."

"Good," I said, perking up as I swept the dirt into the dustpan. "So, let's start with the laundry."

"I can—"

"What, carry the laundry while opening doors? If you want to load up the basket, pour in the soap and softener, and set the timer, be my guest. But the rest? That's for someone with two functioning arms."

He frowned, and I felt a moment of panic that I'd gone too far with my flippancy. "Softener?"

I opened my mouth, then closed it, smiling. "Oh, my big friend, let me introduce you to a whole new world of soft clothes and less wear and tear."

He blinked at me owlishly, but I could see the curiosity in his eyes that told me that, for now, we had a decent start.

JULIAN

Isaiah was a neat freak. There was no way around it. In only a week, he'd somehow managed to make my apartment look halfway decent. He had come over every day like clockwork. At first, someone else had driven him, but after he'd been cleared for work again, he drove himself. Each day it seemed he had some new project to busy himself with.

Not only had he scrubbed the entire kitchen in a couple of hours, but he'd also glued parts of the peeling linoleum down. Another day, he'd shown up with bottles of something and promptly scrubbed the living room. I don't know what he used, but by the time he was done, the cheap floors looked almost new and not nearly as cheap.

I looked up at him, blinking as he stretched to reach the corner. The bottom of his shirt rode up, showing a flash of skin before he pulled his arm back, covering himself again. An uncomfortable flutter rose in my gut, and I pulled my eyes away, annoyed with my body's reaction to something benign.

One thing I'd come to learn about Isaiah, he was pretty

fond of talking. I usually tried to avoid people like that, but I couldn't while we were both in the apartment. Well, and he wasn't really all that bad. As much as he liked to talk, he had never rushed me or acted impatient when I took a while to answer or when I didn't say much.

It was a strange experience, realizing someone wasn't expecting me to talk constantly. At first, I'd been wary of how talkative he was, but after a few days, I learned he was perfectly content just doing his thing and letting me do mine. To his credit, he didn't talk nearly as much with me as I had seen him do with others, but I also wondered if all these cleaning projects were a way for him to funnel his energy elsewhere. I hadn't thought about how much it was costing.

"Money's important," I said out of the blue.

He glanced at me curiously. "Is it?"

I shifted uncomfortably as I tried to piece together what I meant. "It matters when…you don't have a lot of it. And you…did."

He smiled a little at that. "So, growing up as a rich kid makes me blind to the importance of money?"

"Sort of."

"That's fair."

Once more, he surprised me, and I silently watched him resume his cleaning. I had anticipated he would take offense to what I was saying. People didn't tend to like the way I saw things, calling it 'too blunt' or 'rude.' Sure, sometimes I didn't say things right, but other times I thought people were too sensitive.

Isaiah had certainly seemed sensitive, but this wasn't the first time he'd simply accepted what I said. Not only that, but he'd accepted it gracefully, thoughtful and as light as ever. Light was a word I'd use for him, even if it seemed strange for a guy who was a few inches over six feet and built.

It fit him, though. It seemed like no matter what he did, he found a reason to chuckle or smile. After a few days of being around him, I'd concluded that my original theory about him the first month at the station was correct. Isaiah was a genuinely happy and friendly person.

That was, except for the odd moment when I could see his thoughts were elsewhere. I didn't know where he went when that happened or what he was thinking. In truth, I couldn't even explain why, but I had the feeling that wherever he went, it wasn't the happiest of places.

"Can I ask a personal question?" he asked, stepping down from the stool.

Wariness flickered through me. "I guess."

"Well, you don't have to answer if you don't want to," he said quickly. "I'm not gonna be upset if you don't wanna tell me your business."

With anyone else, I might not have believed them. But, considering how easy Isaiah had been at accepting every one of my other frustrating habits, I was willing to see if he was telling the truth. "Okay."

"Why did you transfer to our station?" he asked, scrunching his nose as he looked over the dirty rag. "I know it's probably not fair to say this, but you didn't seem very happy to be there."

"I wasn't," I admitted.

"Well, I guess my suspicions were spot on then," he said with a soft snort.

"Does that bother you?" I asked.

He looked up, his brow pinching even as he smiled. "It stings a little to hear. I like the station, the guys, and the chief, so it isn't great to hear someone's not happy to be there. *But*…I'm also reminding myself that I don't have to take it personally. Maybe you simply didn't like it there, and that sucks, or maybe you had a reason for being unhappy."

I didn't think I'd met anyone who gave such candid peeks into their process until Isaiah. It felt like such an...intimate thing to do, particularly with someone you barely knew. I didn't know if he did that with everyone, but from what I'd seen at the station, he didn't do it in regular conversations. Perhaps he only did it when he was alone with someone.

"You guys are fine," I finally told him. "It was transfer or get fired."

His eyes widened slightly. "Oh. I see."

I could see him struggling, and I couldn't help but smile. "You can ask."

Struggle gave way to surprise, but then he laughed softly. "Caught me. Why would you get fired?"

"I broke another guy's jaw."

"Another...firefighter?"

"Yeah."

"At the station you were at?"

"Yeah."

Isaiah whistled. "That's...wow, yeah, that would do it alright. Not every station has quite the family-esque style we do, but they're still generally pretty close-knit."

"Yeah," I said, shrugging my left shoulder again. I knew that, and it had been true there as well. Not that I had participated, but it had been true for the rest of them...for the most part.

"Okay, so I have to ask why you hit the guy? As grumpy as you seem, you don't strike me as the sort of guy to do something that extreme without a good reason," Isaiah said, propping a foot up on the stool while he watched me.

It was strange being given the benefit of the doubt by someone who barely knew me. I was used to being distrusted, but I knew I didn't do myself any favors by keeping myself separate from others.

"He...was cheating on his wife," I began slowly, trying to

force the words out. It wasn't just that talking didn't come easily to me. This story was still fresh for me despite the months that had passed. "With a sixteen-year-old."

Isaiah's eyes widened. "*What?*"

"She was fifteen when it started," I continued. "He...joked about it at the station."

"Christ," Isaiah muttered, disgust plain on his face. "Quick question, why didn't anyone report it?"

"I did," I said. "Did it anonymously."

"Why anonymously?"

"People don't...trust me. Better if they didn't know it was me. Thought it would be enough. Nothing happened, so I tried again, but this time not anonymously. Since I was a member of the station, I guess they thought they had to look into it."

Isaiah shook his head. "Of course, once it's 'real,' they have to look."

"Didn't look that hard," I admitted. "But I guess a cop talked because the guys at the station heard it was me. The guy was pissed and cornered me in the breakroom. I didn't care, but...something he said set me off. I punched him. Broke his jaw. Captain Bones gave me the choice, here or nowhere."

"Do I want to know what that guy said that set you off?"

"Something not right...about the teenager."

"Mean or crude?"

"Referred to her as...the pussy he was getting. And I shouldn't run my mouth because I was jealous."

Isaiah gave the ugliest snort I'd ever heard. "Yeah, okay, he deserves a lot more than his jaw broken."

I peered up at him for several seconds. "You...believe me?"

"Do I believe you? Yeah, I believe you," he said with a

frown. His disbelief at my question made me feel bad for even doubting him. "But it sounds like no one there believed you. Wait, does the chief know about this?"

"Borton knows…about the fight. He knows I hit the guy first. I thought it was weird that he offered to transfer me here, but I guess Chief Bones asked him as a favor. Dunno why."

"Maybe your last chief suspected the reason," Isaiah said with a shrug. "And even if our chief doesn't exactly know why you did it, I know he suspects there was a good reason."

"Why do you say that?"

"Because I know the chief. He's a hardass and doesn't put up with shit, but he takes care of us and keeps an eye out for trouble. If he believed for a minute you were some violent jerk willing to hit a coworker, favor owed or not, he wouldn't have transferred you to us. I can guarantee that," he said, pointing a finger at me.

I hadn't given it much thought, but I could see the logic behind it. Borton wasn't what I would call a sentimental man, but he cared about the other guys at the station. I had simply thought Borton had brought me on grudgingly because Bones had asked. I'd never considered he might not have done it at all if he thought I was a threat.

"And for the record," Isaiah said, stopping as he walked past me to lay a hand gently on the top of my head. "That also means he considers you one of us, so congratulations, you've been adopted by the world's grumpiest father figure."

His hand was gone a second later, but I could still feel the lingering pressure of his touch. People didn't touch me unless I was taking them home for the night. The contact had been so casual, as though Isaiah hadn't even thought about what he was doing. It was brief, but it left me sitting there in thought.

What a strange man. Even stranger was…I didn't mind it. I avoided talking to people, but I didn't mind when Isaiah did it. I avoided touching people unless it was absolutely necessary, but here I was, not flinching in the slightest when Isaiah casually laid a hand on me.

And I wondered if his underwear were all bright colors and if they all hugged his thighs the way they—

My heart thumped heavily in my chest, and I pushed the absurd thought away. I tried to ignore the warmth I felt flush my cheeks and focus on the TV instead. It had been playing the whole time, but once distracted by Isaiah, I'd lost track of the movie I'd been watching.

"So I was thinking," Isaiah said as he returned to the living room.

"Okay," I said, torn between wanting to avoid eye contact with him and wanting to stare at him.

"I ain't havin' no sissy for a son!"

"You alright?" Isaiah asked, bending down to reach a hand out toward my face. "You got a fever or—"

"I'm fine," I said, leaning away from his hand. God, the last thing I needed was for him to touch me again. My father's fury and outrage still echoed in my head, and I just… didn't understand why.

"Right, okay," he said, pulling his hand away and failing to cover up the hurt in his expression. "So, I was thinking. Since I've been here so often and shared some meals, well, groceries are in order."

"There's food," I said with a frown.

"There's three eggs, two things of ramen, and half a pound of hamburger in the freezer," he said dryly. "We need to get some more food. You wanna come with me while I grab some?"

I couldn't argue. I'd known I needed to get groceries even before my arms were broken. I had been living off what little

I had simply because I hadn't wanted to leave the apartment. Isaiah had been bringing his own meals with him, though I'd noticed he always seemed to 'accidentally' bring more than he could eat, forcing me to take his leftovers.

"Don't really have the funds at the moment," I had to admit.

"Oh no," Isaiah said with a light laugh. "I'll get the groceries since I'm going to dig into them too. With how much time I've been spending here, it only seems fair."

"No," I said, frowning.

"Look, I have plenty of extra money."

"I…" I stopped, looking at him. "How?"

"What?"

"How do you have extra money? We get paid the same."

Something strange flickered across his expression before a faint smile covered it. "I could say the same thing to you. We do make the same money, so you should be able to live in the better apartments closer to the station."

"I send money to my mom to help her," I said quietly. I didn't know why I felt the urge to tell him the truth, but it was out in the open anyway.

"Oh, I was expecting you to get a little mad."

"Really?"

"Well, yeah, I was being kind of bitchy."

"It was a fair question."

A genuine smile curled on his lips. "You're an interesting guy, Julian."

"Am I?" I asked in surprise.

"Yeah. And sweet too. Giving up a chunk of your income to help your mom like that," he said. "She's lucky to have you."

I said nothing, turning my head to stare at the floor. "So, why do you have extra money?"

"Because," he began, and I looked up again at his hesitation, "I get an allowance. Monthly. From my parents."

"Oh," I said, frowning. "But—"

"But what?" he asked, a stiffness on his face.

"You said you aren't in contact with your family. Why lie?"

"I didn't lie. I'm not in contact with them."

"But they send you money," I said, feeling slightly bitter at the idea. It must have been nice to know that no matter what you did, you'd always have rich parents to keep you afloat. "I guess I was right before."

"About?" Isaiah asked, voice even.

"You not understanding why money is a big deal. You're getting money all the time. You probably don't even have to work. Of course, you can afford groceries for someone else. Must be nice."

"Must be nice?" Isaiah repeated. "I'm sorry, but was that a touch of *judgment* I just heard?"

"A little," I admitted with a shrug. "Just must be nice. And easy. Explains a lot."

"It explains precisely fuck all," he growled.

I looked up in surprise at the sudden shift in tone. Isaiah was glaring down at me, arms crossed tightly over his chest. It was immediately apparent I had finally managed to find Isaiah's limit, and once more, it was because I could be too blunt about the truth.

"I lied a couple of minutes ago when I called it an allowance," he said tightly. "You wanna know what it actually is? It's a bribe. They pay me monthly to ensure I don't get any ideas. So I don't try to be part of the family again. So I keep quiet, live a quiet life, and don't draw attention to myself."

"Because you're—"

A sissy.

"Gay?" I asked, swallowing hard.

"That's exactly what it is. Can't have me ruining the family's good name. So they offered me this 'allowance' instead. And you know, I could have told them no, I could have done it all on my own, and I know I could. Because I know me, and I know what I'm capable of," Isaiah continued, his eyes flashing dangerously. "But you know what? Fuck that. I would have avoided them anyway, but if they want to pay me for it? Fine, I consider it restitution for having ignorant shitheads like that for family."

I said nothing, only stared at him while he gesticulated sharply. I had never seen Isaiah more than irritated, and even those odd moments came and went in brief flashes. I had not only irritated him, I'd set him spinning into indignant outrage.

"So yeah. I have extra money, money I could live off if I wanted. But instead, I do what I want with it. Throw it at the city fundraisers because I love this stupid little town and its nosy people. Throw it at the station because I love those idiots like they're my real family, and I don't want them to want for anything. Throw it at charities because they're good causes, at my house because, fuck them, I deserve to live comfortably, and hell, throw it at bar nights because it would burn them up if they knew the money was going toward their homo son going to gay bars, and for sex toys, condoms, and lube."

I felt my face warm and briefly wondered what toys he'd bought over the years. I found myself once more having to shove the uncomfortable thought away before it showed on my face. That and I was getting an earful from him and...I probably deserved it.

"And now I want to use it to help you and, screw it, buy myself a few extra goodies while I'm here. I take that money because it's the only justice I'm ever going to get from my blood," Isaiah said, unwinding his arms and gesturing toward me. "So I'd appreciate it if you showed me the same courtesy I've shown you so far and not fucking judge me."

I swallowed. "Okay."

"Okay," he grunted.

What I had thought was a blunt truth poorly taken was, in fact, just blunt judgment...taken badly. In his shoes, I probably would have done the same, though maybe that was because I was used to poverty, so having extra money would be worth the indignity of being bribed. This wasn't a case of a spoiled rich kid still being funded by Mommy and Daddy. Isaiah's 'allowance' was probably a monthly reminder of what his family had done to him, and I'd gone and stuck my foot in my mouth.

At this point, I wouldn't have blamed him for telling me to go fuck myself and leave. It wasn't like there were many reasons for him to stick around, especially since it had only taken me a week before I offended him.

"Now get your ass up off that couch," he huffed, walking past me toward the front door. "We're going to the grocery store, and I'm buying."

"What?" I asked, startled.

"You heard me," he grunted as he yanked on his shoes. Even more surprising, he snatched up my tennis shoes and brought them over. "We're also buying you some sandals while we're out. That way, you can just slide them on."

"I can..." I reached down with my left hand and quickly found that maneuvering my fingers just right so I could undo the laces was more difficult than I thought. I managed it, however, getting both of my shoes on and then staring at the laces once more. Undoing the laces had been one thing, but tying them wasn't something I could manage with one hand.

My right-hand fingers were still practically useless from the full cast. "Okay...I can't."

Isaiah made a soft noise, crouching down and making quick work of the laces. "There, now c'mon."

Still a little confused at this outcome, I tried to get up. That was easier said than done, as I'd found many things lately were. I never realized just how much I used my hands and arms until I no longer could. Perhaps in a few more weeks, I'd be able to push my hand against the couch to help propel myself up, but for now, the hand was still too tender. Instead, I had to dig my elbow into the arm of the couch to push myself upward.

However, I forgot about my ankle, placing too much weight on it. Pain jolted up my leg, and my knee buckled instinctively to take the weight off my injured ankle. I pitched forward. Had it not been for Isaiah, I would have collapsed onto the floor, or worse, I would have tried to catch something with my broken arms.

"Woah," Isaiah huffed, wrapping an arm around my middle so his body took the brunt of my weight. "Bad ankle, remember?"

"Do now," I grunted. I knew he was strong, but it was still impressive that he caught and held me with little difficulty. I had about four inches on him, but I knew I had at least sixty, if not seventy pounds on him. I had always been the biggest guy in the room since pretty much the start of puberty, but even with the surprise of my collapse as a factor, Isaiah hadn't so much as flinched when he caught me.

Isaiah leaned back, and I could feel his arm around me shift slightly as he took the measure of whether or not I could stand on my own. When his eyes shifted to my face, I felt him freeze. For a moment, we stood there, faces inches from one another as he watched me. I could feel the heat of his arm against my back and the way his fingers slowly curled against my shirt as though preparing to grip it.

My heart began to hammer as I stared down into his eyes. Even in the dim light of my apartment, I could see how bright the hazel coloring was. My left hand had come to rest on his side, and I could feel his warmth and how his chest began to rise and fall quickly. There were scant inches between us, and despite the rumble of my father's voice in the back of my head, I wanted no space between us.

I watched the way Isaiah's adam's apple bobbed as he swallowed hard. "You uh, you able to stand?"

"Yeah," I said roughly, jerking my hand off his side as though it had suddenly grown barbs. "Thanks."

"No problem," he said, patting my side companionably, but I noticed he stepped away from me quickly once he was sure I could stand.

Well, now I had a strong suspicion Isaiah had some sort of feelings for me. I'd wondered when I caught him looking at me a little too long at the station, but now I was almost completely sure. Not that I minded. It wasn't like he was constantly hitting on me. Plus, it tracked that if there were women who found me attractive enough to want to sleep with me, there were bound to be guys out there who did the same.

The idea that he was attracted to me had never bothered me before. And it didn't bother me...well, maybe it did bother me a little now. I couldn't say precisely why, but the squirming in my gut wasn't *just* uncomfortable. It was something else.

"You sure you're okay? You've got a weird look on your face," Isaiah said, squinting up at me.

"I'm fine," I said quickly. "You sure you want me to go with you?"

"Yeah, I'm sure," he said, turning to grab his keys. "You

need to get out of here once in a while, and you definitely need to be walking around. Just because you can't bench-press me at the moment doesn't mean you shouldn't be getting at least some exercise."

"Yeah," I agreed, wondering what it would actually be like to try to bench-press him. I could lift more than either of us weighed, but the idea was kind of funny, and I wondered if I should tell him when I could use my arms again.

Thankfully, getting into his car proved to be easier than getting off the couch. Having at least one arm meant I could buckle myself in without trouble. However, figuring out where to put my right arm proved to be something else entirely. Eventually, I had to settle for twisting slightly so I could lay it in my lap so it wouldn't thump against the door.

Isaiah waited until I was ready before backing out of the parking spot. Despite his seemingly normal conversation earlier, I could see a shadow in his expression that hadn't been there before. I had clearly struck a nerve, and now I was beginning to suspect I knew where his thoughts went when he sometimes checked out.

"About...earlier," I began, trying to find the right words. "What just happened?"

"I didn't mean to cop a feel," he said quickly, glancing at me. "I'm not trying to come onto you."

"I-I know that," I said, a little startled. "Is that what you were thinking about?"

"A little," he said, sounding embarrassed. "Okay, I was definitely thinking about it a lot."

"Well, you caught me," I told him.

"Right. I know. I did. I just...you know." He cleared his throat.

The situation had been strange, I had to admit that much. Yet it had never once occurred to me to suspect he was doing anything but trying to help me.

"Did you..." I began and then stopped, thinking better of it.

"Considering how straightforward you are when you talk most of the time, I don't see any point in you stopping now," Isaiah said with a half smile.

"Did you...like that?"

"Catching you?"

"Are you attracted to me?"

"Okay, I take back my previous comment. There might be a point to stop being straightforward."

"Oh."

Isaiah sighed, reaching up to run his hand through his hair. "Okay, so I'm just going to put this out there. If you don't like it...well, I'm guessing you'll make that known. But yes, there *is* some attraction. And if you need me to explain why someone into guys might be into the living embodiment of masculinity, then I don't know how to help you."

"They don't all like that," I said, frowning.

"What?"

"Gay guys. It's not always about being into masculinity. Just into guys."

Isaiah glanced at me, the road, at me, and then back at the road with a laugh. "I'm getting schooled on tolerance about my own sexuality."

"No. Just saying."

"I know, but it's funny to think about. And you're right. I know a guy a few towns over who loves drag queens. But my first crush was this handyman who always came by the house when I was a kid. Big guy. Calloused hands. Arms as big as my waist at the time. It unlocked something in me and... anyway!" he said hastily, and I tried not to smile when I saw his face turning pink. "My point was that, yes, there's sexual attraction there. And yes, that moment was kinda weird. Felt a little like we should kiss. Don't ask me, my brain's weird."

I didn't think it sounded all that weird, but now I understood why the moment had felt off. It felt like we were going to kiss, so I could see why it would be weird for Isaiah, who was in the middle of admitting he was attracted to me. The only weird part left, however, was that I had felt the urge to...well, follow up on that feeling. It had been brief and disappeared quickly, but it had still been there.

Which didn't make sense. I wasn't into guys. I had always been with women and only wanted to be with women. I didn't care about whatever Isaiah or other gay guys did. That was up to them. But I wasn't—

Sissy.

Gay.

"But I'm not going to suddenly start trying to get into your pants or...whatever," Isaiah added hastily.

"So, you're attracted to me."

"Yes."

"Sexually."

"Yes. Is this you trying to understand, or are you enjoying watching me squirm from sheer embarrassment?"

"This is embarrassing?"

Isaiah glanced at me, frowning. "Seriously? Yeah, it's embarrassing. I'm admitting I have the hots for a straight guy, one I'm supposed to be trusted to help take care of."

"You *are* helping me," I pointed out.

"Well, okay, sure. But I don't want there to be any room for doubt. I'm not going to use moments like that as an excuse to touch you."

"There isn't."

"What?"

"Room. There's no room for that. Because you aren't. You're gay, not a molester."

"I...yeah, okay. I mean, yes, thank you," he said, stumbling over his words. "Sorry, I shouldn't be making it out like you're the type of person to act like that. It isn't fair to you."

"People have done it to you before," I said.

"More than once," he said with a laugh that sounded *too* light. "Comes with the territory of being gay, you know? All too often, a straight guy finds out I'm gay, and suddenly it's all, 'oh, just so long as you don't hit on me' or something like that. As if I wanted to hit on them in the first place, like I was attracted to them."

"Except this time, you are attracted to the straight guy."

"I knew it!" he yelped and, to my surprise, reached over and swatted my chest. "You *are* getting a kick out of this!"

"A little," I admitted with a laugh, rubbing the spot where he'd hit me. It hadn't been hard, but I felt the need to chase after the touch all the same.

"Dick," he grumbled, settling back in his seat and continuing to drive. Then he glanced at me and smiled. "You have a nice laugh, by the way."

"Oh," I said, unsure what else to say. It wasn't something I did often, and I couldn't recall anyone ever saying that about me.

"And a nice smile too. Not that I'm saying you should smile more, but it's a nice one."

"I don't really smile."

"You do. Or at least you have a few times. It's nice. But I'm not expecting you to suddenly become all sunshine and rainbows just because I said you have a nice smile."

"Thank you," I said simply, wondering if I might start trying to smile and laugh a bit more. Honestly, with how good Isaiah had been with me, the least I could do was smile more. "And uh, sorry."

"For what?"

"That's what I was trying to say earlier."

"I'm still a little confused."

104

"When I said something about what happened earlier. I meant me pissing you off."

Isaiah stopped the car in a parking spot, then turned to stare at me. "You weren't talking about that weird moment when I caught you?"

"No."

His face burned. "Then why did you let me talk about it!"

"I was curious."

"Ugh," Isaiah groaned, slumping forward to let his head bonk into the steering wheel. "So I made an ass out of myself for no good reason."

"You didn't."

"I did!"

I smiled as he moaned pitifully. "I don't think you did. It doesn't bother me."

Isaiah sighed heavily, turning to look up at me. "If it was anyone else, I'd accuse you of saying that to make me feel better. That's not really your style though, is it?"

"I'm not good at making people feel good," I shrugged, agreeing.

A thoughtful, almost sad expression crossed his face. "Is that so?"

I looked away, knowing that if this continued, I would get more distracted. I couldn't believe it, but I'd finally found someone I could not only talk to but who could take me off track. I wasn't sure if it counted as a superpower, but if it did, it would certainly be Isaiah's.

"You were right. I judged you," I said, staring out at the grocery store parking lot. "I shouldn't have done that. My whole life, I've always been...poor. I looked at you as just some rich kid. I thought I was telling the truth, but I was being a dick."

"A little," Isaiah said, but the gentleness in his voice told me maybe I hadn't completely pissed him off.

"You're not," I said, turning to look at him. "Just some rich kid. You're a good guy. And you're better than your family. I'm sorry they hurt you by pretending you don't exist and made you feel bad about something stupid like being gay. But I'm also not sorry."

Isaiah watched me, curious. "Why's that?"

"Because I'd rather they sent you away and paid you money to stay away instead of keeping you around and treating you like they would. They don't deserve someone like you around them. They're cunts."

Isaiah's face slowly morphed into a wide smile. "Has anyone ever told you you have a really good way with words?"

"No," I said, wondering what I'd done to deserve sarcasm.

"Well, you do. You might not be tactful, you might not always be nice, but you know how to get right to the heart of something and call it," he said, straightening up. "Even if you're not always right, you've got a unique sort of truth that I respect."

"I'm not always right," I said, unsure how to handle the rest of what he'd said.

"Correct, because you've been wrong about something else in this conversation."

"What?"

To my surprise, he reached over and gently took my fingers in his hand, giving them a light squeeze. "You made me feel good, so maybe you're better at it than you think."

Another squeeze, and he was already pulling away to open the door and let himself out. For a few heartbeats I could only stare after him, wondering just what the fluttering in my chest could mean. I was still locked in silence when I finally undid my seatbelt to follow him. Isaiah waited patiently outside the car, primed to help me if I asked, which

I wouldn't, or if I desperately needed it, but never insisting on helping.

He waited until I was out before he turned and began walking. I noticed he was walking slower than he normally did, allowing me to keep pace with my injured ankle without being too obvious.

The realization sent another flutter through my chest and...I didn't push it away right away.

ISAIAH

"You never apologized."

After just over a month of spending every day with Julian, I was used to his non-sequiturs. He was the sort of person who spent most of his waking hours in his own head. At first, that meant he would take his sweet time to savor something before he spoke, but that had started to change. More and more, he would simply blurt out something that clearly made a lot of sense in his head, as he'd been there for the entire thought process but made absolutely no sense to anyone else.

I looked up from the sizzling pan of bacon. "Context, Julian, context."

"When you chewed me out."

I thought about it and then turned to face him. "That was like…two weeks ago."

"I know."

"We talked about it already."

"I know."

I snorted softly, turning back to the pan, not at all surprised by the pattern of the conversation. I had come to see that Julian simply didn't care much about the normal ebb and flow of a conversation. Instead, he said what was on his mind, which happened a lot more often now, with no frills. Sometimes that made him a little rough around the edges, but other times, it was refreshing.

"What was I supposed to apologize about?" I called back, curious. I knew what 'chew out' he was talking about, considering it was the only one, but now I was wondering just what was going on in his head.

"Nothing."

"Um...okay."

He appeared in the doorway, filling it with his bulk. Despite my assurances that I wasn't going to be weird about the whole attraction thing, the sight of him still sent a squirm of arousal through me. In a twist of cruel fate, my telling him I found him attractive had not helped kill the attraction. In fact, that, along with his nonchalant acceptance of it, had only made it worse.

But no, I was *not* going to obsess about the tank of a man standing a few feet away, looking too damn good, and tempting me to climb him like—

"You weren't supposed to apologize," he continued cryptically but thankfully, tearing me from my thoughts.

"Well, you can officially consider me still confused," I admitted as I took the bacon out of the pan to drain on a few sheets of paper towel.

"You didn't apologize," he repeated.

I sighed, turning to face him. I looked him in the eye and shook my head. "This is making sense in *your* head. Make it make sense in mine."

I saw the frown cross his face before I turned back to the grease-filled pan, cracking a couple of eggs into it. I could tell he needed a moment to think through things, to make it make sense to someone other than him. I wasn't perfect. I couldn't read his mind and instinctively know what he meant. But I could acknowledge that he sometimes needed time to make his words make sense.

"I just…you chewed me out. Then didn't apologize. People usually apologize after they yell at someone."

"They do when it's uncalled for," I agreed, taking some grease out as I threw butter into the pan. "And you deserved to get checked. So I wasn't going to apologize."

"I liked it."

"Me yelling at you?"

"No. You not apologizing because you were right."

"Well, uh…" I wasn't sure what to say about that. As much as I'd grown more used to his eccentricities, that didn't mean I was an expert.

"You're just…nice, is all."

"And this is connected to you appreciating the fact that I didn't apologize?"

"Because it meant you're nice, but you can still stand up for yourself. I like that. It's a good combination."

Julian wasn't one to compliment casually, and I smiled at him. "Well, thank you. That's nice to hear."

"Sure," he said, shrugging his one shoulder. It amused me that the gesture was so ingrained in him that even with two broken arms, he found a way to shrug. I wondered if he'd continue to shrug with only the left shoulder after he got the full use of his arms back. "What are you doing?"

I glanced at him before turning my attention back to the pan, where I was dumping flour in while whisking it gently. "Making a base for the cheese sauce."

"I thought you were making something with bacon."

"Bacon covered mac n cheese. There will also be bread-crumbs on top."

"Oh."

"You should try it with some chopped tomatoes too. I always do."

"Really? That's a little weird."

"Why? You eat pizza, don't you? Cheese, tomato, and starch."

He leaned against the counter, staying away from me as I poured milk into the pan. "How's your friend?"

"My friend?" I asked in confusion.

"Yeah. That guy, you know, the cop. You told me a few weeks ago he was going through a hard time."

"Oh! Bennett," I exclaimed, eyeing the bechamel carefully. I nearly forgot I'd mentioned needing to visit Bennett a few weeks before. The comment had been in passing, and I hadn't thought twice about it afterward. "Yeah, I went over to his house. Turns out we had to have a little intervention."

"He okay?"

"Yeah, he's fine," I said with a snort, shaking my head. "Now his 'no longer as straight as everyone thought' boyfriend got his shit together. His baby momma, ex-wife, whatever, came back into town, and Bennett got weirdly dramatic about the whole thing. I guess they're staying together. Adam's gonna move in with him, and Adam's ex-wife is going to stay in Fairlake so they can raise the kid. At least that's the last I heard."

I honestly didn't know what to think about the whole situation. It sounded wild, and I knew I didn't have the whole story. Personally, I wasn't all that sold on the idea of dating a formerly straight man, but this was the happiest I'd ever seen Bennett. Which was pretty impressive since Bennett, by his very nature, was one of the perkiest people I knew. So as long as he was happy, and Adam didn't suddenly decide his little bit of fun was over, I was more than ready to be happy for my friend.

"Wait," Julian said slowly, pulling me out of his thoughts. "This Adam guy…is straight?"

"Uh," I grimaced, pouring the cheese into the mix and beginning to fold it in slowly. "Well, that's…complicated."

"Is it?"

"Well, he spent his whole life being straight. Then he came back here after living in Boston for years and reconnected with Bennett."

"They were friends?"

I snorted, glancing at him with a small smile. "They were the *best* of friends. Like, attached at the hip, where one was, the other was sure to be. Like, they were *that* quintessential bromance to end all bromances. Then Adam left. Then he came back. Now it's a bromance without the bro part."

"But I thought he was straight?"

"Yeah, so did everyone else, including Adam and Bennett. I guess he learned new things about himself, including a love of dick," I said with a chuckle. "Huh, I wonder which one tops and which one bottoms? Pfft, knowing how buddy-buddy those two get, they probably decide over matches of Tekken or something."

It was only as I finished rambling that I realized Julian had grown quiet, or the very Julian-specific quiet I'd started to recognize. True, even though he was talking more than ever, he was still quiet. Yet I had learned there was a specific type where he wasn't just being quiet but was actively thinking about something.

I glanced at him as I grabbed the pot of pasta and carried it over to the sink to drain it. "You alright?"

"I've never heard of that," he muttered. "Just…turning sexualities like that."

I laughed softly, shaking the strainer a little more before dumping the pasta into the cheese sauce. "It's not 'turning' sexuality, not really."

"Then what is it?"

"Well, like I said earlier, it's complicated."

"But you understand it?"

"A little," I said, glancing at him and smiling gently while I mixed the pasta. "No offense, but you're like...purely straight, right?"

"Right," he said quickly.

"Well, I get it a little better than you because I've struggled with my sexuality. Sure, things are a lot better for gay people, but there's still issues, and there were a lot more when I was a kid and had to work my way through things. Suddenly here I am, clearly thinking and feeling things I'm not 'supposed' to be feeling, surrounded by people who aren't going through the same thing," I said. "I mean, some people, like Bennett, were lucky in that regard. His family couldn't care less who he's attracted to, so long as he's happy. He also had his best friend who, for a while, simply didn't care and wanted to be Bennett's friend no matter what, and Adam's family, who are like a second one to Bennett, were just as accepting."

Julian hunched forward. "But not you."

I laughed softly. "Yeah, not me. My family weren't open about the fact that they're homophobic, but there were more than enough hints for me to grow up 'knowing' my feelings were wrong. So, it didn't come as a terrible shock when my parents reacted badly when they found me with another boy."

"You...were caught?" Julian asked slowly, his tone strange enough to earn a curious look from me.

"Yeah," I said with another laugh. "Friend of the family was visiting us for...some reason. I don't know. I was fifteen and couldn't care less about business shit. But they had a kid about my age, cute. Grew up cute too. Oliver and I weren't doing much, just making out and above the clothes touching, but we got caught all the same. My parents lost their minds, I was in deep trouble, and that family retreated back to Nevada and haven't been back since. Bonus though, Oliver grew up not only handsome, but from what I've seen, his family doesn't have the same hang-ups about him being gay, been with the same guy for about five years now."

Julian's brow furrowed, and I thought what I saw wasn't just frustration but confusion. "Why do you do that?"

"Do what?" I asked, grabbing the pan and setting it down to pour in the mac n cheese.

"The stuff with your family bothers you. Enough for you to get worked up when they come up," he said, and a glance told me he was watching my face closely. "Why do you laugh about it other times?"

"Well, that's less complicated," I said with a laugh, smoothing the surface of the mac n cheese so it would cook evenly. "Fact is, life isn't always great, and my life hasn't always been kind to me. But when things suck, or I'm feeling a little hurt, there are only a few choices. I can get mad about it, I can get depressed, or I can learn to find the humor in it."

"I don't see the humor in it."

"I'm sure a lot of people don't. But it makes me feel better to laugh. And if you ask me, the world needs less crying and more laughter. Or...maybe that's just a good excuse for avoiding dealing with my problems by laughing them off. It's kind of a toss-up which one it is." I shoved the pan into the oven and set the timer before turning around to find Julian watching me closely. "What?"

He shrugged again. "I guess we all have our ways of dealing with things. I never understood why people laughed and smiled when it seemed like they shouldn't."

"What's your coping mechanism?" I asked, crossing my arms around my middle and leaning back against the stove.

His lips thinned, and I wondered if I was pushing too deep into his private business. I appreciated how much he had been trying to open up, but it was obvious he wasn't used to doing it. The last thing I wanted to do was make him more uncomfortable with it than he already was.

"I don't...talk," he finally said.

"I noticed," I said with a small smile.

He glanced up and returned the expression. "I don't talk about things. I just keep it in my head and don't tell other people about it. Makes things easier."

"Easier, how?"

"Easier because...people don't have to deal with my stuff. I don't have to deal with...explaining things."

I thought about his story about the coworker he'd punched and the reaction of everyone around him. I thought about the way everyone else at the station treated him alright, but with barely veiled suspicion. I thought about the fact that he was only at our station because someone had asked a favor, and he had spent his time believing he'd been shunted aside, made someone else's problem.

"People probably don't believe you very much, do they?" I asked softly.

His eyes flickered to my face, and I could see the surprise written into his features. Then, after a few heartbeats, he looked down at the ground. "No."

My shoulders slumped at the soft admission. "Not even your family?"

It was fascinating and unnerving how obvious it was when the shutters came down in his eyes. For a brief moment, I could actually see the pain and frustration. The moment I brought up his family, however, I could see him lockdown, retreating into his shell. Now there was only Julian, the grumpy, quiet man I'd known from day one.

"You didn't finish telling me why Adam doesn't confuse you," he said, flat gaze on the fridge rather than me.

Right, mental note, don't mention his family. I suppose that should have been obvious. I'd already seen how little he talked about them. I knew a few things, like he had a mom he helped take care of and a younger brother going to school. His father was *never* mentioned, not even in the most benign and casual sense, which spoke volumes about Julian's past. Other than that, I knew he talked to his mom on the phone occasionally, but never when I was in the apartment.

"Well, uh," I said, trying to remember what I'd been saying before we got sidetracked by coping mechanisms. "I guess my point was, I get not being sure about your sexuality. Maybe there was a time when Adam questioned himself and pushed it away, putting more weight on the 'straight' side of his bisexuality."

"Is he bi?"

"I mean, he's currently experiencing a happy romantic and sexual relationship with a guy, so clearly, he's a little bi. Maybe just enough to be attracted to Bennett, using the emotional relationship they already had to bridge the gap. I don't know the exact reason, but whatever it is, they're doing their thing."

Julian turned his gaze up toward the ceiling thoughtfully. "I just...it seems weird that it was so easy for him."

"Who said it was easy? All we can see is that they're together and happy. No one but Adam, and probably Bennett, got to see what went on in Adam's head," I said with a shrug, opening the fridge to grab a couple of beers. I opened both and handed one to Julian, who took it carefully with his left hand. He'd had a few weeks to adjust, but I could see he was still clumsy using his left hand.

"Sure," Julian said, taking a drink. "He just...it makes sense that you...struggled. You were surrounded by people who made you feel bad about it. I don't get how he couldn't know that he would have been alright to be openly bi, especially with the way everyone reacted about Bennett."

It was my turn to shrug. "Brains are weird things, and

people are even weirder. Sometimes we lie to ourselves and other people about ridiculous stuff. And sometimes, it feels like our brains keep things hidden from us, even though they're *our* brains. So maybe he didn't know, or maybe he did on some level but kept unconsciously pushing it down, afraid of what it would mean."

His eyes flicked to me, holding for a few heartbeats before he looked away and took a deep drink of his beer, downing nearly half of it. I raised a brow at the reaction but said nothing, unwilling to guess what was going through his head.

The timer went off, and I turned around to pull the mac n cheese out. I grabbed the bowl of breadcrumbs and coated the top, and then crumbled the bacon over the top before placing it back in.

"'Scuse me," I said to Julian, pointing to the counter behind him where the cutting board I'd brought sat, with a couple of tomatoes on it.

He grunted, shuffling out of my way, and after a moment's hesitation, disappeared back into the living room. He would either drop himself in front of the TV or pick up his phone and scroll for hours. I rarely paid attention to what he did on his phone, but I couldn't help but be curious about what he found so fascinating.

Other than his phone, the TV, and his hobby with electronics, I wasn't sure what else he did while he was home. Then again, he was probably better at focusing on a single task than I had ever been, so I couldn't question it too much. Honestly, there was something impressive about how he could simply focus on one task for long periods without any sign of restlessness.

When the timer went off again, I turned around to grab the pan from the oven and set it atop the stove. I finished chopping the tomatoes and then wiped things down behind me.

"Where'd you learn to cook?" Julian asked, making me jump out of my skin.

"Goddamn, you're so quiet," I hissed, tossing an oven mitt at him.

It hit his chest and flopped uselessly to the ground. His expression didn't change, but his eyes glittered with what I thought was silent laughter. "Sorry."

"Somehow, I don't believe you," I snorted, snatching the mitt up before scooping out servings for us. "It was, uh, a bit of TV, but a lot of internet.

Well, it was either that or live off frozen meals and sandwiches for the rest of my life. My family had left Fairlake behind when I was nineteen, and by that time, I'd already been on my own for almost a year. I could have afforded to have premade meals brought to me or get a cook, but I had been bound and determined to learn. I'd wasted more food than I wanted to think about, but I had learned the basics and expanded ever since.

"Are you alright?" I asked, noticing he'd managed to grab another beer while he was in the kitchen. They were twist-offs, but there was a bottle opener on the wall next to the doorway, which would work just as well. "I've noticed you standing and sitting funny."

Julian's left shoulder rose and fell in sharp motions. "My bed sucks. Sleeping with these casts sucks."

That I could believe. "Forced to sleep on your back?"

"Yeah. Not used to it."

"Back hurts, huh?"

"Yeah," he said, shrugging again as he scooped food into his mouth. "This is really good."

"Thanks," I said brightly, pausing long enough to swallow a bite. "I might be able to help with your back."

"I don't want any pills," he said without looking at me.

"And I'm not going to offer you any," I said with a

chuckle. "But I could probably dig deep and massage some of those muscles loose."

He paused chewing, glanced at me, then swallowed. "You know how to massage?"

"Uh, yeah," I said, scratching my neck nervously. "I had a guy I was dating once express an interest in being massaged. I thought he meant the normal type of massage because who wouldn't want to have a partner who could relax your muscles, right? Well, he meant the sensual kind, and I learned the practical kind. Whoops."

Of course, he and I had discovered that *any* massage could be sensual if you're willing to make it so. I was quite aware of just how strange an offer it was. Most people tended to hear 'massage' and associated it with sexual intimacy that didn't *have* to be there.

I shrugged, trying to hide my nervousness. "I just thought it might help a little. I'm sure your back is knotted to hell and back right now."

"Probably," he said slowly, still watching me closely. "Were you...any good at it?"

"I got the job done," I said, knowing I was being cryptic. Finally, I winced. "Look, I know it's kind of a weird offer, but it's not...not me being creepy or sexual. Massages don't have to be weird or sexual. They can just help when your muscles are messed up."

"I know you're not," he said quietly, looking away. If it weren't for the fact that Julian wasn't the sort to say anything without a good reason, I would have doubted his words from that reaction alone. "But...sure, maybe we can try."

"Uh, after we eat?" I offered, a little surprised. In truth, I'd expected Julian to say no based on the physical contact aspect alone. The few times I had unthinkingly touched him out of friendliness, there had always been confusion about him afterward.

119

"Sure," he said, turning his attention back to the TV and taking a big drink of his beer.

There was honestly no way in hell he would follow through on the idea. Not only was he the sort who seemed uncomfortable with the idea of being touched, but there weren't too many straight guys I knew who were down for being massaged by another guy, even a professional, *especially* when I'd already let him know I was attracted to him.

Admittedly there was a good reason for being attracted to him. As I wasn't exactly a small guy, I couldn't very well seek out big guys for my love of size difference easily, yet Julian managed to fulfill that desire. Plus, now I realized he didn't hate everyone, it was easy to be charmed by his quiet gruffness and the steadiness with which he went about everything.

Grimacing, I forced another bite of the food into my mouth. No, I could not afford to sit around and start... obsessing. I had managed to avoid forming any attachment to a straight guy in the past, at least anything past 'yeah, I'd hit that if it were possible.' I wasn't going to break that streak just because the hot straight guy in question also showed more of himself to me than who knew how many people before me.

Plus, doing so felt like a violation. Like feeding my attraction was somehow taking his trust in me and, well, not quite using it against him, but it felt close to it. Julian didn't trust easily, and I was slowly being given little pieces at a time. A *friend* is what he needed right now, and not one who drooled over his tree trunk thick biceps and thighs that could squash my head like a—

I cleared my throat roughly, suddenly realizing my underwear was growing tight. If I could have got away with it, I would have got up to leave the room. Sadly, I had grown comfortable spending my off hours at Julian's apartment and was wearing loose pants. Even with my underwear, I was sure I would give away my physical condition. And while Julian wasn't going to be checking out a guy's junk anytime soon, he was pretty attentive to things around him.

"Done?" he grunted, making me look at him.

I looked down at my bowl and saw it was empty. "Oh, yeah."

"Here," he said, hooking his fingers around the lip, brushing against my knuckles before pulling it toward him. I tried to ignore the absurd flash of arousal that he managed to pick up and hold the heavy ceramic bowl with only two fingers.

His ankle had finally recovered, so he was far more steady. Julian hadn't said anything, but I'd noticed he could put more weight on his left arm. He probably still had another month or so before the cast came off, but at least he wasn't quite as fragile. There was absolutely no hope of getting any use out of his right arm, but at least he could do more than before.

Taking a deep breath, I pushed myself up from the chair and checked myself out. Once I was sure I wasn't going to walk in, boner on display, I entered the kitchen as he closed the freezer door. I glanced around to find another open bottle of beer on the counter, but nothing else to signify what he was digging around in the freezer for.

"Oh," he grunted, opening the fridge to grab a beer, open it, and hand it to me.

"Thanks," I said, taking a drink and stepping around him. It was only then when I had to walk past him, that I caught the brief but distinct smell of liquor. I remembered a bottle of whiskey in the freezer that had gone untouched since I'd seen it on my first visit. Apparently, Julian was in a pretty good mood if he felt it was safe to hit the harder stuff.

At least, I hoped it was a sign of a good mood.

Well, good mood or bad mood, I decided to keep my observation to myself. He was a full-grown man, and if he wanted to have an extra shot or two of liquor on top of his beer, I wasn't going to get in his way. And I suppose I was curious what someone like Julian was like once they had a little extra alcohol in their system.

"Shit," he grunted, opening the freezer and dropping the bottle on the counter. I couldn't remember how much had been in there the last time I paid attention, but it looked like he'd taken more than a single shot. "Want some? Probably not your thing, but—"

"Why? Because it's whiskey, and I'm gay?" I asked with a chuckle.

"Because it's cheap."

More curious than anything, I glanced at him. "So, are you assuming that because I've had all this money, I've never suffered through cheap liquor?"

His brow furrowed, and I tried to follow the emotions before they disappeared. There was wariness there, as well as confusion. I couldn't be sure, but he was trying to decide the right answer to the question.

"There's no trap in the question," I told him lightly, dropping the bowls onto the counter next to the sink to wash properly later. "I just like trying to figure out what's going on in your head. To see how you work."

"That's…what I meant. Yeah." He grunted, but I could see from the way his fingers wrapped tightly around the neck of the bottle he was still bracing himself.

I snorted, grabbing the bottle and gently tugging it out of his hold. "Well, you'd be absolutely correct. But, truth be told, I didn't like the idea of making myself suffer through cheap food or drink…well, *bad* cheap food and drink."

"A philanthropic epicure," he said with a small smile while I unspun the top of the liquor bottle.

That took me off guard, and I looked at him in surprise for a few seconds before chuckling. "I guess that's one way of putting it."

"Did I say something wrong?"

"Well, I wouldn't call myself philanthropic," I began, opening up the cabinet to find one dusty shot glass in the back. "But it was, uh, the phrasing you used."

"What's wrong with it?" he asked, then his eyes shifted to the shot glass. "You can just wipe the mouth of the bottle off."

"First off, I am accepting your hospitable offer to partake in your private store of liquor, but that does *not* mean I'm going to drink out of the bottle like some half-feral animal," I told him with a wink as I dropped the shot glass onto the counter, pouring a shot. "And secondly, there was nothing wrong with it. I told you that. It's just not how you normally talk. It took me by surprise."

"Oh," he said, and against all logic and to my total surprise, he looked down bashfully. A moment later he glanced at the bottle. "I've had a bit of that already."

"And it got you talking more openly than before," I noted, finger rubbing gentle, slow circles against the still full shot glass.

"My own personal pebbles."

I hesitated to take the shot. "Your what?"

Inexplicably, he continued to look embarrassed. "Uh, Demosthenes. Politician in Greece. Plutarch once said that he managed to get over his stutter by shoving pebbles into his mouth to help him speak clearer."

"Did he?" I asked in mild surprise, finally tipping the shot back. The taste was rougher than I would have preferred, but it went down smooth enough, only lighting up with intense heat once it hit my stomach. "So, the alcohol is your pebbles to remedy you not showing that you sit around reading all day?"

It had been an intuitive stab in the dark, but the surprise on his face told me I was spot on. "I...yeah. A lot of old stuff mostly. Don't really like anything written in the past fifty years."

"History and philosophy?"

"Fiction too. But yeah, mostly."

"And yet you like old westerns and cheesy 80s action flicks."

Julian smiled a little at that. "I didn't think you paid attention to what I do on my phone."

"I didn't and don't. I don't wanna pry," I admitted, deciding to pour another shot. "But it occurred to me that even formally educated people wouldn't use epicure. That's the kind of thing writers, or people who read a lot, use. Though I guess they're kind of the same thing."

"Readers aren't always writers," he said, pointing at himself. "But I'd bet all writers are readers."

"True, true," I said, taking the next shot and wincing. I could already feel a lightness in my limbs, and I checked the bottle to find out it was 100 proof. "A bit like a composer having never experienced music in their life. Possible, but not a good idea."

Julian grinned, taking the bottle and drinking as much, if not more, than my two shots. "I used to get books like that out of the library all the time. Started with Greek mythology, but then I started learning their history."

"War stuff?" I guessed.

"Some," he said with a shrug. "But just...their government. Their history. The rise and fall of eras, how they formed, how they split. How they became the Romans. The Romans defined modern civilization. Even after they fell, what was left, what was remembered, shaped the modern world into the way it is now."

"Wasn't China a massive civilization for like…millennia?" I asked, trying to remember the world history my teacher had attempted to bury in my skull. Not much of it had taken, but bless them, they had tried.

"Yeah," Julian said, eyes glittering. "But they were in the east and pretty isolationist."

"Well, that's certainly changed," I noted, fascinated by this change in him. The former taciturn and quiet man was almost entirely replaced by this rapid-talking, enthusiastic man. "In the modern-day anyway."

"That's new, though," he told me, holding up his hand in a gesture I didn't understand. "Japan is more with the modern world because of World War Two. They only got into that war in the first place because of ancient viewpoints dragging them into trouble. After that, they decided things needed to change if their people were going to survive."

I sorely wished I had enough knowledge to be able to keep up with him right now. His enthusiasm was downright infectious, and at the very least, I wanted to keep him talking. "And all of this came from the way things were back in Roman days?"

"Well, no. Yes, but no. The Roman Empire changed the landscape of practically everything in the Western world."

"Really? I'm now getting a clear picture of this little redhead kid, sitting in the middle of his room, maps all over the place."

"They were all in a book, but you're not wrong. I used to study it forever until my dad saw me one time and—"

The effect was instantaneous. It wasn't just shutters coming down. I watched the lights switch off in his eyes, and his expression hardened. I didn't know if it was the memory that had come back to him or the mention of his father.

Whatever it was, the exuberant Julian was gone, replaced by hard-faced mimicry.

"Yeah, I read a lot. It's mostly boring history stuff," he said with a shrug, grabbing the beer and taking a sip.

"That…wasn't very boring sounding to me."

"Do you know history?"

"No, not really," I had to admit.

"Because you find it boring," he said, turning around to walk away.

"Well, it didn't sound boring when you were explaining it to me," I said, a little frustrated. I desperately wanted the Julian I'd just gotten a peek of to come back and show his face again. I would be willing to place all my allowances for five years to bet that who I had just seen was the real Julian.

Julian hesitated a moment before shrugging and disappearing into the living room. I sighed heavily, my hands dropping to my side as I stared at where he'd just been standing.

I would bet another five years of those same allowances that he'd been taught that his interests were ridiculous, stupid, or, as he said it, boring. His infectious enthusiasm for a topic had been squashed, and not just once. That was the reaction of someone repeatedly and mercilessly stepped on. It was hard to picture someone as big and tough as him being treated poorly, but…everyone was a kid once.

Sighing, I grabbed the beer bottle and prepared to enter the living room. I didn't know if it was smart or not, but I wanted him to understand that I *did* want to hear what he had to say. Maybe I wouldn't always understand what he was talking about, and sometimes I'd be lost, but I still wanted to hear it.

Yet instead of walking in to start my speech, I stopped immediately as I found him pulling his shirt up over his head. It took him a moment to get it over his whole arm cast, but that just meant I was granted the full display of his back. My mouth went dry as I stared at miles of skin stretched over hard muscle. Even in the low light of the living room lamp, I could see freckles dotting the skin of his shoulders and upper back, and I briefly wondered what it would be like to run my fingers...or lips over them, connecting them.

"W-what are you doing?" I managed to get out, only slightly stumbling over my words.

He glanced at me in confusion. "You said you wanted to try rubbing me."

"Phrasing," I muttered, thinking that wouldn't help my situation.

"What?"

"I'm going to get some lotion," I said quickly. "Otherwise, it's just going to be a bunch of skin-on-skin friction."

"Is skin-on-skin friction a bad thing?" he asked, raising a brow.

"Uh, for this particular thing, yes," I said and then darted out of sight before something else was said that went straight into the gutter part of my brain. Considering how often I'd been coming over, I'd brought a few of my own things to keep if I needed them. I inevitably returned to my own house to sleep; otherwise, if I wasn't working or sleeping, I was here, so it was good to have my own stuff.

That meant using the lotion I'd brought over the week before. Working at the station meant a lot of scrubbing, cleaning, and water all over the place. Chapping and peeling skin wasn't as bad during the summer, but as the weather turned toward autumn and winter, lotion treatments were necessary.

"What the hell?" I muttered as I picked up the bottle and gave it a shake. I spun the bottle open to find there was nothing in the bottom of it. "Well, *shit*."

"What?" Julian called from the other room.

"Uh, nothing!" I called back, grabbing my toiletry bag to see if I had a small sample bottle. Only to find...lube. "Uh... well, that—" I returned and looked at him on the couch. "I don't have lotion."

"Oh," he said, his brow furrowing.

"But," I said with a wince, holding up the bottle. "I have this. This would work if you're okay with it."

"What is that?"

"Lube."

"Oh for—"

"The massage," I insisted, eyes going wide.

The corner of his lips twitched. "Okay."

"This would probably be easier if I had more room to work."

Julian looked around and shrugged. "We can use my bed. It's not big. But it's bigger."

"Yeah, sure," I said faintly, trying to keep my voice light as he pushed himself upright.

"Do you need light?" he asked as we stepped into the bedroom.

"No," I said quietly, thinking it was probably better to see as little as possible. I was still reeling, not just from the absolute bait that had been seeing him on display but from the fact that he was actually going through with this. I was almost sure he would let the topic go unmentioned again.

"Alright," he grunted, kneeling on the bed. I waited while he used his left arm to balance himself as he stretched out face down. I could see how this would be an awkward position to sleep in. His right arm was pretty much stuck at an angle, and it was probably easier to sleep on his back with the arm resting against his hip. "Show me what you got."

Lord help me, I could actually hear the looseness in his voice from the liquor settling in. He might not have been the bouncy, free man I'd seen in the kitchen, but he was looser than usual. Now all I could do was hope my body didn't decide to betray me while I was trying to do this one thing that was supposed to be an innocent favor.

With a silent prayer, I took a deep breath and stepped forward.

JULIAN

Turning my head, I watched him approach though I couldn't make out his features in the dark. Very little light from the living room leaked into the room, and I had the curtains drawn on the windows. With the warmth of the liquor floating through me, it would have been relaxing, laying there in the dimness with a little heat in my gut.

Except I wasn't alone, and my back felt like someone was constantly tweaking and twisting the muscles.

I was surprised when his hands finally touched my skin, slick but warm. Apparently, Isaiah had thought ahead and warmed the lube. It occurred to me then that I probably should have asked if I needed to be shirtless. It was possible to do this with a shirt on, but as far as I knew, this was how things were done. Isaiah hadn't seemed to mind, except I hadn't given him a warning, and he'd been slightly surprised.

Then again, if I walked into a room and found someone taking their shirt off for no good reason, I probably wouldn't have been any less surprised. The difference was Isaiah tended to wear his emotions on his face, much like his heart lived on his sleeve. Once, I might have found it confusing and maybe a little annoying, but Isaiah could pull it off and still be endearing.

"Harder or softer?" he asked as his fingers worked across my skin.

"Harder," I said without hesitation. Truth be told, it *had* felt like he was holding himself back unnecessarily. His fingers were moving quickly, but that made sense, considering he was using lube. It was an odd choice, but after a few minutes, I had to admit it was pretty effective.

"Sure," he said softly, fingers digging in deeper.

There was a twinge of pain, but a zing of odd pleasure quickly replaced it as he found something in my back that both loved and hated the attention. I had never had a massage, professional or amateur, so I wasn't sure how this was supposed to feel, though I suspected it was a good feeling.

"You're going to ask me to go harder, aren't you?" he asked after a few minutes.

"I was thinking about it," I admitted. The sensation was pleasant, his fingers working into my skin and muscle, but I felt like there had to be more to it than just a few zings and tingles.

"Uh, okay, well—"

I glanced over my shoulder, frowning. "If you can't, that's—"

"Well, no, I definitely can, but I need more leverage," he said with a light laugh that made me want to smile. "But this isn't exactly what I would call a massage table, so it, uh—"

"What?" I asked, confused as to what he needed. It wasn't like anything in the apartment could be used as a fill-in.

"I need to...straddle you, so I have the right angle and leverage to go harder," he said quietly.

Now I understood why he was so awkward about the whole thing. That would mean he would probably be sitting on my thighs or even my ass. It would be a very…intimate position. Considering what we'd already talked about, I understood why he was acting so strangely. Even then, it still made me frown because I knew he wasn't taking advantage of anything. If I had genuinely suspected that Isaiah had the slightest inclination to take advantage of me, I wouldn't have let the massage start in the first place.

Even if the idea of him straddling me was…odd sounding.

"Okay," I said instead because the last thing I needed was to scare him off more than he already was. I was enjoying this, and I was enjoying that it was Isaiah doing it. I didn't usually trust anyone to touch me for anything other than professional reasons, so feeling like I could trust someone for something as intimate, if innocent, as this was enough for me.

"S-sure," he muttered, and there was a long enough stretch of nothing that I wondered if I might have to say something. Isaiah had become pretty good at sensing what was going on with me in my silence, but he didn't seem to do as well when silence met *his* wants.

Then I felt the bed shift, heard it creak, and felt the soft fabric of his pants against the back of my leg before he got himself comfortable. I felt his weight on the back of my thighs, and I took a moment to evaluate the sensation. It was a little strange since I knew it was Isaiah, but I found it neither uncomfortable nor painful. He was probably balancing himself, so the worst of his weight was on his curled legs, but I didn't mind him there.

His fingers pressed into my lower back with far more pressure than before. It felt like they were digging directly into the heart of the tight muscles of my back and ripping them out. The muscles in question screamed in protest even as a wave of pleasure wrapped itself around them. There was no stopping the low groan as his thumbs continued to dig in, drawing alternating waves of pleasure and pain.

"Too much?" he asked, fingers stopping.

"Fuck no," I muttered. I had no idea how the hell his fingers managed to cause pain that made me want to beg him never to stop. It was unlike anything I'd ever felt before, and it made me wonder if maybe those pain-loving people had the right idea.

Then he eased up, using his fingers in tandem as if he were gently kneading bread. It didn't have quite the same zing as the deep tissue grinding he'd done before, but it worked as a contrast in intensity and sensation. It was simply relaxing, a low-level thrum of gentle pleasure that made my shoulder ease up. For someone who'd acted like they weren't confident in what they offered, he definitely knew what he was doing.

"Julian?"

"Mhm?"

"I know this is a touchy subject for you and all, but I get the feeling that you, uh, had a pretty shitty childhood and… yep, there's your back going rock tight. Let me finish before you get ready for a fight, will ya? I'm working hard back here."

That made me snort, and I tried to loosen up a little. "I guess you could say that. I probably haven't been subtle."

"Not really. Even just casually mentioning your dad does that. But usually, my fingers aren't pressed against your muscles when it happens."

"Sorry."

"No, I'm touching the touchy button. I'm not surprised you're being touchy."

"While literally being touched."

His fingers stopped, and Isaiah snorted roughly. "I love those little moments where I see you have a sense of humor. I would have thought it was dry, but it's actually a little goofy, isn't it?"

I shrugged as he dragged his fingers down my back on each side of my spine, sending chills through me. "Never bothered to find out."

There was a pause before Isaiah spoke again. "He wasn't a very good person, was he?"

I knew who he meant. "No."

"It's…good that you know that. I've known people with bad parents who don't realize it."

"Yeah."

"But I've also known people who knew a parent was bad and continued taking everything they said and did like it was gospel. Still blamed themselves for it, took all their insults, the shit they did, and took it to heart, even years later."

I closed my eyes, mentally fading for a moment. I was eight years old again. One minute I was giggling, leaning forward to kiss my best friend on the corner of the mouth. I didn't know why, it just felt like the right thing to do at the time. The next thing I knew, there was my old man, and all my giggles and the bubbly feeling in my chest were gone. Instead, I stood there, hands clenched into fists at my side.

He'd dragged the boy out of my room, tossing him out of our ramshackle trailer, and I never saw him again. I'd known what was coming, and I stood there, staring up into his face. Looking back, I could see now that I was staring into a face that was eerily like my own. The same strong, almost square jaw, the slightly too long nose, the thick brows, the same bright green eyes and brilliantly red hair. Except, unlike him, my nose didn't have little rivers of broken blood vessels, and my eyes weren't thick with bags or bloodshot.

"I ain't havin' no sissy for a son!"

His bellow had rolled over me and might have knocked me back if his palm against my cheek hadn't done it first. It was one of the worst times he'd taken his hands to me. He'd split my lip twice and my brow as well, broke my nose and dragged me to my closet until the next day. After that, he'd insisted I take boxing lessons to make sure I "became a man."

Back in the present, I let out a low sigh. "Are you talking about me or you?"

Isaiah's fingers twitched against my back, and I briefly wondered if I'd gone too far until he chuckled. "I sometimes forget how insightful you are. But I guess I was always warned about the quiet ones."

"I thought that was about sex."

"Yeah, that too, I guess."

The thoughts connected in my head, and I wondered what it would have been like if I'd met Isaiah long before this. Isaiah reminded me a little of that boy whose name I couldn't remember. But I could remember his bright eyes and how he laughed, even with a black eye or the occasional split lip. He had been my best friend, and while I couldn't remember his name, I could remember how bright his smile was.

"He's dead," I told Isaiah. "No one else knows. Not my mom. Not my brother."

"When?"

"He died about five years ago. I found out two years ago."

"Why don't they know?"

"It would break my mom…more than she already is. And my brother was too young, he didn't know. He just…" I closed my eyes. He blamed me, and though she had never said it outright, my mother did too. Shortly after the kissing incident, he had found his little fling and decided family life wasn't for him, "didn't understand."

"What did you do?" Isaiah asked, his fingers flaring to rub down my sides, and I sighed. The sensations alternated between light and easy, dancing and tingling, and the occasional crashing spike of pain and pleasure. Whatever Isaiah was doing, I wasn't sure if it was doing the job, but my whole body was starting to feel good.

"Asshole changed his name. Probably to avoid any child support demands," I said, hardly able to summon the anger I'd felt back then. "I found his gravestone, though. Went all the way out to Ohio to find it. Tiny little plot. Not even a quote on it. Guess he died alone."

"And?"

"And I sat there for a couple of hours. Had me a bottle of Maker's Mark, decided to treat myself to decent whiskey for once. Had a little talk with him. Told him about things. Then I figured there was only one way to cover everything I felt."

His fingers stilled on my back. "What?"

"I pissed on his grave. Had a lot stored up from all that drinking, and considering how much he liked to drink, it only seemed fair."

I heard Isaiah's breath catch, and I tensed, waiting for the inevitable. That detail had been one of the biggest reasons I hadn't told anyone. All too often, people who should have understood still condemned me for doing something like that. Either because he was my dad and it was disrespectful toward the dead or for other reasons.

I practically jumped out of my skin as Isaiah burst out laughing. Shocked, I turned my head around to see him bent over as he laughed into his lap.

"Isaiah?" I asked slowly, wondering if I'd somehow managed to break him psychologically.

"Th-that's brilliant!" Isaiah wheezed. "God, you drank a bunch of liquor and pissed on his grave. I hope he was thirsty. Though, probably a good thing you didn't tell your family about that."

"You...don't even know if he deserved it," I said slowly. "That was my dad."

"I know what it means to have shitty parents who treat

you like dirt," he said with a sudden savagery I'd never heard in his voice before. Gone was the lighthearted man who trod carefully around people's feelings and smiled when I knew he should be showing pain. Now his voice was all teeth and claws. "And I also know what I saw. What happened in your kitchen. So yeah, if that was because of him, then piss away, Julian, it's the least he deserves."

I hesitated. "What did you see?"

"What I saw," His fingers began rubbing again, and I relaxed despite how strange this conversation was, "was a man who found something he was passionate about. I watched you light up as you talked about something *you* cared about. But the minute you were reminded of your dad, you immediately shot yourself down, said that the whole thing was boring, and shut down."

"Oh."

"Yeah, oh. And one thing you should know."

I opened my eyes. "What?"

His hands went flat against my back, and I felt his weight bear down on me. It wasn't until I felt his breath against the back of my neck that I realized he was leaning closer, his voice low. "I *want* to hear what you have to say. Even if it might sometimes hurt my feelings or even piss me off, I want to hear it, got it? You've got a lot locked up in that head, and from what I've seen, I'm enjoying what I see."

"S-sure," I said, not sure what else to say. However, it seemed to content him, and I felt him pull away to resume work on my back.

"Good," he said, voice light and carefree once more.

I, however, was still feeling the tingle of his breath on the back of my neck and could still feel the intensity of his voice. The sheer earnestness and insistence had been apparent, but more relevant was the feeling of heat it left behind. It had gone from my neck and ears to slowly drip down into my stomach, becoming a tight curl of heat.

No, not heat, *want.*

Suddenly I was incredibly aware of the weight on my thighs. I could practically feel the whorls of his fingertips as he worked them into my back, seeking out muscles and kneading them into submission. I could feel how his thighs tightened when he tried to work into a deeper muscle. And if I paid attention, I would swear there was more pressure on my thighs than before when he leaned forward.

"Shoulders?" I asked without thinking, feeling my face burn at the suggestion.

"Uh." And I swore I heard him swallow hard. "Sure. Focus on my fingers. That way you can tell me where it feels good and where not."

I almost believed that was the reason until he was forced to lean forward. It meant more weight on his knees and legs, but it also meant my suspicions were confirmed. My breath stopped as I felt the hard press of something first brush along my thigh and then between my ass.

At that moment, I learned that not only was Isaiah hard and doing quite well at hiding it, but Isaiah…was not a small man. Inexplicably that realization sent a jolt of under-standing and anticipation through me just in time for his fingers to clamp around my shoulder muscles. It hurt worse than any other part of the massage, but somehow I felt the sensation of his dick pressing on my ass morph into pleasure.

"Fuck," I groaned, unable to help myself. Only for the sound to choke off when I felt his hips *and* dick twitch.

Worse yet, I heard the way Isaiah's breath caught as his fingers stilled on my neck. He wasn't in a position to draw away from me. In fact, he held himself still, the press of his dick against the bottom of my ass. For a brief moment, we were both unmoving as he sat there, and the sensible part of my brain tried to remind me he was probably panicking and attempting to get control of himself.

However, this new part of me reminded me that if Isaiah was trying to get control of himself, that meant there was something to get control of in the first place. Not that it should have been a terrible surprise since he *had* admitted he was attracted to me. Then again, I would have expected that to come in the form of him...well, him not grinding on my ass.

Then again, what did I know about the dynamics of sex between guys? All I knew was that my partially drunk, relaxed, and emotional brain was fixating on the fact that a guy's dick was hard, both for me and on me. Particularly that it was *Isaiah's* dick.

Isaiah cleared his throat roughly before he backed up enough to continue rubbing my shoulders. There wasn't enough space for him to entirely back his hips off, so I could still feel the occasional brush of his dick against my ass, but it was no longer pressing against me.

An idea bubbled up in my head, bringing my father's voice into my thoughts. I could hear that same ugly tone, with its ugly accusation. The words meant to encompass so many nasty things...and for what? People like Isaiah? Who could call him a sissy when he'd learned to live with being hated simply for who he was? For someone who could live his life honestly despite all that and find a way to remake his life into what *he* wanted it to be.

For one of those rare moments in my life, my father's voice shut the fuck up.

"Hey, Isaiah?" I asked softly, and it was only then I felt myself pressing against the bed, cock throbbing with the frantic beat of my heart.

"Yessir?" he asked in a clipped voice I thought had more to do with nerves than any true professionalism.

"My chest has been a little tight too, probably because I can't use it that much," I said, which sounded true to my ears. "My back feels like jello, so you must be doing a good job."

"Uh, I can…massage your front if you want," he said slowly.

I knew what he meant, but I still felt a thread of anticipation in me tighten at his words. "Okay. I need to roll."

"Sure," he grunted, lifting himself up so I had free movement.

I had already committed myself to the full reveal, and with a deep breath, I moved. It meant shoving my left arm under me and using the weight of my right arm and its cast to swing me around, but I managed it somewhat gracefully, if not smoothly. I was wearing a pair of loose shorts, however, not having bothered with underwear since my accident unless I was leaving the house. Which meant there was absolutely no question about what was going on with me as I settled onto my back.

Isaiah knelt beside me, and despite my previous thoughts about the low light, I could see more than before. His eyes were wide, flicking between my crotch and up to my face as if wondering if I could see the same thing he could. Even if I couldn't feel it, I would have been able to see it. From what I'd felt, Isaiah and I would be hard-pressed to say who was packing more, so I knew he could see the pitch of my shorts.

"Julian?" he asked in a higher pitch than usual.

"Yeah?"

"You…you sure?"

"Sure."

His breath sucked in sharply, but after a few heartbeats, he straddled my thighs again. This time, however, he leaned in as he placed his hands on my chest. To my surprise, there was no hesitation on his part as he shifted, pressing our covered cocks together as he leaned forward.

Immediately, my eyes locked onto his as his fingers dug firmly into my chest muscles. At the same time, I felt the shaft of his cock press against mine as his weight lowered. Pleasure from both ends of my body shot through me.

"Julian?"

"Yeah."

It was a testament to his ability to speak that he said nothing but ground his hips forward. He was secretly an evil shit too because he also found something in my chest muscles to dig his fingers into. The result was that bizarre mix of pain, discomfort, and pleasure that dragged a groan out of me.

To my surprise and growing arousal, I could see how he smirked when he heard me. Someone completely different had apparently dropped into my bed as he repeated the same gesture. Before I could recover, his fingers found my nipple, pinching lightly before giving a little tug. A jolt ripped through me, and I found myself shoving up into him with a grunt of surprise.

"Noted," he said, with the same confidence he had used the night we'd been pulled to that farmhouse fire. That night, there had been no patience and tactfulness, only a man who knew precisely what needed to be done and wanted to know whether I would back him up.

I had, and I would again, and right now, I wondered if I always would.

"And here I had you pegged for the dominant sort," he muttered.

"What?" I asked, the haze around my thoughts making it too difficult to make sense of what he was saying.

His hands slid up my chest to grip my shoulders. "I'm going to kiss you. You good with that?"

It was a question, a command, and a statement of fact all in one. "Sure."

A smile curled his lips, and he bent forward, the full realization of what was going to happen landing on my lap.

Sissy!

I could feel his breath against my lips and the grip of his fingers.

Queer!

I felt the barest brush of his lips against mine, the way his fingers tightened.

Faggot!

I couldn't move as his lips pressed against mine and, for a moment, did absolutely nothing. The boom and bellow of my father's disgust and hatred echoed through my skull, locking my limbs to my side and freezing my muscles.

And then, perhaps unconsciously, I heard the slight sigh of disappointment...betrayal? It came from Isaiah, and I could feel him pull away. Alarm, sharp and blaring, resonated through me. I could hear the snap of something in my head, and my father's berating fell away, dropped into the canyon of my thoughts where I couldn't hear him anymore.

I grabbed the back of Isaiah's head to pull him to me, forgetting what I was doing and cracking him in the head with the cast. He grunted, hunching forward as I yanked my hand back, and pain radiated down my arm.

"Ow!" we both yelped.

"Sorry!" I grunted almost immediately.

"It's okay," he said quietly and didn't hesitate to place his lips on mine.

This time I felt the soft brush of his lips and reached up with my arm so only my fingers made contact with his skull. I pulled him to me, holding him close as our lips parted. A jolt shot through me, and I held him as tight as possible without banging him with the cast again.

There was the excitement I remembered.

The bubbly pops inside my chest threatened to lift me off the bed.

But unlike then, there was a fierce heat inside me, yanking me forward and demanding my attention. I could feel how hard and strong his body was, and I could feel the insistence of his lips on mine. His cock was still pressed tight against mine, I remembered how it felt pushing against my ass, and a shudder passed through me.

"Fuck," I muttered, wishing I had the use of my hands. I wanted to run my hands up and down the planes of his body, to see and feel everything he had to offer.

I wanted...him.

"Not sure you're ready for that," he added with a chuckle full of mischief, delight, and so much heat I didn't know what to do with it.

"Isaiah?" I asked quietly as he pulled away.

"You can *always* say no, or stop," he told me.

I was confused for all of three seconds until his fingers curled at the hem of my shorts and began to pull. My eyes widened as he gave another tug, only to reach in with his other hand and, without hesitating, wrap his fingers around the base of my cock. His touch was electric, and I jerked at the feel of his grip as he set it free, letting it slap lightly against my stomach.

"Oh, someone would feel this," he said in a low purr that went straight to my groin. "Hey, Julian?"

"Yeah?"

"Know what a gag reflex is?"

"Yes?"

"Funny. I don't."

Again I was reminded how the lighthearted, somehow shy Isaiah was gone. There was a low rumble to his voice as he inched himself down and positioned himself. I was helpless to do anything but watch as he lowered himself slowly.

Only as his lips reached the tip of my dick, I realized what he had meant.

"Isaiah?"

His words about 'stop' and 'no' rang through my head as his mouth closed over the tip. Not that I would have summoned either of them beforehand, but now? I could only groan at the unexpected pleasure of the warmth closing around the sensitive head. With a low moan of pleasure, he slid forward, taking more of me into his mouth. A strangled noise escaped me as I felt his tongue swirl around what he had in his mouth, adding a shock of pure pleasure to the whole experience.

"Oh, God," I pleaded as he slid further down until he was almost impossibly low. At least now I fully understood what he meant about the deep-throating thing. By now, most of my previous partners would stop or back off.

He hummed, sliding back up to just below the head and stopping. I watched, my eyes widening as he drove forward, pushing past the point he'd been at before and taking me all the way to the root. Pleasure and shock rocked through me, and I felt my hips buck in surprise.

"Fuck!" I barked as I felt his throat muscles close around the shaft and sensitive head of my dick. Which is when I was convinced that under all that cute sweetness, there was an evil mastermind because he groaned hard enough that the reverberations traveled down the length of my dick.

He slid back up and resumed repeatedly going from head to base. All I could do was throw my head back and lay there, bound to what he was doing and unable to do more than be a victim of his skill. I didn't think I'd ever been as vocal and desperate as I was at that moment, bound by the pleasure he kept repeatedly tying me to.

Which is precisely when the finger slid into me, and I shot up off the bed in surprise. Perhaps if I'd had full use of my arms, I might have, but the best I could manage was a fumble.

There was *something* inside me.

Well, it wasn't a dick.

It felt good.

But it was something.

Well, there was a guy currently sucking my dick.

But something—

"Isaiah," I breathed as he held still, as if afraid to move or just being patient. I couldn't tell.

He pulled his mouth off me but didn't remove his finger. "I'm not trying to fuck you."

Technically no, but he was definitely the first person to have *ever* been inside me like this, even if it was only his finger. "Sure."

"Focus," he told me, voice low and careful. "Does it hurt?"

"No?"

"Is it uncomfortable?"

"A little."

"Physically?"

"Not...really."

"Then why?"

Sissy.

"I shouldn't—"

"Shouldn't?"

"Isaiah—"

He took a deep breath, and I shuddered when he kissed the innermost part of my thigh, somewhere I didn't think anyone had ever touched. "You're still allowed to say no or stop, and I will. But if you give me just a few minutes, trust me."

"Sure. Yeah." It sounded like me but didn't feel like me. Nerves and anxiety shot through me from every corner of my brain, and I could hear *him*, hear his insults, hear his hate and—

And Isaiah's mouth was back on me, and his finger didn't move. It was there, but it didn't move in the slightest. Just like with his conversation, I could focus on the good he was doing and not obsess over the fucked up things in my head. I could feel the way his lips shifted over the head and down to the base, the way his throat muscles squeezed enthusiastically. In no time, I was groaning for more before I even knew what hit me.

At some point, I felt his finger begin to move. I tensed, but I heard his words. I could still back out at any point. Of course I could. Isaiah...wouldn't. Most of all, he knew better than I did about how all this worked. If he thought I could get through this without trouble, I definitely could.

Just as I began to settle, I felt his finger shift and hit...*something*. A whole new sparkling wave of pleasure washed through me, and I felt my voice choke in my throat as I held myself in one place, staring up at the ceiling in surprise. His mouth and finger began to work in tandem, and I released a shuddering gasp.

Jesus. Was this something guys went through when they were fucked?

The thought came with repeated answers, and I gasped as I felt another finger added. This time the sensations came with a feeling of being *opened*. Maybe it should have felt like a violation, but all I could do was lay there in wonder as his second finger opened me up further. There was no pain, only a sense of *stretching* as his fingers unerringly found whatever point inside me had threatened to undo me.

The third finger was added, and even as I felt the same aching pleasure of being filled, I came to a realization. This was precisely the sort of thing someone would do if they were preparing for anal sex. This kind of slow build, with patience, lubed fingers, and adding pleasure, was just the sort of thing that would help someone to...bottom.

Oh, God, there was no way in hell I would *ever* be ready for someone of Isaiah's caliber. That wasn't even covering the fact that a guy's mouth on my dick and his fingers in my ass was one thing, but his dick inside me?

Sissy

A popping sound broke through the room, followed by Isaiah's voice. "I'm not going to try to fuck you. You're way too tense for that, trust me. I'm not in the business of hurting my partners."

"Are you a top?" I asked, remembering the terms I learned years ago from a short-term girlfriend's best friend.

"Baby boy, I'm whatever I want to be, so verse works just fine," Isaiah said with that same cocky swagger that threw me off even as it attracted me. "I'm whatever you want me to be."

I tried to laugh, but then his mouth was on me, and his fingers *curled* inside me. I cried out in earnest this time, not even caring that the shitty walls in this apartment were paper thin. All that mattered at that moment was the feel of him wrapped around my cock, pushing up inside me. Both together, driving pleasure through me in ways I hadn't known were possible.

Honestly, it was a miracle I'd lasted as long as I had. I hadn't found time to find a way to take care of myself in a month, and now the single most erotic thing was happening to me. I could feel the tightening of my stomach and the hard tingles in my thighs to signal the end.

"Isaiah," I managed to gasp out, knowing there wasn't much time but still feeling compelled to warn him.

I shouldn't have been surprised when he didn't change what he was doing. Isaiah continued, pushing and then launching me over the edge of the abyss of pleasure. I cried out once more, my hips jittering upward in shakes as I felt myself come harder than I had probably ever done in my life. The sheer pleasure threatened to rip me from consciousness as I jerked upward, spurting hard into his mouth and throat.

With a shuddering gasp, I collapsed back onto the bed, staring up at him. My eyes widened as he pulled his fingers from me, only to rear up with surprising speed. Helpless to do anything else, I watched as he knelt and began to fist his cock. My breath caught as he grunted, his body giving a jerk. Isaiah pointed his cock down, and I felt a splash of warmth against the shaft of my cock as his hips jerked and swayed with each pulse from his orgasm.

Eyes wide, I watched as Isaiah, still fresh from his orgasm, bent forward and took me into his mouth once more. I *should* have been too sensitive, but some part of my brain knew what was happening. He had just swallowed my cum, coated my dick in his, and was doing the same to his own load. The thought overrode the sheer agony of oversensitivity, and I groaned pitifully as he once more took me throat deep before slowly pulling back.

Right, so, not as straight as I thought, *and* a new slight kink unlocked...good to know.

"Holy shit," I breathed once he freed me from his mouth.

"Shh," he said. "Let me get a towel."

I wasn't really in a position to argue. Even without my broken arms, my whole body felt like one big limp noodle, and I let him get up without an issue. He tucked himself back in his pants before hurrying out, showing up again a few seconds later with a washcloth. The gentleness took me by surprise as he wiped down my softening cock and then down into my ass.

"You okay?" he asked.

"Pretty sure," I said with a small smile.

"You going to be okay later?"

Good question. "Not...sure."

He looked up, a small smile on his face. "I love that you're honest with me. Even when it's not always the 'best' idea, you still do it."

"Don't know how else to be," I admitted. "Except to not say anything at all."

"Huh," he said with another gentle swipe. "Is that why you're always so quiet around people?"

"Sometimes," I said.

"I'm sure there are other reasons," he said, but I could tell he wasn't prying for more answers. That was one of my favorite things about him, he understood so much, and while he was willing to ask about the things he didn't, he never pushed too hard, and he never pried.

"Hey, Isaiah?" I said softly, closing my eyes. There was such warmth in my body, I didn't know whether it was from the alcohol, the sex, or some combination of the two. All I knew was it was definitely something worth relaxing and maybe even falling asleep on.

"I kissed a boy before you," I confessed.

"Oh, yeah?"

"Like you. I was younger, though. Got caught by my dad."

"Bet he didn't like that."

"Broke my nose."

"Of course he did."

"Made me take boxing lessons the next day."

"Of *course* he did."

I laughed at the derision in his voice, it sounded so foreign coming from him. "It's okay."

"Why's that?"

"Because it meant I knew how to break that fucker's jaw. He deserved it."

"He did."

"Also meant it was more believable that I broke that asshole's skull, not Tristan."

"Tristan?"

"My brother."

I drifted a little after that, my thoughts in the past and the present. On some level, I knew I was starting to fall asleep, but it was the best bit of drifting I had done in a while. My whole body felt made of loose pudding in the best way, and there was a warmth I didn't remember having before.

"Isaiah?" I grunted, almost sure he had to have left by now. "You can stay here. With me. Tonight."

"You sure?"

"Sure."

I immediately felt a weight against my body and realized it was Isaiah. It was that weird soap he insisted on using in the shower that was so strong but could only be smelled when you got a shade too close to him. It reminded me of the incense they burned in the corner store near the trailer park I'd grown up in. Not unpleasant, just rich and thick, yet always at the edge of my senses.

I felt a weight against my stomach on the left and his body shimmy up against my side. Smiling, I wrapped my arm around the presence, pulling it close, and finally decided, you know what? It was okay just to let myself drift for a bit longer. I could leave all the other nonsense at the back of my head. Let it come for me later.

For now? I was more okay than I could ever remember being.

ISAIAH

"So, I have a question," I muttered into the phone, glancing toward the apartment door.

"Sure, you know you can talk to me about anything," Bennett chirped back, far more cheerily than anyone who'd been woken up five minutes before had any right to. "But you can start by telling me why you're smoking again."

"I'm not," I protested, flicking ash from my cigarette into the parking lot outside Julian's apartment. The early hour meant the apartment complex was quiet, almost haunted, as I stared through the fog covering our town.

"I can hear you exhaling sharply. I haven't heard you do that since you quit five years ago," Bennett pointed out.

"Fuck you, Livington," I muttered. "This is why no one likes cops. Nosy asses."

His laugh was as rich and boisterous as ever and made me smile. "Love you too, buddy."

"Yeah, yeah," I muttered. There was only one small convenience store in the whole of Fairlake. It wasn't quite twenty-four hours, but it stayed open late and opened early. A perfect place for the town's high school students and night owls to find a part-time job. It was also there that I had found the pack of cigarettes, glad that the bored, pimply-faced girl behind the counter hadn't shown the slightest flicker of recognition at my face.

"Alright, you dragged me out of bed from the man of my dreams for a reason," he said lightly, but I could hear the pointedness of it. Not irritated, that wasn't Bennett's style. Probably because, from what I learned, he could go back in and flop onto Adam without the slightest issue if he was feeling needy.

No, he sensed something seriously wrong, and I *might* be dancing around the issue.

"So, what, uh…was going through your head when you slept with Adam the first time?"

"Define slept with."

"Did something sexual with him."

"I mean, other than 'Jesus, I was right, he does have a big dick'?"

"Yes," I said with a heavy sigh.

"Because that was definitely in my head…and my mouth."

"Bennett."

He laughed. "Fine, I might be willing to tell you. But you've got to tell me why you're asking."

"What? I can't ask my friend what was going on in his head when he slept with his straight friend?" I wondered.

"You sound like Chase."

"You take that back!"

Not that Chase was a bad guy. The same as when I'd first met Julian, I didn't quite understand him. The man seemed made of all hard lines, sharp edges, and gruff tones. He was more talkative than Julian, but most of that was grunts, growls, and, especially with Bennett, sharp-tongued commentary.

Yet this was the same man who had been the first to show

up at Bennett's house after we'd all caught wind that something was wrong with him. And after I knew he and Bennett had argued about…something. I knew Chase wasn't as mean and rough as he seemed, and he cared despite how much of a dick he could be.

But hey, I didn't deserve to be compared to him.

"Would this have anything to do with a certain redheaded newbie to the fire station?" Bennett began, and I hated how much amusement there was in his voice. "Who is somehow bigger than Chase and Adam, looks meaner than Chase, talks less than Adam, and has spent a while pitbulling you every chance he gets?"

"I…pitbulling?" I asked in confusion.

"You know, guarding you, standing near you. I've seen him do it. He *really* hates it when I flirt with you."

"You flirt with anything good-looking that has a pulse."

"I did, yes."

"Oh, Adam the jealous type?"

"Nope," he said cheerfully. "Just don't see the point in flirting, even harmlessly, as I did before."

"Aww, someone's in love," I teased.

"Damn right," he said without hesitation. "Did you suck that grumpy man's dick or something?"

My face burned. "Or something."

"Oh, ho! Well, now we're getting to the truth."

"Bennett?"

"So let's see, you messaged me a little while back about how you screwed up and he got hurt. And, of course, this being Fairlake, I heard about what happened. You got it in your head that you had to help him to make up for what was not your fault to begin with. You've both been spending a lot of time together, learning about each other, and…his dick was in your mouth."

"Why do you assume it was his dick in *my* mouth?" I

contested hotly because there wasn't much else I could protest about.

"Because you and I tried to make a go of things, and I've never met as enthusiastic a cock sucker as you," he said affectionately. "And he doesn't exactly scream 'bottom' to me."

"Ehhh," I hummed doubtfully, remembering how Julian had reacted. Sure, he hadn't exactly been enthusiastic about something in his ass, but I had felt his physical reaction in my mouth. Not to mention, for all his outward toughness and bravado, he had *really* responded when I'd been aggressive and dominant with him.

"Oh? A big bottom? Emphasis on big," Bennett chuckled.

"I can't tell if you being a perv is because you didn't get laid last night or because you did," I muttered.

"Oh, I did. Don't you worry about that. Absolutely wrecked my—"

"Yes, thank you," I said with an eye roll. Hearing about him having sex didn't bother or arouse me, but if you didn't catch Bennett before he started, you were in trouble.

"He bottoms."

"Adam? The…former straight guy?"

"All that kinda goes out the window when you realize that having your prostate slapped around feels amazing."

I couldn't help my laugh. "Alright, that is pretty convincing."

"Exactly. Now…I have to ask, is Julian Adam 2.0 but not?"

"It's," I thought about what Julian had told me the night before about his father. "No, not really. Sorta, but not really."

"Vague, okay."

"I-I don't want to say too much."

"Because it's hard to say or because it's Red's business?"

"Julian," I corrected, although I was relieved that he understood my reluctance to talk. "And the last one."

"Gay in denial?"

"Bi and…sorta denial?"

"Oof. Self-hating?"

"I—"

"Right, right, that's probably answer enough for me. Jesus, Isaiah, what have you stepped in?"

"A very good question," I muttered, running my hands through my hair and glancing toward the door. I was probably safe from Julian waking up soon despite how early he had gone to bed the night before. I probably wouldn't see him for another hour.

"Is this like…" Bennett hesitated. "This is especially unfair for me to ask, but is this a serious thing for you?"

I couldn't help laughing at the question, but at least he was self-aware enough to know. If there was anyone I could accuse of having commitment issues, it had been Bennett. Before Adam, I'd never seen him be with anyone for more than a few months, and even then, there were signs things were going to fall apart.

Yet even I had to acknowledge this time was different for him.

"I don't know," I admitted, glancing back toward the door again. "I mean, I like him, there's no denying that, but—"

"There's a difference between liking someone and *liking* them," Bennett grunted in understanding, making me smile. It was just what I could have said to him and expected to be understood. Both of us had always been pretty good at communicating with one another on an intuitive level. "How badly is he going to take what happened?"

"I don't know," I sighed. "He's…hard to predict sometimes. It's like someone took Adam and Chase, then scrambled them up and popped out Julian."

"Christ, that bad?" Bennett asked with a laugh.

"Well, he's as serious as Adam but doesn't seem *quite* as, uh—"

"Grumpy as Chase?"

"Yeah," I snickered. "I can picture him glaring at me for calling him grumpy."

"Chase *is* grumpy, even Devin admits that, and he's crazy about the surly lug." Bennett snorted. "But I don't know, man. From what little I've seen of Julian, he seems pretty grumpy."

"Naw, he just lives in his head, like...*a lot*. He hasn't come out and said it, but I think he doesn't know what to do with people. It's like they confuse him."

"Shit, I know that feeling."

"Bennett, that's like saying *I* know the feeling. We're both ridiculous *people* people."

"People persons?"

"That sounds weird."

"So does people people."

I rolled my eyes, knowing full well I needed to get the conversation back on track before we both got lost. "My point is, he doesn't know how to handle people. He's got more comfortable with me, but—"

"Clearly," Bennett snickered. "How's he look, by the way?"

"Like he's got broken arms," I said dryly.

"You are no fun."

"He looks like the living embodiment of sex."

"Can't be. I already have that in my bed right now."

"You in love is disgusting," I said, even as I grinned.

"Yeah," he sighed wistfully. "So straight guy who might not actually be straight and probably has hang-ups about that, looks like a sex god and is managing to have a real human connection with someone in this town for the first time. Does that sum it up?"

"I know it's corny to say, but God, it sounds so...weak when you summarize something so big into something so small. Do *not* make an anal joke about that."

"Wouldn't dream of it," he assured me, the filthy liar that he was. "But even summarized, I'm not sure what to tell you."

"Okay, well, what if he wakes up and freaks out?" I asked nervously with another glance toward the apartment. "Shit. I really should *not* have done that. He was vulnerable. He's *been* vulnerable. He's been trusting me more and more, and I—"

"Listen to me. When Adam and I first fooled around, he'd been drinking, and like, thirty seconds before I kissed him, I punched him in the face."

"I...you what?" I asked, not having heard the details before.

"He deserved it," Bennett assured me as if that was supposed to help. "Right, but then I kissed him. I freaked out, ran into my house, then he came in, talked to me, and asked me to do it again."

"I...that's a new one."

"Right, also hot. Then one thing led to another, and boom! Dick in my mouth."

"You missed your calling as a storyteller," I snickered. "Jesus."

"My point is that sometimes things in life don't happen neatly and easily. Not even things that turn out to be fantastic. I mean, look at Adam and me. Bastard ran away to Boston and practically forgot all of us. Married some woman, then comes crawling back here. I punch him, and suddenly we're like rabbits—ow!" Bennett yelped, making me arch my brow. "Well it's all true!"

"Who are you gossiping to?" I heard Adam's deep voice rumble, somehow carrying through the phone.

"Isaiah. He found another 'straight' guy in town to give a blowie to."

"Bennett!" I protested.

"It's not like I'm going to tell him details. I wouldn't do—"

Adam snorted. "That Julian guy?"

157

"How the hell?" I asked in shock.

"I'm kind of wondering the same thing," Bennett asked, and I could hear the frown in his voice. "How does the man who hates the nosiness of everyone in Fairlake know enough to make that guess?"

"Well, unless there was some other guy he's been halfway living with while playing caretaker," Adam grumbled. "Come fetch me when you're done. I need to take a shower."

"What, you don't know how to operate the shower" Bennett called after him, then snorted. "Horny bastard."

"He's...really comfortable with being with a guy, isn't he?" I asked, a little surprised.

"That's the weird thing about Adam. It can take him *forever* to realize something about himself or his life. But once he does? He thinks it to death for a little while and then does something about it. All his second-guessing comes before he makes his decision," Bennett explained, and I would bet he had that stupidly dopey, romantic smile on his face. "And he decided to be with me, so he's giving it his all."

"I have the feeling things aren't going to be that simple on my end," I said softly, thinking of what Julian had told me.

"Well, every situation is different. At this point, the best you can do is wait to see how he reacts. I know you're freaking out at the moment."

"Only a little," I said weakly.

"But remember, last night is bound to be a bigger deal for him than it is for you, even if you are catching feelings for him. Maybe you should have held yourself back, or maybe taking the opportunity he presented...he did present it, right?"

"Kind of a mutual sort of presenting," I muttered, unsure why I was acting so bashful. Although Bennett and I were just friends, it didn't mean we hadn't had a bit of fun in the early days. We'd happily shared a few guys in the past, so it wasn't like I had any reason to be weird about sharing my sex life.

"Even better. Point is, you're not going to know what direction to go until you talk to him," Bennett said, being far too reasonable. "So, get him to talk if you can. I can't help you deal with him, though, because I know next to nothing. You're probably the closest to an expert on him this town has. Unless you can contact an old friend or family."

"That's not happening," I said with a snort. Julian most certainly would be unhappy if I tried to contact his family.

"Then, you'll have to navigate this based on what you know about him."

"That...sucks."

"Sure does! But if you need anything, you know how to get ahold of me."

"Yeah," I said with a heavy sigh. "I suppose it would probably be dumb to take off like the coward I feel like, huh?"

"If he needs space, I'm sure you'll figure that out soon enough and can give it to him. But to take off before dealing with it? Yeah, that feels like a really bad idea."

Like I'd be abandoning him.

"Yeah," I agreed. "I just don't know what to do."

"You've got good instincts, and you've got good friends if it doesn't work out," Bennett said with a chuckle.

"One of those things is debatable."

"Which...which one?"

"I'm going to get off this phone and let you try to figure it out."

"Actually, what I'm going to do is get off the phone and then probably get off with my boyfriend in the—"

"Byeeee, Bennett," I called to drown him out, snorting as I hung up the phone.

I wasn't so sure about the instincts part, but he was right about the friends at least. In truth, I could fall back on

Bennett and the guys at the station whenever I needed to. However, I wasn't so sure that falling back on them for something like this was such a great idea, even if it would be worth it to see some of their faces.

With a sigh, I shoved my phone back into my pocket, turned and walked into the apartment, glancing around.

There was no sign of Julian, but that didn't mean much. It was absurd that, despite his size and weight, Julian could move with unnerving quiet. It wasn't even like he moved with grace, but he still somehow managed to make the barest noise even when he was fussing with something. Impressive considering his current handicap, the man was probably like a ninja with the full use of his arms.

I listened for a moment before forcing myself to take a deep breath and sitting on the couch. I dropped the phone on the makeshift table and turned on the TV. There wasn't much on, but I managed to find old reruns of Tom and Jerry and settled on that. It was perfect, requiring next to no thought, entertaining enough to keep me distracted, and with just the right dash of nostalgia to ease my nerves.

Which lasted about half an hour until I heard the soft shuffle of footsteps in the hallway. It was followed by a gentle click as the bathroom door closed, and I forced myself to take a steady breath. I was going to figure out just what kind of mental state Julian was in soon, but the anticipation was going to kill me. I suppose when he didn't come barreling out to chase me from the apartment was a good sign unless his bladder took precedence, and then he would kick me out.

My heart leaped at the sound of the door, and I sat there, eyes on the TV, while he shuffled out. He glanced at me as he passed, and I looked back and found no answers on his face. How the hell the guy managed to keep his face so unreadable was beyond me. Either he had years of practice, or he had some unheard-of superpower.

"Morning," I called softly as he shuffled into the kitchen.

The only sound was a returning grunt, and I wasn't sure if it was just normal morning grumpiness or a bad sign. I didn't know what he was like in the morning since he had time to wake up properly before coming in for a shift at the station. Then again, I hadn't seen him after a guy had sucked him off while shoving his fingers inside him, so there was that.

There was a soft thump and clink of glass, then the sound of running water. Finally, after a few moments, the familiar gurgling of a coffee machine. Trying not to be *too* obvious, I glanced toward the doorway to see the shadow of movement in the kitchen.

I didn't know how much time had passed, but eventually, he reappeared with a cup in his hand. I blinked when he walked away after setting it beside me, immediately reappearing with sugar and a half-gallon of milk, which he also put down before disappearing. Curious, I watched until he reappeared with a steaming cup of coffee and sat in the armchair.

"What?" he asked after a few seconds, his voice thick and rumbling from sleep.

I glanced at the sugar and milk on the table beside the first cup of coffee. "I, uh…thanks."

"Don't have creamer," he grunted. "But you always take yours with a lot of it."

"I…do," I admitted slowly, touched by the fact that he apparently paid a lot more attention to my habits at the station than I'd given him credit for. Before that could sink in, I saw his eyes dart to me again as he quickly snatched up the sugar and milk to add to the coffee. It was probably a good sign, and I had to take the gesture for what it was.

Flashing him a smile, I took a sip of my coffee, which I had accidentally made sweeter than usual intentionally. I winced against the taste but settled back into the couch to watch the TV while I drank. Unable to help myself, I occasionally glanced toward him as the slapstick cartoon comedy played before us.

After several minutes, he finally spoke. "You...want to talk?"

Taking a deep breath, I sighed and said what sounded best. "I think you...need to talk."

I spared a glance his way and watched as he stared down at his coffee cup, frowning. Not for the first time, I was struck by the idea of the gulf that existed inside him—the gap between the things going on in his head and what he could speak aloud. There were probably so many things he left unsaid, and I couldn't help but ache at the thought.

"Sorry," I muttered into my cup, suddenly conscious that I was probably asking more of him than he had ever given before.

"No," he said quickly, then frowned down at his cup thoughtfully. "You're right. I just—"

I opened my mouth to answer and quickly shut it, chiding myself. I knew full well that, given time, Julian could say whatever he needed to say. He didn't need me cutting across his thoughts, attempting to put words into his mouth. Maybe I understood him enough that I could sometimes help him feel comfortable, but that didn't mean I needed to appoint myself as his personal translator. Especially not with something as...different as this situation.

"I don't," he began, then stopped again, scowling at the floor.

"Hey," I said, fingers twitching as I felt the urge to reach out to him but stopping myself.

He slowly looked up at me, still frowning. "Yeah?"

"Take your time. I've got coffee. I've got good cartoons.

I've got plenty of time for you to put your thoughts together," I assured him, hoping my smile was reassuring.

He blinked slowly, glancing at the TV and cocking his head slowly. "I...never really watched this before."

I smiled, turning back toward the hijinks on the screen. "My grandfather was big into old cartoons. He made sure I got to see all the old stuff."

"Your...grandfather? You never mentioned him before."

"I was kinda young when he died. But I was old enough to see these cartoons and remember watching them with him when I was like six, maybe seven, before he died."

"How did—?"

"Liver failure," I said with a sad smile. "He was fond of his gin. Had been for years."

"Oh. I'm sorry."

"It's okay," I told him. "From what I learned, my father, hard-nosed, homophobic bastard, didn't fall far from the tree that was my grandmother. Whereas my grandfather was a gentle, loveable sort, she was...less so. Gin was probably his way of easing the sting of her personality. Kind of a shame that I didn't get a dad that took after his father, but that's life."

"Oh, and your mom's parents?"

"Eh, distant. Other side of the country. Did their own thing. Made sure to send gifts, and we'd see them once every few years while growing up," I said with a wave of my hand. "Not knowing them is...quite easy."

"But not knowing your parents?"

I took a drink of my coffee before pulling my gaze back to the TV. "Harder. They're shit parents, but...they're parents."

"You didn't want to go back?"

"To my parents?"

"Yeah."

"Of course," I answered immediately. "So much of my life was trying to get their approval, trying to, I don't know, finally get them to see me. But at some point, I just...stopped. That instinct is still there, like a small voice in the back of my head that catches me at odd moments, but it's not important. *They* aren't important. Well, they are, but they don't determine my life anymore."

"Oh."

"Sorry, I know I'm running in circles."

"No."

"No?"

"It still hurts. You carry that hurt forever. But you don't let the hurt control you as it did once."

I stopped, setting my cup gently into my lap as I turned to stare at him for a moment. I'd never managed to summarize what was going on in my head quite as well as he had just done. Perhaps Julian wasn't quite as disconnected as other people thought, and especially as much as he thought.

"Sorry," he muttered, looking down at his lap.

"No," I said with a slow smile. "Don't be. You didn't do anything wrong. Actually, you hit the nail on the head so well that I'm a little surprised."

"Oh."

"Not surprised because *you* did it. Surprised because I've never had anyone call me out so well before."

"I wasn't...no."

I chuckled softly. "Wrong phrasing. You didn't call me out. You understood me."

His eyes darted up to me, down to his lap, back up, and down again. I managed to bite my tongue to keep myself from saying anything further. Once again, I felt it was more important that he said whatever was on his mind rather than force my own into the conversation.

"Oh," was all he said, but I smiled all the same.

"Yeah," I shot back.

"That's...good," he said softly.

"I'd like to think so," I smirked.

Finally, I felt we were approaching the topic he really wanted to talk about, namely what happened last night. I'd thought he might want to address it immediately, but I wasn't surprised to see he was slowly working his way there...if he would at all.

"Are you okay?" he asked finally.

I blinked, surprised by the question. "Oh, uh, yeah. I mean, a little nervous, but—"

"Yeah. Me too...a little."

"Well, considering what happened last night and what you told me about when you were a kid, I can't say I blame you."

"Yeah."

I shifted slightly, sensing I might be able to get away with a little nudge. "Other than being nervous, are you okay?"

A crease formed on his brow. "I...don't know."

"Right, okay, that makes sense," I said, taking a deep breath. "But uh, I don't really know how to help you maneuver through this without you telling me a little more."

"Yeah," he grunted. "It was...weird. I mean, it was good too! You were...good."

I managed to smother the worst of my smile, hopefully enough to show my appreciation. "Well. That's good. Both things are good, actually. Glad you enjoyed it, and I was good enough to make it enjoyable."

"You did," he said, eyes darting up to my face before looking back down at his lap. This time, however, there was a little color on his face, and I would have paid a fair bit of money to know precisely what thoughts he was having at that moment.

"But," I said, pulling the topic back on track before one or both of us got distracted. "There's clearly some things about it that weren't so good. And I'll guess it has to do with your dad."

I expected more than the barely visible flinch and wondered if talking about it as much as he had, while comfortable, had helped him to talk or hear about his dad in other circumstances. It was certainly worlds apart from the reaction I'd seen yesterday when he'd completely shut down and locked himself away from the world.

"I kept...hearing him," Julian explained softly, face scrunching up as he gestured vaguely toward his head. "The whole time. I could hear the things he said back then."

"I can probably think of a few words he used," I said, keeping my voice even. "Did he use all of them, or did he favor a certain one?"

"Does it matter?" he asked, sounding curious rather than irritated.

"It might. It worked for me. If I could use the words without wanting to flinch away from them, then they didn't have as much power over me," I explained, shrugging. "But that's me. Everything that works for me isn't always going to work for you."

"Feels weird, saying them aloud. I've never done it."

"Because you thought it was cruel to use a word you didn't think applied to you, or because you were afraid it applied to you?"

He flinched again, his lips thinning. "Both. Neither. I don't know."

"Well, I'm not going to push you," I told him gently, giving in to the urge to reach out. I laid my hand over his. "This is something you have to do on your own and only when *you* are ready."

Julian gazed at my hand, and I could see myriad emotions flitting over his features. They flared to life and died away too quickly for me to be sure what I was seeing. But I was sure I saw fear, resentment, anger, pain, terror, and longing. This was a man at war, both with himself and a past I was sure he'd never been able to leave behind.

I may still carry my pain, but I suspected Julian had never stopped hurting in the first place.

"He talked...about people like that," he said. "Guys into guys mostly. Didn't really say much about lesbians."

"No offense, but I'm not surprised," I said, unable to help my dry tone. Homophobes could spread their heat across all spectrums, but I'd long since noticed that some were pickier along gender lines. Both men and women could be homophobic, but I'd noticed homophobic men tended to aim at gay and bi men, while women did the same toward their own gender. "Probably liked the idea of two women together."

Julian frowned. "Well...so do I."

I took a moment, mostly to prevent myself from snorting. "Julian?"

"Yeah?"

"You, uh, clearly like the idea of two guys together too."

"I...yeah."

"Alright, just wanted to make sure you were at the point of admitting that."

"Faggot," he whispered.

Surprise, more than anything, made me lean back, raising a brow. "What's that?"

"That was what he called...them...me?"

"Oh!" I said, letting out a little laugh. "Sorry, sorry. I was taken a little off-guard."

"Queers."

"Right."

"Fairies."

"Classic."

"And—"

I waited a few heartbeats, sensing we were reaching the heart of the issue. Finally, I gave his fingers a squeeze. "Yeah?"

"Sissy," he breathed, the word coming out so tightly it sounded like it had to be squeezed through his throat.

Ironically, the one word I didn't hear very much growing up, if at all. Yet I could tell it had all the meaning of the other words combined and was still somehow more potent. It took me several moments with him staring at our hands before I thought I might have finally figured out the problem.

"That's what he called you," I said softly in understanding. "Your dad, when he caught you kissing that boy."

"Yes."

"And it was...sissy?"

I froze as the sound of his voice shifted, growing...not deeper, but curt, quick, and sharp, all like the crack of a serrated whip. "I ain't havin' no sissy for a son!"

For a moment, I could only stare at him as I watched his shoulders drop, and he let out a low breath, taking it slow. It was only when I watched his face ease that I realized I had just watched the closest approximation I was going to get to who his father was and what he'd sounded like to a young Julian. The sheer vehemence and disgust had been like a slap across the face, a spark of the old accusations and arguments I'd had with my own father.

"Sorry," Julian finally said, sounding tired. "But it's him. It's always him running through my head. My mother worried about...everything. She's always so *worried*. Everything has fallen apart for her, constantly, all the time. She lost my dad, and I was always getting into trouble, and my brother's the only thing she can trust."

"And you worry," I said, without thinking.

"Yeah," he grunted, pulling his fingers away. "I feel like her sometimes—little thoughts. Things at the edge but always there. Always pestering me, bothering me. Reminding me just how wrong things are. But sometimes I'm...*him*. Like I'm just so angry, like I just want to break everything around me and—"

I could see the way he was beginning to amp himself up, the spiral of his internal emotions finally taking hold of him. Without thinking, I slid from the couch and knelt before him. I could have stood up, but instinct screamed that this was the best way to approach it. His words cut off almost immediately as I knelt between his legs, reaching out to gently place my hands on his chest.

I met his eyes. "Julian?"

A couple of heartbeats. "Yeah?"

"You? Are not your parents. You came from them, and they shaped you, but you are not them. You can choose to take what you've got from them and make it something else entirely for you, you hear me?" I told him, my voice low but as urgent as I dared make it. "There is no destiny. There is no inevitability."

"Even history shows us there are cycles, that we always end up right back where we started," he said with a hollow smile.

"That's about people as a whole. That's society. I'm talking about *you*," I said, my fingers tightening against his chest. "I'm talking about what the *person* can do. We can be so much more than what we're given, what we're told is going to happen to us, or what we'll be. You hear me? You don't *have* to be them, and I can tell you right now you are *not* your father."

Julian stared at me for several seconds but I instinctively reached out, gently closing my hand over his to draw it back into his lap.

"And from what I've seen, you're one of the toughest, strongest, and hardheaded people I've ever known," I continued, feeling the fingers of his left hand close over mine as though without thought. "You're not the person your father accused you of being, and you're better than he ever dreamed of being, alright?"

"Sure," he said after a moment, closing his eyes.

"I mean it," I insisted, laying my head on his thigh and taking a deep breath. "We don't have to be the people we think we're supposed to be."

I could feel the tension in his body as I lay there, letting my eyes close as I listened to him suck in a deep breath that shuddered through him. A moment later, I felt his cast against the back of my head before I felt the curl of his fingers in my hair.

"Sure," he grunted, his voice steadier than it had been moments before. "Sure."

"Good," I said, hearing how steady he was. "Good."

"I'm not…" he began, then hesitated.

"What?" I asked immediately.

"Not…totally okay."

"Of course not."

"But what happened?"

"Yeah?"

"Last night."

I almost laughed at the clarification but held it back. "Yeah."

"It wasn't bad," he said with a sigh.

"No," I agreed. "But it doesn't have to happen again either. I don't regret it, and I liked it a lot, but that doesn't mean you have to—"

"Are you always like that?"

"Er, like what?"

"That, uh…*confident*."

It was probably the first time I'd ever heard him say something that wasn't direct but vague enough and carried meaning behind it. I remembered how I'd been when things started, and I smiled, picking my head up to meet his eyes.

"Confident? Yes. But I kinda sensed that you needed that."

"I," he began and then breathed in deep, "guess I did. I liked it."

"You did," I agreed, sensing the mood of the moment changing, shifting ever so slightly.

"Could you do it again?" he asked, and I had to appreciate the bluntness of his words. "More often?"

I finally gave in and laughed, bringing my hands down to rest on his waist, my fingers spreading out so my thumbs brushed against his groin. "That, I can definitely do."

His eyes burned with unspoken desire. "*Good.*"

JULIAN

It had only been a couple of weeks since the interesting night I'd shared with Isaiah. On the one hand, it felt like everything between us had changed in ways I could barely keep track of, and on the other, it felt like nothing had changed in the slightest. He continued to come over and spend time with me, watching TV, curled up with his own book, or napping between his shifts at the station.

I was rarely able to fall asleep unless I was in my own place, whereas Isaiah seemed to have little difficulty. Watching someone sleep was something I'd never considered doing before. But, then again, I'd never had more than a night with someone. Although Isaiah and I weren't technically anything, it was clear we shared something.

Which was probably why I found myself watching Isaiah as he napped on my couch. It wasn't a huge couch or particularly comfortable, but there he was, sprawled across it with his legs dangling over one of the arms. His head was tucked against the other arm, and I could just see half of his face as he slept. I hadn't realized how animated his face was until I'd seen him asleep.

The absence of emotion was a little strange, but there was no denying how peaceful he looked. He was wearing the loose pants he'd brought with him and an unmarked shirt. The shirt had risen up when he'd tossed his arm over his head, and it was strange how that little slip of skin was enough to send a jolt of thrill and anticipation through me each time I noticed it.

In all honesty, wanting to touch him was something I'd been experiencing a lot more in the past couple of weeks. Usually, I held myself back, feeling that balled-up knot of something awful inside me that made me too scared to cross the distance between the two of us and make contact. It usually came down to Isaiah to initiate contact, though I had a sneaking suspicion he didn't do it nearly as often as he would have preferred.

However, the desire was still there, and I found my attention drawn back to his sleeping form repeatedly. Glancing between him and the television, I felt the fingers on my left hand itch with the desire to reach out. Chewing my bottom lip, I leaned over in the armchair, moving carefully, so I didn't disturb him.

The tips of my fingers brushed along the locks of his hair, and I stopped when he took a deep breath. Then, when he didn't do more, I let my fingers slip into his hair completely, pushing gently against his scalp. Isaiah let out a soft sigh as I let his hair play through my fingers and brushed it off his forehead.

Without warning, Isaiah's eyes slid open. Squinting against the light from the afternoon sun that filled the room, he tilted his head to peer up at me, a slight furrow forming on his brow.

"Hey," he said, voice a little rough from sleep but smiling.

"Hey," I said, pulling my hand back.

He hummed softly, closing his eyes and readjusting himself on the couch. "Felt good."

"I wasn't trying to wake you up," I said hastily, feeling a stab of guilt. I knew just how important it was to get as much sleep as possible when you were between shifts.

"You didn't," he mumbled. "I've been drifting in and out for a little while now."

"Floating," I said.

"Hm?"

"It's what I always thought of it as. Not really awake, not really asleep. Just floating between the two."

"That's a good one. I'll have to remember it. Sounds nice, which is good. I kind of like that feeling."

"Me too."

"Had a dream about you," he said after a few moments.

"Yeah?" I asked, unsure if I should ask what it was about. Then again, if it had been bad, he would have probably clarified. Isaiah was pretty good at communicating precisely what was going on in his head, which made things a lot easier between us. "Good?"

"Pretty good," he said, pushing up from the couch to arch his back and stretch his arms behind him with a low groan. That same slip of skin made another appearance, and I felt the same heated jolt zip through me as I stared. When he stopped, I looked up and found him watching me, a slight smile on his face. "Not *that* kind of dream."

"Oh. Right," I said, jerking my eyes away and feeling my face warm. It wasn't like I could exactly pretend there wasn't a shared attraction between the two of us. Turned out, Isaiah wasn't just sweet and lively, he had a pretty healthy sex drive.

"You're clearly thinking something along those lines, though," he said with a chuckle, and I grunted. I knew I was being difficult, especially because he'd already figured out I was a fan of those moments when he got cocky and direct.

I'd never considered whether I preferred to lead or follow, though I generally avoided being in charge. I took orders at work because that was how it worked, but in every other aspect of my life, I preferred to be left to my own devices. Yet Isaiah could come in and take charge, whether to improve my eating habits, make sure I wasn't trying to do something I shouldn't with my arms, or initiate something sexual, and I had no issue with it whatsoever. Honestly, it was nice to feel like someone was willing to take the lead when I was probably useless, especially when it was Isaiah.

"Sorry," I muttered without thinking.

"Don't be," he said, and I could tell from his tone he wasn't entirely done with me yet. "Are you just being horny because you felt like it, or did seeing me drooling on myself get you going?"

I snorted, shaking my head. "Uh, no. You didn't drool."

"Good. Because if that's what did it for you, I'd be a little worried."

I smiled again because he was really good at getting that sort of reaction out of me. "Just...when you were sleeping, your shirt uh...came up. Saw a bit of your stomach. Random, I know."

To my surprise, he chuckled. "Not weird in the slightest. There's probably a term other people use, but I prefer the Tummy Peek. Clever, I know, but it's what I call it."

"I didn't know that was a thing," I said thoughtfully. "Any other time I was, uh—"

"Turned on?" he offered, winking.

"Yeah," I said, still not sure if it was 'right' for me to talk about being turned on by other people, especially women. "Uh—"

"Tell me," he said, reaching up to adjust his hair, which was sticking up a little from his nap.

"It was always just...direct stuff. Touching. Kissing. Maybe seeing...parts of them. But not something so...little."

"So, you were still attracted to these women. You just experienced it differently than you are with me."

"Yeah. I guess. Is that weird?"

Isaiah snorted, shrugging his shoulders. "You're asking the wrong person if something is weird. I think sexuality is a bit like anything we like and want, or don't like and want. You'll have different things you like, but that doesn't mean you like everything the same way. For example, maybe you like chocolate and steak, but you prefer to have chocolate only once in a while, but you could eat steak all the time. Or, in this case, you're still attracted to women, but there's a reason you're attracted to me differently."

"Like what?"

"Hell if I know, I don't live in your head."

"Probably for the best."

He cocked his head, eyes sweeping over me before he slid off the couch. Not for the first time, he knelt between my legs as I sat in the chair, his eyes intent on mine. The stirring in my stomach grew stronger, and I felt my jeans tighten. He reached out to set his hands on my waist and, using his thumbs, nudged my shirt up about an inch, revealing my stomach and the trail of red hair that ran up to my chest.

"I've found myself enjoying the sight of a tummy peek on you more than once," he said softly, running a finger along my hip to rest on the strip of hair. His finger dipped down to brush along the waistband of my pants before running up again to push the shirt even higher. "And I don't just mean in the past couple of weeks either."

"What do you mean?" I asked, curious about what he had to say as his fingers slid further up my stomach.

"There were a few times when I first came here to try to help you," he said, looking down as though he found his hand movements just as interesting as I did. "Where I caught myself looking at you."

"Kind of like you are right now?" I asked through a tightened throat. Even though I could still hear that fearful, angry voice chiding me for what I was allowing to happen, it was a lot quieter whenever Isaiah looked at me.

"I probably would have died on the spot from embarrassment if I'd let the look reach my face," he chuckled, inching forward. "And there were definitely a couple of tummy peek moments that threatened to make me forget myself."

"I kind of want to say it's a shame you didn't, but it's probably good you didn't," I admitted with a wince.

"You think that's bad?" He chuckled, fingers continuing up my shirt to rub my chest gently. "I thought you were pretty good-looking when I first saw you, your first day at the station."

I remembered seeing him that first day as Chief Borton escorted me around, introducing me to everyone. Everyone had been friendly enough, if a little curious at my impromptu addition to the station, except for Isaiah, who had been lounging in the break room when we'd entered. He'd been kicked back in his seat, immediately slamming all four legs onto the floor when Chief Borton walked in, grinning sheepishly.

A week later, when Chief Borton snapped at him for balancing on two legs again, I realized why he'd acted so strangely. Yet he'd recovered quickly, bouncing up to give me the biggest smile I'd received that day, and took my hand without hesitation. Everyone else had been almost wary of getting close, perhaps reading something on my face that so many others had before and drawing away.

Not Isaiah, though, and that open greeting had stuck with me ever since.

"What about it?" I asked finally, trying to understand what he was driving at.

"Oh, there was a time in that first week. I decided it was time for me to shower before my nap while on shift," he said, spreading his hands wide to run them down my sides slowly. "I didn't realize someone was in there until you came out, with your damn towel thrown over your shoulder like you weren't giving a view people happily pay for on the internet."

I blinked at the description, inwardly cursing as I felt myself warm again. "What?"

"Look at this," he said, running his hands up my body for emphasis. "This? This is the most eye candy that ever eye candied. I saw you stroll out, water still on you, and I about fell over. It's a good thing the shower rooms are shaped like they are, all I saw was your back, but that was enough to send me to gay heaven right then and there."

"Seriously?" I asked, my humor finally winning out over my discomfort. It was so *strange* to have someone so effusively compliment me, even if it was about my looks. Especially someone like Isaiah, who could easily pull any person he wanted, guy or girl. "That's...a lot."

"Yeah, so was that back and ass. Honestly, I'd have a hard time picking my favorite part of you," he said, and I blinked when he bent down to kiss my stomach. I felt his breath gust against my skin, making my own catch in my throat. Then his lips, soft but urgent, pressed against my skin before he backed up. "But for the record, your dick is equally impressive."

"Glad to hear it," I said, smiling a little.

"But," he said, pushing himself upright and into my face, "it's your smile that takes the top spot."

"I...what?"

"Your smile. Get that look off your face. It's a good smile."

"I don't...smile much."

"Maybe, but sometimes that can make something all the more special. Especially because I'm pretty sure I've seen you smile more in the past ten minutes than anyone else in town has seen you smile since you arrived."

"That's...true," I admitted. I'd yet to meet someone as good at pulling a smile out of me as Isaiah.

"So, that's special," he said and leaned in close, pressing his lips against mine. Thankfully, kissing him wasn't nearly as difficult as it had been the first time, and after a couple of weeks, I reached up to hold the back of his head as gently as I could.

Sometimes I wondered what it would be like to do things like this when I had full use of my arms again. To be able to wrap my arms around him and draw him closer, to hold him and run my hands freely over him.

"Mmm," he hummed happily, and I felt an absurd pride that I had somehow managed to make that happen. "Now, let's see what we can do about putting food into our stomachs. Then maybe I can help you shower again later."

A phrase that would have previously irritated me, but considering how he 'helped' the last time, I could only smile. "Sounds like a plan."

AT HIS WORDS, I froze, leaning back and letting his cock slip from my mouth. Even after a month of the two of us being more than just friends, sucking dick was still strange and unfamiliar. Probably didn't help that I didn't have full use of my limbs, but the whole experience was still surreal. Then again, I was willing to get over that, considering how much fun Isaiah seemed to be having at my fumbling attempts to pleasure him.

"I said," he began, pushing himself upright to sit on the

edge of the bed. He was completely naked, his clothes on a pile next to the bed where he'd thrown them. There were little wisps of light hair on his chest, matching the trimmed patch of chestnut brown hair at the base of his dick. "If you're willing, I'd be down to do more than just blowjobs."

Not that the thought hadn't crossed my mind, but this was the first time it had really been addressed. I knew enough about the mechanics to understand how it would go, and I'd fantasized a few times about it. However, the difference between fantasy and bringing it up as a possibility was worlds apart. Every time I thought about bringing it up, I felt myself quickly backing away before even so much as a sound could escape my throat.

"Hey," he said quickly, reaching down to where I knelt to run a hand gently down my face. "I'm not going to push you into anything you don't want to do. Because trust me, this mutual blowjob thing is a blast, but I figured it would be a good idea to offer you something else if you wanted it."

"I do," I said quickly, then clarified after a moment. "Want it. I just—"

I really didn't know what I was supposed to do. The entire thing felt too big for me to comprehend, and it felt like I was trying to wrap string around a boulder. All I got were bits of string and an untouched boulder. I didn't know the first thing about what that meant, even though I knew it was a big step in…some direction.

And that wasn't even covering the other big thing, only inches from my face. Isaiah wasn't as big as me, but not by a whole lot. I had already figured out that when it came to sex, Isaiah was probably going to take the lead, and that meant something more than just the few fingers he'd gotten into me over the past month, well, a few fingers and one toy, shaped in such a way it left me feeling like I was made of electricity and fire when I came like a geyser.

His eyes followed mine, and he chuckled. "Babe?"

The term ripped through me in its gentle affection, and I couldn't help but look up at him in wonder. "Yeah?"

"I'm not talking about me fucking *you*," he said with a smile. "I don't think you're quite ready for that, especially without use of your arms."

"My arms?"

"Being able to move might make you feel more secure. And that's if you're ever mentally ready for bottoming."

Immediately I realized that I *wanted* to be ready, but he was right, I wasn't ready, not yet. The fingers and the toy had been phenomenal, and I was more than happy to see them make a return. But that had opened the door for a lot more than that possibly going inside me. Now I could easily picture Isaiah, full of cockiness and command, taking control as he put himself inside me. The thought was equally terrifying and arousing, but the arousal was winning more every day.

"Wait, you want me to—" I glanced down at my cock, jutting out between my legs, sagging slightly from its weight. "But—"

"Look, I know you're bigger than me, definitely thicker," he said with a shrug. "But I can take it."

Not that I doubted his words. Isaiah wasn't the sort for empty bragging. I just knew in the past my dick had occasionally been a problem with other people. And I had *never* been allowed to put it into someone's ass, which I knew could be a far more painful experience.

"Sure," I said after a moment, not knowing if I was agreeing with him or the idea. "But my arms—"

"Your arms haven't stopped us with other things," he chuckled. "Now get your ass up onto that bed and lay down if you're really sure. I'll do most of the work this time, but when you get your arms free soon, we'll see what you can do with full movement."

With a slow nod, I used my left arm on the bed to pull myself up as he got up, giving me room to move. I hesitated, dick bobbing as he went toward the bag he always brought, usually filled with new clothes or shower supplies. There was enough light from the table lamp that my eyes could follow the lines of his body, then down to the curve of his ass. Isaiah wasn't shy about complimenting me on my ass, but I had to disagree with him on one thing, it was *his* ass that was the best in the world.

"I can feel you watching me," he said, just in time for him to bend over as he rummaged through the bag.

"Shit," I muttered as I watched his leg muscles tighten and got a full view of his whole ass. I knew damn well he was doing it intentionally, but the throb from my dick told me I didn't care in the slightest. This man could taunt me as much as he wanted as long as I continued to see things like this.

I was still a little in awe of how quickly my mindset had changed in the past month. True, the fear my dad had given me was still there, always ready to find a weak point to claw at, given a chance, but it was always losing. In moments like these, I could barely hear him and could only see Isaiah. And hell, soon, I would be feeling Isaiah in a way I never had before.

"So," he said, his dick still sticking out in front of him as he returned to me, a bottle in hand, along with two other things I couldn't make out right away. "I know the chief makes sure we get routine checkups, including STI panels."

"Oh. Yeah," I said, trying to focus on his face but repeatedly finding myself distracted by the rest of him.

Isaiah reached out and gently pushed me until I realized what he was doing and let myself fall on my back. We were only, hopefully, a couple of weeks from my casts coming off, and the impact of falling didn't hurt like it would have weeks before. I was left to stare up at him as he smirked down at me.

"Anything I should potentially be worried about?" he asked, and I realized the other object was a condom.

"No," I said, swallowing hard at the implications. It had been months since the last time I'd slept with anyone, and there had been plenty of tests in between. "Nothing."

"Me either," he said, cocking his head.

"Sure," I croaked.

"Sure," he said with a smile. "So, no condom? Or condom? I won't take offense either way."

Once more, I found myself amazed at the trust he was willing to put in me with what seemed like no effort on his part. "N-no condom."

"Best way possible," he said, tossing it onto the bedside table. "Especially for your first time. I want this to feel as great as possible for you."

"I want you...to feel good," I said with a frown.

Isaiah laughed softly, the sound bubbling up from his chest as he crawled onto the bed. "Oh, trust me, I know how to make sure it feels just fine for me. You just lay back and let me show you what's possible."

There was no way in hell I was going to argue with him and watched as he straddled my waist. He opened the bottle and let some lube drop onto one hand. With the other, he held himself steady on the bed, propped up next to my shoulder. At that moment, I was so damn glad he insisted on keeping a light on for this as I watched his eyes latch onto mine. The faint scent of his earthy cologne hit my nostrils as he leaned in closer, catching my lips with his.

Isaiah moaned, and I realized, with a flash of pure arousal, that he was fingering himself like he'd done to me several times before. My lips parted, and I accepted his tongue into my mouth, reaching up to steady him with my left arm. His body relaxed against mine even as he let out another guttural noise of pleasure.

"By the way," he said in a low purr. "I wasn't kidding about making this as good for you as possible."

"W-what?" I managed, mind awhirl with what he was doing and what was going to happen very soon.

"Didn't see what I had with me, didn't you?" He chuckled, and I finally had to pull my eyes from his face to see what had fallen with the bottle of lube.

"Oh," I said, eyes widening as I saw the toy he'd used a few times on both of us. It was narrow and angled slightly, with a hilt at the base that spread out to end in a ball. He'd called it a prostate massager, and all I had known was the sensations while he'd taken me in his mouth had been beyond description.

God, he wanted to do that *while* I was inside him?

I was going to have a stroke, guaranteed.

"You're trying to kill me," I told him as he leaned back, pulling his hand free from himself to snatch up the toy and add lube to it.

"Oh, there are far worse ways to leave this mortal coil," he intoned while somehow reaching behind him with the toy and finding his target.

As always, there was a moment of resistance as the fear in my head reached a fever pitch because *someone* was trying to enter my ass. It was only a moment because that person was Isaiah, and I knew full well I could trust him there. I also knew it was a lot easier to take even that narrow toy when you weren't tensing up.

The toy began to slide into me, and without warning, I felt warmth against the head of my dick. Jerking my head back, I realized he was holding the base of my cock as he hovered his ass over me. My eyes widened, and then I groaned when I felt the toy slide in. The curve of its tip almost immediately found the bundle of nerves inside me that threatened to light me up from the inside while the hard ball at the base pressed just below my balls.

"Fuck," I grunted when he hit the switch, and immediately the low but strong vibration of the toy began. Pleasure, slow and deep, began to build inside me.

"That's the idea," he breathed, and he shifted, putting pressure on my dick.

For one precise moment, there was nothing but pressure and faint heat. Then I let out a choked cry of pleasure as I felt heat and grip unlike any I'd felt before wrap around my cock. I watched Isaiah tense, shoulders straightening before a shaky smile spread over his face.

"Probably should have used more than three fingers," he said with a snort. "But that's okay. I'll adjust."

I couldn't find the energy to try and argue with him as he let himself slide down another inch. Some part of me knew that he knew what he was doing, even if I wanted him to avoid hurting himself. The rest of me was locked onto the sensation of him wrapping himself around my dick, slowly rocking as he worked himself down.

No words could have escaped me when I felt myself fully encased inside his body. The toy inside me was vibrating furiously, sending potent sparks of pleasure through me that arced up to my dick and exploded with ecstasy I'd never known before. I couldn't believe I was now completely inside Isaiah, who took a deep breath before pushing himself up and easing himself back down.

"Fuck!" I grunted, arms flopping uselessly against the bed. There was no way in hell I would manage to last for more than a couple of minutes, and that was if I was lucky. "Isaiah, please! I can't—"

"Don't worry about what you can or can't do," he said,

leaning forward and kissing my lips gently. "Just enjoy it."

"Like I have a choice," I grunted as he began to move his hips.

It felt like I was losing my mind as he worked his hips, driving me into him as I felt the vibrations in my ass run through my entire body. I couldn't help but try to reach out, unsuccessfully, with my right arm, but at least managing to rest my left hand on his hip as he worked himself into a rhythm that threatened to untether me from reality.

Maybe I'd been doing things wrong all these years, but I had never known it was possible to feel so much pleasure. For the first time since we'd started, I was incapable of hearing the inner voice of panic and worry. Instead, all that existed for me at that moment was the sight of Isaiah as he rode me, his cock bobbing as he put his hands on my stomach to hold himself steady. On every downstroke, his dick came down, slapping against my stomach and leaving a shining puddle of pre-cum behind.

"Shit. Fuck. Fuck. Isaiah," I groaned as I felt my stomach tighten even more.

"C'mon," he hissed, his voice so full of desperate pleasure and need that I could only shudder at what he was probably feeling.

My hand be damned, I gripped his hip and shoved him down as best I could, sheathing myself entirely inside him. My back arched as I instinctively tried to drive myself deeper as my orgasm burst through me. White filled my vision as I poured into him, crying out without regard to the apartment's thin walls or even my own self-control. Every inch of my nerves felt alive with pleasure as I gripped Isaiah as best I could.

"Shit, shit," Isaiah swore, and I watched him grab his dick and begin pumping. It took only seconds before he cried out, and I not only felt him tighten around my cock, but felt the warm splatters of his cum as it reached my chest, chin and my cheek. I tried to hold onto him for as long as his body was taut before he finally hunched over, letting out a low, satisfied huff of breath.

"Hey, uh, Isaiah?" I croaked, trying not to move too much and risk messing with him.

"Yeah?"

"Could you, uh…that thing is still on."

"Oh!" He let out a soft laugh and pushed himself upright, twisting around. My attempts not to move were sorely tested as I felt him moving while still keeping me inside him. It didn't help when he shifted the toy before gently easing it out. "My bad, sorry. I was a little, uh, distracted. Here let me—"

I let out a soft whimper as he pushed himself upward. I was only half hard, and my dick slumped to slap against my stomach with a soft noise, and I let my head fall back again. "Yeah, I get that. That was—"

It wasn't the first time in my life that I wished I had a better grasp of the spoken word. That had easily been one of the most intense, satisfying, and intimate moments of my life. I had trusted Isaiah to know what he was doing, and he had delivered in spades, and now I was still trying to remember my name and where we were.

Isaiah chuckled, patting my stomach affectionately. "While you try to remember how to breathe, I'm going to go clean this up real quick."

He snatched up the toy from the bed, and I smiled when I saw him wobble a little as he walked. It was good to know he'd followed through on his full promise and made sure the experience was pleasurable for him as well. I could only hope that when I had full use of my arms and could do most of the work instead, I could return the favor.

I closed my eyes and smiled, realizing I had thought of a

'next time' without the barest internal flinch. Most of my life, I'd given very little thought to the idea of other men, at least sexually. Whenever anything of the sort threatened to make me think too long about it, my father's voice would rise up and crack like a whip, reminding me what I wasn't allowed to be.

Sure, the voice was there, and part of me suspected it would always be, no matter what I did. Now though, I could think of Isaiah standing in the bathroom, completely naked, my cum inside him, and feel mostly contentment...and maybe weak arousal. I knew he'd come back into the room and probably insist on curling beside me for a little while.

I was looking forward to it.

* * *

"THANKS FOR THIS," I muttered, a little uncomfortable as I looked toward the driver's seat.

Chief Borton glanced at me, raising a thick brow before turning his attention to the road. "Was a little surprised that you messaged me, but you're welcome."

I looked down at my arms, now cast free. The doctor had let me wash my arms, but there was no hiding the fact that my entire right arm and my left forearm had been hidden away from the world. Between the occasional shopping trip with Isaiah and attempts to go on a daily walk after my ankle had healed, the difference in skin tone was obvious, even with my pale complexion.

"I didn't wanna tell anyone that I was going to see the doctor today," I said with a shrug, smiling when I could finally do it with both shoulders. "I wasn't sure if they were going to cut off the casts or not. Didn't want to get anyone's hopes up."

"Isaiah."

"What?"

"You said 'anyone,' but you meant Isaiah. It's not as if there's anyone else you've seen while recovering."

"You stopped by," I said, glancing out the window. It had only been a few times, but it was enough for me to understand that perhaps Borton cared a little. Not as much as he did for the others, but I had never really gone out of my way to involve myself with everyone else.

"But you were willing to disappoint me if your casts didn't come off?"

"I didn't tell you it could happen until it was."

"Yeah, I remember sitting there for an extra twenty minutes while they did it."

"Sorry," I muttered, staring down at my hands and flexing them. It was so strange to see them again, and I kept wiggling them or picking at things just to prove I finally had them back.

Borton snorted. "You ask for a lot less than those other idiots do. But ya know I'm not taking you home, right?"

"What?" I asked, looking up and realizing we were heading in the wrong direction.

"Taking you to the station. Might not seem like it, but everyone's gonna wanna see you with your arms free. Plus, we should probably have a little talk about you coming back in a couple of days and what you're allowed to do when you get back," he said, glancing sidelong at me.

"Oh. Right. Yeah."

"Gotta say, this is the most I've heard you talk in one sitting. At least without sounding like it's the most painful thing in the world anyway."

I held my arms up, giving him a small smile. "I have a reason to feel pretty happy."

"Yeah, probably be nice to wipe your ass without worrying you're gonna make a mess."

That didn't exactly rank high on the list of reasons I was glad to have my arms back. "I guess there's that."

"I probably don't wanna know a few of those reasons."

"Uh—"

"So, how's it been having Isaiah around all the time?"

The timing of the conversation was strange, and I shot him a confused look. "What?"

"Well, the man's practically been living at your apartment for weeks. And seeing as how you two haven't killed one another yet, I guess it's pretty good."

"He's...nice to have around," I said slowly, choosing my words carefully. There was absolutely no way I was going to get into what was going on between Isaiah and me. Only in the past few weeks had I grown comfortable enough when it was just the two of us, so the idea of the rest of the world knowing brought back that old panic.

Borton glanced at me again. "He's got a good heart. Been through a lot of stupid shit in his life, but he's never stopped trying to do things for other people."

"His family didn't deserve him," I muttered.

"He told you about that, eh? Well, I'm not surprised. He doesn't go blabbing it around, even if most people know about it to some degree or another. Can't be the only Bently left in Fairlake after the rest flew the coop and not hear some things. I want you to keep what we just talked about in mind in case you get another fool idea in your head."

I looked up, frowning. "I told you already. We were doing our job. There's—"

"Not that. I already gave him hell for that and gave you some too. I'm talking about why you got transferred to me."

"Oh. That."

"Yeah. Bones filled me in on some things when he called me up. The rest I heard from others."

My choice might have got me in a heap of shit, but the

alternative, keeping my mouth shut and head down while everyone ignored what was going on, was even worse. Maybe I should have handled it differently, but I'd seen his smug face and knew exactly where to plant my fist.

"Okay," I said instead, glaring out the window.

"Listen," he said, pulling into the station's parking lot. "I know enough to know that what you did was justified."

I looked over slowly, frowning but saying nothing until I sighed. "Isaiah?"

Borton scoffed. "You really think he'd tell me anything? All he said was that he thought I should look into that situation a little more closely. And if I found anything 'interesting,' I might want to start making contact through the right channels. That was it."

"Bet you liked that," I chuckled.

"Told him to mind his own business, then did as he asked. Didn't tell him, but after a few calls to some people I trust out that way, I'd heard enough. So, you'll be happy to know I made a few more calls, and they're investigating. Of course, that means they're gonna be looking at Bones too, but he's an idiot or a prick for letting that happen under his watch," Borton told me gruffly.

"Oh. That's...good," I said, feeling a flutter in my chest. "Thanks."

I was going to have to thank Isaiah too at some point. I couldn't believe he'd found a way to help me without spilling everything.

"That said," Borton turned off his truck and turned to stare at me. "You find yourself in a situation like that again, you come to *me*, you got it? It's my job to take care of shit around here when it goes wrong, so you let me do my job. Don't go off and get yourself into shit again. It's just going to get you thrown out on your ass, and you'll have nowhere to go. Then I'll have to deal with Isaiah moping around here because his new bestest friend is gone. I do *not* want to deal with a moping Isaiah, you hear me?"

"Yeah, I hear you."

"Good. He's been through enough shit already. Maybe you can add something good to his life."

"Sure."

He hesitated. "And maybe he can add something good to yours."

Isaiah had already done that, but I couldn't bring myself to say it. Instead, I indulged in the pleasure of opening the passenger door with my right hand instead of having to twist around and fumble with my left. Sliding out, I hit the ground and closed it, smiling at no longer having to fumble with everything all the time.

The back door opened, and one of the twins stepped out, a large garbage bag in his hands. He stopped when he saw us, cocking his head. "Well, hey there, Julian. Chief."

"Hey," I said, shoving my hands into my pockets.

"Looks like they let you out of your cocoons," he said, eyeing my arms.

"Yeah. Just a little bit ago."

"Bet that feels nice."

"Best I've felt in a while."

"Probably makes jerking off easier."

I shook my head. "Yeah, thanks, Larry."

He blinked. "How'd you know?"

"You're the perv," I said with a shrug.

Borton snorted, waving Larry off. "Just because the man don't talk much doesn't mean he's blind and brainless. Get back to work."

"At least now I know why the pizzas are here," Larry muttered, walking toward the back dumpster. "Good seeing you again, Julian."

"You too," I said, following Borton into the back hallway.

"Pizza?"

"When I found out you were getting cut out, I called over and had Zach order some pizzas for everyone. Told them no one was allowed to touch them until I got back," Borton said, sounding smug. "I'm sure there was a lot of whining and grumbling while they waited. Drama queens."

Ignoring his good-natured grumbling, I followed him toward the break room. Almost immediately, I heard Zach pipe up, "Thank God. Rich, the next time you make me order food for a bunch of hungry firemen, make sure you're around to fend them off. I've had to threaten them at least once, and Isaiah thinks he's a fucking ninja, and I can't see his goofy ass trying to sneak some."

"All lies!" Isaiah called from in the room.

"I was held up," Borton said, stepping out of sight. "Picking up the guest of honor."

"Guest of..." Zach began and then stopped when he saw me, glancing down. "Well, hell's bells. Nice tan lines."

"What the hell!" Isaiah yelped, and I spotted him at the back of the room, hopping up from his seat. He practically elbowed Zach out of the way as he reached out, taking hold of my forearms and pulling them toward him. I blinked as he stared down at my arms before turning his head up to frown. "When did they do this?"

"Earlier. In the past hour," I said with a shrug.

"Why didn't you say anything?"

"I didn't know if they were going to do it or not. Didn't want to get anyone's hopes up."

"You ass," he said softly enough that I knew he wasn't upset. "I would have taken the shift off to take you."

"I know," I said with a shrug. "Borton took me instead."

His eyes crinkled at the corners. "Well, it's good to see your arms back. Even if it is a little weird to see them without casts after so long."

"I could always go back and have them put back on if that would make you feel better," I offered, smirking a little.

"Don't you dare," he snorted.

"Did he just make a joke?" Zach asked. "Did…Julian make a joke?"

Which was all it took for us to be reminded we weren't alone in the break room. With a flash of embarrassment, Isaiah pulled his hands back from my arms. Smiling, I ducked my head and put my hands back in my pockets. It was strange to feel his hands on my forearms, and I was itching to have them back.

"Can we eat now?" Terry called from where he'd been sitting next to Isaiah. He had apparently been working out before we'd arrived, wearing a muscle shirt with a cut down each side. When he pushed up, I found myself a little distracted by the sudden view of his sides. They were toned nicely, and I could see the way his muscles flexed as he moved. Considering he and Larry both followed the same routine, I could imagine his twin looked much the same.

Warmth flushed my face at the realization that I had just felt…attraction toward Terry and, inevitably, Larry. Clearing my throat, I pulled my eyes away as everyone crowded around the pizza. Everyone that was, except for Isaiah, glancing at me with a smirk.

With a sense of panic, I grabbed Isaiah by the arm, calling out so everyone could hear me. "I'm borrowing him for a second. Be right back."

Borton looked up from the pizza boxes, raising a brow. "Fine, but I paid for this shit, so get back here soon so you can have some."

We turned just in time for me to slam into Larry, who stumbled backward. I reached out to catch him, pulling him closer to me to steady him.

"Woah," he chuckled. "Where's the fire?"

"Sorry," I grunted, letting go of him immediately, feeling Isaiah's eyes on the back of my head. I couldn't recall a time in my life when I had ever felt as awkward as I did right then. I shuffled to the side, avoiding eye contact with Larry and letting him pass, thankful there was enough room that we didn't brush up against one another.

Clearing my throat, I walked into the hallway and thought about where I wanted to go for a moment before heading toward the locker rooms. I flipped the lights on as we entered, instinctively glancing back toward the shower rooms before turning to face Isaiah.

His brow was raised. "So, wanna tell me why you checked Terry out and then acted like you'd never checked anyone out in your life?"

"You saw that," I said in a strained voice.

"I did, yeah," he said with a snort.

"Shit. I didn't want you to."

"You are aware of the fact that I'm aware of the fact that other people are, in fact, attractive, right?"

"Do you think they're attractive?"

"Eh," he wiggled his hand. "When I first met them, yeah. Had *a lot* of twin fantasies running around in my head."

"But not now?" I asked, trying desperately not to let his words take root in my imagination.

"I worked to more or less put a wall between me and them in that regard. From the looks of it, though, you've got some work to do in that area."

"I've never..." I glanced around. "Sorry."

He reached out, tugging one of my hands free from my pocket and wrapping his hand up in mine. For a moment, I only stared down at our joined hands. It was the first time he'd been able to do more than just hold my fingers, and the sensation of his hand in mine was novel...and welcome.

"You've never been attracted to another guy before? Other than me?"

"Not that I know of. And I didn't want to do it right in front of you."

"Julian."

"What?"

"It doesn't bother me."

"Sure."

"I mean it."

"I know," I said because I did. "It's just...weird."

"Well, maybe you just locked all of it way, all the way down the bottom, so you didn't even know you were bi until everything happened between us. Now that you went and opened Pandora's Box, it's all starting to come out."

"I don't want to sleep with them," I said.

"No," he said, then grinned. "But I'm sure you had some fun ideas about twins at that moment."

I warmed. "Isaiah, don't."

"Trust me, I won't hold something like that against you. Even someone who's used to feeling attracted to people is going to have thoughts and is going to look. You're allowed to look, and you're allowed to feel attracted to people."

I pulled my other hand out of my pocket to grab him by the waist with my right hand, pulling him close. His eyes widened, and he reached out with his free hand to brace against my chest. Fulfilling one of my many wishes over the past month, I wrapped my arm around his waist and held him close.

"I want *you*," I said quietly, giving his waist a squeeze. "Even if I feel...other things for other people. I want you."

"For what it's worth, I know that you having thoughts isn't the same thing," he said softly. "But it never hurts to hear that you're wanted."

Reveling in my regained bodily freedom, I pushed him

until his back hit a row of lockers. Isaiah tilted his head back, and I caught his lips with mine, immediately deepening the kiss. He let out a low groan of pleasure as I pinned him in place, and I felt just how pleased he was by the sudden presence of his cock pressing against my leg.

"Don't you dare tempt me to do something I shouldn't be doing with the building full of guys," Isaiah grumbled at me, even as he ground against my leg.

"Coming over tonight?" I asked softly, even though I knew the answer.

"Damn straight," he chuckled. "Emphasis on the coming, I hope."

"I'm sure we can manage," I said, grudgingly pulling away from him. We would have plenty of time later tonight, and less chance of being discovered, after his shift was over. "Borton's talking about bringing me back."

"Oh?" Isaiah asked, frowning. "Bringing you back how?"

"Probably light stuff for a few weeks," I said with a shrug. "Not what I'd like, but it beats sitting around my apartment for days on end."

"You didn't seem to mind it too much. You looked pretty comfortable," Isaiah said, cocking his head.

"Probably because you were there to keep me company… and stop me from going insane."

"I'm sure there were other benefits too."

"If I'm not allowed to tease you, you're not allowed to tease me," I told him with a scowl, opening the locker door.

Isaiah laughed, the sound echoing off the walls of the hallway. "Fine, fine, I'll be good. But if you're tired of your apartment, you're always free to come to my house. I really can't believe it took me this long to offer."

"I never thought about it," I said, then shrugged. "Sure."

A smile curled at the corners of his lips as he squeezed my hand. "Sure."

ISAIAH

"I hope you aren't expecting anything fancy," I told him as we drove down my street. It had been a week since I'd made the offer to come over before Julian finally took me up on it. Not that it was an excuse for him to see more of me. Nothing in our patterns had changed. Sure, I didn't need to be around to help take care of things anymore, but that didn't mean I didn't have reasons to be around him.

His eyes were on the neighborhood, a quiet little slice of Fairlake that sat at the southern end of the town. It contained some of the older houses built before what would eventually be the town center was raised north of my neighborhood. Considering its historic nature, a lot of effort went into the homes, both by those who lived in them and because Fairlake itself wanted to keep its oldest suburb as well-kept as possible.

"Nicer than where I live," he said quietly, eyes flicking over a two-story house, the lawn lined by a wrought-iron fence that looked like it had been bought yesterday.

"Well," I began and realized I didn't know what to say. I could tell there was no bitterness or anger in his voice, but I still felt a twinge of guilt. There was no denying that comparing our two living places was comparing night to day.

The shadow on his face passed, and Julian looked over, smiling softly. Reaching out, he took my hand in his, squeezing it. I took it for the comfort it was probably meant to be, setting our twined hands on my thigh as I reached my house.

It was one of the smaller houses on the block, mostly because I didn't need much space for myself. It sat on a slight incline, but thankfully whoever had the house before me had squared off the lawn, so the property didn't dip down the hill. It was small, longer than it was wide, with a large window at the front where my living room was. A small porthole window was at the top where an attic had originally been. I wasn't much for yard work, but the yard was clean, and I'd made sure the blue paintwork of the house had been maintained, thinking it added some charm.

Pulling into the driveway beside the house, I turned my car off and stepped out.

"C'mon in and make yourself comfortable."

The kitchen, much like the house itself, was long rather than wide. It was amusing to see Julian come in and look around, probably unaware of just how much his bulk filled the narrow space. I kicked my shoes off, leaving them by the back door, walked past the breakfast nook I had put in the living room, and turned on the lights.

"Leather," he murmured, running his hands over the plush couch I had in the center of the room. There was a sturdy shelf under the large front window that I often spread out on while I read, but the couch was a close second for my favorite lazy spot.

"You're going to find a lot of leather and wood," I said, tapping my socked toes on the floor. "And stone. The house mostly came like that, but I've just fed into it."

"Looks nice," he said, smiling at the shelf under the window where I'd left a book and an empty mug of tea behind.

"It's also insanely easier to clean than fabric," I said with a smirk. "I like things clean, but that doesn't mean I want to work my ass off cleaning it."

He peered around, spotting the doorway. Smiling, I led him in, nodding toward the door directly across from me. "Bathroom. That's literally one of two rooms in the whole house I had someone come in and change."

"Like what?"

"Like the fact that though I'm not part giant like you are—"

"You're not small."

"I'm still not exactly little either," I finished, opening the door to reveal the large shower I had installed. "There's enough space in there to fit a cow if I want…well, maybe not a steer, but anyway. Plus, multiple showerheads."

"Why?"

"Because I don't like to feel like I'm showering in a tiny box?"

"Why multiple showerheads?"

"Oh. Well, we'll have a shower later, and you'll figure it out quick enough."

That made him smile, and I pointed toward the door to our left. "That is the guest room. Don't usually have much use for it, but hey, it's better to have and not need than to need and not have, right?" I turned and pointed at the door on our right, which was open, and I could see my large desk with my absurdly expensive computer sitting on it. "And this is where I do most of my screwing around. Got a whole fancy gaming computer, enough space to do some VR, and where I keep some of my books."

"I didn't know you played games," he said, then glanced around. "Wait—"

"What?" I asked.

"Where's…your room? This is all the rooms."

I winked. "See, that's where the second room I changed comes into play. This is the fun one."

I walked to where a door sat in the ceiling. Stepping to one side, I pulled the chain, bringing the attic door down. After unfolding the ladder, I motioned for him to go up. He shot me a curious look before taking the ladder carefully as he tested its strength against his bulk. Apparently satisfied it wasn't going to shatter under his weight, he climbed up, giving me the perfect sight of his ass.

"Nice ass," I called up, smirking when I heard him grunt in response. Julian was *terrible* at accepting compliments, which of course, meant I went out of my way to give them. That it just so happened to be a fantastic ass was a nice bonus.

As I reached the bottom of the ladder, I heard him. "Oh."

I climbed up, far more confident in the ladder's strength than he was, and pulled myself up. I found him standing in the middle of the room, looking around with big eyes. I flicked the switch, turning on the strings of lights I had draped along the rafters of the attic. The entire space had been scrubbed thoroughly, and I'd had power routed upstairs to more than just one bare bulb.

The beams were exposed but kept their dark color, which shone in the sunlight. There was the original small porthole window facing the front of the house, but at the back, I'd installed a large window that looked down on my yard and, coincidentally, the woods and Rockies in the distance. There were shelves lined with books of all sorts, a small seating area near the porthole window, and my large, plush bed positioned under the large window.

"This is," he spun around slowly, gazing around, "cozy."

"Yeah, it is," I said, grinning. "I had the idea after living here for a few months. Had to go through a handful of changes to get it done, but I don't regret it for a moment. C'mere."

I grabbed his hand and pulled him toward the bed. Then, with a light shove, I pushed him onto his back. He hit the mattress with a frown, only to freeze and gaze around.

"Right?" I asked with a laugh. "That mattress is probably the most expensive thing I own after my gaming computer. I don't regret a single cent spent on it, though. I get the best sleep in the world on it."

"I can see why," he said, pushing himself up so he could properly sprawl across it. "I can't believe you chose to willingly sleep on my bed when you had this thing waiting for you."

"Well," I said, slinking forward and adjusting slightly before launching myself at him. His eyes widened as I came down, grunting as I landed on his barrel of a chest. "Probably because the company in your bed was a lot better."

He raised his hands, wrapping his arms around me and holding me against him. I slid down so I was on the bed but still pressed against him. The familiar comfort of my bed combined with the scent of his woodsy cologne that always hung around him, even lingering on his clothes a few days after he'd taken them off. I breathed deep, letting myself take respite in the warmth of his body and the feel of his strength.

"I wonder what it would be like to raise a family in a place like this," he said quietly after several minutes of silence.

He had never mentioned a family before, and I peered up at him. "Do you want to raise a family?"

"Me? No. Not a good idea," he said quickly. "I was just...I grew up in places like my apartment. When my dad was around, he drank most of the money. Didn't get much better after he left, though. My mom didn't take him leaving very well. She was always worrying, constantly smoking, and could barely hold a job most of the time. It didn't improve until I could get a job and help out."

"Help out? Is that your way of saying you handed over everything?" I asked softly, watching his face.

Julian's face scrunched, sighing heavily. "All of it. Yeah."

I nodded. It fit what he'd told me before. Even now, he was caring for his mother even though it severely affected his quality of life. A firefighter's income wasn't amazing, but it was enough that he should have been able to help her and afford a better apartment in Fairlake. "What about your brother?"

"He...Mom wanted him to focus on school," Julian said, shrugging his broad shoulders and jostling both of us in the process. "Not that he really wanted to do that. He wanted to spend time with his friends, date, and party. It was usually me who had to go pick him up when he got himself into trouble."

"Because you couldn't tell your mom," I guessed.

"No. She worried about enough as it was. The last thing she needed was to know that not only was her one son barely getting through shit, but her better son was also screwing around."

"Ah," I said, keeping my opinions to myself. It was better that he did the talking.

"He was the one with the best chances, even if he was screwing around and risking it," Julian said, closing his eyes. "It's why I...when Tristan broke that guy's jaw at a party. I was the one who..."

He stopped, and I realized what he was trying to say. "You took the fall."

"Yeah."

"How, if you weren't even there?"

"I was there, just too late to stop it from happening. Everything happened so fast, and people were pretty drunk. It wasn't hard to stand there and say it was me when you had a bunch of drunk teenagers who didn't know up from down. Guy pressed charges, and it wasn't like I had plans for anything that a felony would keep me from. Tristan had college waiting for him, scholarships he barely managed to make, a whole career."

"Okay," I said slowly, taking stock of everything. "Which meant you were kept from any job that would have looked at your record…which is all of them."

"I said it didn't make a difference."

"You did. Which meant Chief Bones knew about it when he hired you."

"Wasn't too happy about it, but I had what I needed, and well, even if I seemed like trouble to him, I'm a big guy. I can handle a lot."

"So you were brought into that station with the specter of your felony, your brother's felony, hanging over you. Which is probably why they treated you like dirt, and no one wanted to listen to you."

"Probably. Makes sense."

"Which is what led to you being the odd man out, hitting that guy, and barely managing to get transferred to our station."

"As a favor."

I took a moment not to lose my temper as I continued. "And now you're living in *those* apartments because you're giving your mom so much money that that's all you can afford. While your brother is, what, off fucking around college?"

"Law degree. He's going to be a lawyer. Mom fills me in from time to time."

Taking another deep breath, I let it out slowly before

pushing myself up to kneel next to him. Julian stared at me in confusion as I reached out and placed my hand on his chest.

"Listen to me," I said to him, keeping my voice calm. "Literally, none of what you just told me is okay."

I could see the way those shutters tried to come down. "Oh."

"No, *listen*," I said urgently, taking his hand in mine. "In no way, shape or form should any of the things you told me be your responsibility. It wasn't right for you to be put in that position. No child should have to forfeit everything, including their future, to take care of their mother and brother."

"Someone had to do it," he said, jaw tightening. "I know you had your own problems, but there wasn't a problem with money or food for you."

"That's not what I'm saying. It's *beyond* admirable that you did all those things and found it in you to be stronger than your mother, better than your father, and more selfless than your brother. But that's my point, you gave and gave and gave for so long, Julian. You've given things no one should *ever* have to give."

"I—"

"Like taking the fall for your brother when it should be him who has to face a life of constantly being treated suspiciously because of *his* bad choices. And don't get me wrong, I'm sure life has been hard on your mother, but from the looks of it, there's a time and place where she has to figure it out. It *should* have been when you were still a kid, but that time is long past. You deserve to have something for yourself. To be selfish and think of *you*."

He made to sit up, and I caught his face with my hands. "I'm sorry if this upsets you, I really am. But all you just did was confirm that you really are a gentle soul, with far more kindness than most of the people I've met. You deserve to feel good. You deserve to be treated well, okay?"

Julian stared at me intensely as I continued to hold his face, not backing off as I saw the storm going on in his head through his eyes. It was one of the few times he didn't immediately shut off his expression, and I was going to take it for the gift that it was.

After a minute, his expression softened, and he leaned into my touch. "You do."

"What's that?" I asked, gently drawing his head into my lap where he could lie peacefully.

"Take care of me. Make me feel good," he whispered, closing his eyes.

I ran my hand down the back of his head, fighting the stinging in my eyes. "I try, and I'm glad I do. And maybe one day, we can get you to see that you're allowed to take care of yourself."

"Maybe," he said, reaching up to hold my thigh and give it a squeeze. "But I want to do those things for you."

"And you do," I promised him. "Don't you worry about that. I'm happy."

"Good," he said, burying his face in my lap and breathing deeply. "Good."

There was nothing left to say to fill the silence, so I simply knelt there while he hid his face. Gradually I watched the tension in his body leave as he gave into the comfort of my bed and my touch as I gently stroked him. For all I knew, these moments were the only ones he'd ever had in his life, and I was more than happy to give them to him.

For as long as I could.

* * *

"CHRIST," I grumbled, pulling at my shirt and sighing at the smell. "That was such a fun call."

Zach chuckled behind me. "I told you not to get too close, but you never listen to anyone."

"I listen," I complained, looking at my filthy hands.

"To who?" Zach asked, hanging his helmet on a hook. "Chief, but only when he's pissed at you. And Lover Boy."

"L-lover, what now?" I spluttered, momentarily forgetting about my misery.

Julian entered the truck bay, wiping his hands and frowning. "What's on your face?"

"Speak of the devil," Zach muttered and then raised his voice. "Someone got a little too close to our barn fire."

Julian's frown deepened, and I could practically see him generating the worst-case scenario in his head. "What'd you do?"

"How was I supposed to know the damn thing would explode?" I complained loudly. "And it was filled with... actual shit?"

"Explode?"

Zach rolled his eyes. "He's being a bit dramatic. It was less of an explosion and more like...a water balloon."

"Full of shit," I added, still annoyed at the idea.

"Which our resident genius here got splattered in," Zach said, gesturing to me. Most of me had been safe, but I knew damn well some of it had managed to get inside my coat and onto my clothes and skin. And even if it hadn't, I wouldn't feel clean until I scrubbed myself raw. "Because he didn't listen when I told him that maybe he didn't want to stand too close."

"I like fires," I muttered.

Julian raised his brow. "I know arsonists are more likely to be firemen, but they don't usually out themselves so quickly to their coworkers."

Zach snorted, patting Julian on the shoulders. "Gotta say, I like this new sense of humor you found while you were holed up, being driven mad by Isaiah."

"Shut up," I said with a scowl, remembering his previous comment and deciding I needed to corner the man later. "Where are you going?"

"It is two o'clock, well past my bedtime. I'm going to go catch a nap and pray nothing else wakes me up," he said with a yawn, stalking off.

I rolled my eyes. "At least he sleeps like the dead unless the alarm goes off, so I don't have to deal with him for the rest of the night."

"You okay?" Julian asked, looking me over.

"Yeah, I'm fine," I said with a sigh. The call had been simple, not even needing to bring in the on-call team. Just a barn that had caught fire. Zach and I had been there more or less to keep it contained. It was pretty easy to do since it was isolated from other buildings and the ground was damp. It was mostly watching until it died down enough for us to kill what remained and let the cops deal with the family. "I am going to go melt myself in the shower and pretend I don't have flecks of shit all over me. Anything of note while we were gone?"

"No," he said, sounding grumpy. Julian had been brought back onto the roster, but considering it had only been a couple of weeks since the casts had come off, the chief was still keeping him on light duty. Which meant that while those on shift could go out on a call, he had to stay behind, manning the radio, dealing with dinner, and other things.

"Feeling antsy, huh?" I guessed, kicking off my boots finally.

"A little," he admitted with a shrug.

Considering the only other person in the building had just walked off to fall asleep, I reached out without hesitation to pull him in for a kiss. "Only a few more hours. Then we can both crawl into bed…or maybe screw on my couch again and fall asleep."

"So you can roll off me and onto the floor when you wake up?" he asked with a smirk.

"That was one time," I told him with a playful swat. "Now, if you don't mind. I'm scrubbing myself raw."

"Sure," he said, watching as I marched toward the hallway.

I passed the break room and dipped into the locker room, opening mine to retrieve the toiletry bag and my big towel. I pulled my socks off, throwing them in the bag I always brought for dirty clothes. In went the rest of my clothes before I hurried to the shower. For whatever reason, every room in the station was perfectly comfortable, but the locker room and showers were always cold until someone got a nice steaming shower going to balance the temperature.

The shower stalls were basic, each stall separated by barriers. Curtains blocked each of the stalls off, but as I'd learned, that didn't really matter. All of us were insanely comfortable with one another, so even if we showered in privacy, that didn't stop most of us from walking around with everything hanging free before and after the shower.

Choosing the stall at the end, I slid the curtain open and left it open as I fiddled with the water, standing off to one side while I adjusted the temperature. Once settled, I opened my bag and pulled out my body wash and shampoo, setting it on the shelf in the corner. I allowed myself to soak in the water for a few minutes, pretending it was getting rid of the memory of a massive splatter of shit striking me.

With that done, I scrubbed shampoo into my hair and covered myself head to toe in the body wash. The amount was excessive, but I didn't care as I scrubbed every inch of my body I could reach before rinsing it. With that done, I turned into the spray, letting it hit my hair and wash it down my back.

"You know," a voice began, startling me. "This was more fun to watch than I thought."

"Jesus," I barked, turning to find Julian smirking at me. Almost immediately, I realized he wasn't wearing a stitch of clothing. My eyes widened as I looked over his completely exposed body, feeling a pulse in my groin when I saw he was half hard. "What…are you doing?"

"Joining you," he said, stepping forward and pulling the curtain closed behind him. Not that it mattered, anyone could look in and see two pairs of feet in one stall.

The idea sent a zing of anticipation through me, but the voice of reason was still inside my thoughts. "Uh, we're not exactly alone here."

"I already looked in on Zach," he said and reached out with one hand to wrap around my hardening cock, giving it a few strokes. "He's out cold, and you know he's not waking up unless we scream at him."

My eyelids fluttered as he continued stroking me. "That's…true."

"And I saw an opportunity," he said, reaching out with his other hand and setting a bottle on the shelf with my supplies. "So I'm taking it."

"Bold," I said in approval pulling him closer so I could kiss him.

After the first few fumbling attempts where he was finding his footing, Julian had grown more confident as the weeks went on. I no longer had to be the one trying to bridge the gap. Instead, I found Julian instigating sex more often than I did. It was certainly a welcome change of pace, and I was all for encouraging him to push for it more often if that's what he wanted.

"Probably shouldn't push our luck, though," he said, his

cock pushing against my hip, slick and sliding against my body easily. "Well, maybe a little."

"I'm listening," I said, reaching down to wrap my hand around his thick shaft.

He plucked the bottle up. "I did a little research."

"Did you now?"

"Found out why our lube was so bad for shower stuff."

"Well, yeah, it's water-based. Washes right off. That's why you get blowjobs in the shower."

"Turns out you can get away with using lube in the shower if it's silicone based."

My brow raised as he turned the bottle for me to see those exact words. "Oh shit, are you telling me you decided the first time we fuck in the shower is at *work*?"

A bit of doubt reached his eyes. "Is that okay?"

"Yes, yes, it fucking is," I told him, pulling him into another fierce kiss. I had no idea where this sudden urge for risky, semi-public sex had come from, but there was no way in hell I was going to turn it down.

I was distracted enough that I didn't notice until his finger slid inside me that he'd been lubing up his digits. A grunt of surprise left me, and I smirked a little when I felt him curl his finger just right to get a low groan out of me. He might have come to having sex with me with very little knowledge, but he was a quick learner and a dedicated student.

"Someone's feeling spicy today," I chuckled, nipping at his neck like I knew he liked it.

"A little," he said, with more heat than I was used to hearing. Something had riled him up, but I wasn't altogether sure it was the idea of fucking me in the shower stall at the station.

"Then forget the prep," I said, backing up, so he was forced to pull his finger free.

His brow furrowed. "What?"

I turned to face the wall, planting my hands on it and pushing my ass toward him. "Go for it."

"I don't...want to hurt you."

"You won't. You'll stop if I say."

Whatever mental battle he had going on inside him was quickly won as he stared at me, presenting myself. He quickly squeezed a decent amount of lube on himself. Then, hunching down, I felt one of his hands come down on my waist while he steadied himself and began to push forward.

I wasn't surprised when the first entry burned far more than before. While I was confident with most partners that they could go in with minimal or no preparation on my part, Julian was a different matter entirely. Only a few weeks fucking had led me to think we might be able to manage it now my body was more or less used to it.

That didn't stop the burning ache as he pushed inside, but I had to admit it wasn't as bad as it might have been. I still had to make him stop a couple of times, but only for a few seconds. It wasn't long until he was sheathed in me completely, and I groaned softly as I could feel just how hard he was.

"God, you're gorgeous," he said, running a hand down my back, fingernails gently nipping at my skin.

"And you feel amazing," I groaned. "Move. I want to feel you come inside me."

It was more my kink than his, as he was pretty content to come wherever, but he also knew it was a sign that I was incredibly turned on. He reared back, bringing his hand down so one was on each of my hips. He pulled me back as he pushed forward, burying himself to the hilt once more.

The fading burn inside flared to life, but at the same time, I felt the surge of pleasure that tried to wipe all thoughts from my mind. I bowed my head with a low groan as he began to work himself up. Normally, Julian took his time, building up into a steady but deep rhythm. Having the use of his arms had made him into a dedicated but usually controlled lover.

This time, however, he began working me far more roughly than he'd ever done. His hips slammed into my ass repeatedly, and I realized just how little he cared about where we were as the sound of our wet skin slapping against each other filled the room. Pressing my forehead against the shower stall, I groaned fiercely as he began to hammer away, having to stop every once in a while to adjust his footing.

Before I knew what was happening, he turned me around to face the low shelf. I knew immediately what he wanted, bending forward so it hiked my ass up, making it easier. With this new angle, he found his rhythm, and my whole body began to jerk with each thrust.

However, there were no complaints from me, not from how he hammered away at my insides or his fierce grip on my hips. My cock jutted out, bouncing with each harsh thrust, and I could see how badly I was leaking. I had no time to adjust to each wave of pleasure with every thrust, feeling like I was being tossed around on a sea of bliss.

"Fuck," he grunted and gave one final, hard thrust to bury himself inside me. Julian was thick enough, and in this case, hard enough, that if neither of us moved, I could feel the pulse of each spurt as he came inside me. The very knowledge of what was happening was enough to make me moan, no longer caring that it echoed off the walls.

He pulled out, leaving me to groan in frustration before he spun me around and knelt before me. My heart hammered in my chest as he brought my cock to his mouth. He had shown frustration in the past that he couldn't deep throat as I could, but I'd never needed it before, and I didn't need it now. He had just spent a few minutes working my ass over with more confidence and vigor than he'd ever done before, and now he was taking my cock into his mouth with plenty of enthusiasm.

I was glad the shelf was behind me as I shuddered, reaching down to grip his hair fiercely. Without thinking, I began moving his head for him, bringing him down as far as I dared onto my dick. I knew it wouldn't take long, but I could still revel in the thrill of using his mouth, much like he'd used my ass.

With a hearty groan, my hips shuddered, and I pulled his head back as I came. The first few spurts landed in his mouth, but I'd pulled back enough that it broke free, sending a couple of sprays into his face. It wasn't the first time my cum had ended up on his face, but I didn't think I would ever get tired of the sight.

"Shit," I mumbled as he stood up, and I pulled him close to lick the corner of his lips. "I don't know where *that* came from."

"Are you okay?" he asked, and I could hear the worry in his voice.

"You're lucky I'm still standing," I chuckled, pulling him close to kiss him gently. "And if I weren't okay, I would have told you."

"Right," he said, now almost shy. A direct contrast to the behemoth who had just used my body.

"I do have to ask, though, are you okay?" I asked softly. "Never seen that from you before."

"Just been...frustrated, I guess," he said with a shrug.

I lay my head against his chest, letting us both soak in the warmth of the shower. "Because of light duty?"

"Yeah. You and Zach went out earlier, and I felt useless. I hate that."

"I know. And you know you're not useless, right?"

"I know. It just feels that way sometimes."

"Well, I for one, love having you around again," I chuckled, reaching down to playfully squeeze his softened dick. "Especially if you're going to start pulling stuff like this on me."

"Feels like I used you a little," he admitted, rubbing my jaw with his thumb.

"I could jokingly say you did, but if you used me, it's because I wanted to be used," I told him gently, kissing his chest. "All I felt was a whole lot of good things. So yeah, if you wanna whip that monster mode out on me again, feel free."

"Sure," he said, bending down to kiss my forehead. "Let's get you dried off. I think you're clean now."

"Unless you count the load in my—"

"We talked about you teasing me after we've already had sex."

"That it might get me sex again a few hours later?"

Julian shook his head but couldn't hide his smile. "We'll see what happens when we clock out."

Somehow, I thought I knew what would happen, but I could wait.

* * *

"I'M SO glad I convinced them to start serving these," I told Julian, holding my bread bowl full of steaming soup out toward him. It was the perfect accompaniment to our walk around town. Although he could just as easily run on a treadmill or just run in general, he preferred to get his cardio by going on walks with me.

I might have got a little choked up when he said that.

"You realize I have one too?" he asked, holding up his own, which was full of chowder.

"Yes, because I insisted they start making them during the

spring, but especially during the autumn. When it gets cold around here, people need warm clothing to warm their bodies, but good hot food and drink to warm their souls," I told him, nodding.

"A shame they didn't use you for their slogans," he chuckled.

"Oh, someone thinks they're hilarious," I grumbled.

"Well, look who it is," a familiar voice called out, and I turned to see Bennett waving from the other side of the street. He wasn't alone. I could see Adam to his right, their hands intertwined. Just behind them on the sidewalk was the dark-haired Chase, who scowled in our direction while the smaller, dark-haired man beside him smiled softly and raised a hand in greeting.

"Oh, hey guys," I called, glancing to make sure it was safe before crossing. "What're you four up to?"

"Bennett decided we should have a double date," Adam informed me, shaking his head.

"You do know it's possible to tell him no, right?" I asked.

"I do it all the time, but no one ever listens to me," Chase grumbled.

I eyed him, not at all fooled by his seemingly foul mood. That was just Chase. "Right, and yet despite all that experience, here you are, doing what he wants."

The other man, Devin, who I had only met once before, laughed softly. "That's what *I* told him, but here we are."

Bennett glanced over my shoulder. "Well, hey there, Julian. Which one did you get?"

"What?" Julian asked, and even without looking, I could see that familiar crease forming in his brow.

"Soup," Bennett said, pointing at the bowl.

"Oh. Chowder, supposed to be clam, but I don't think it is."

"What else could it be?"

"Probably seafood that's easier to get. I don't mind. It's good."

"Lyre's food is pretty legendary around here," Bennett agreed. "What are you guys up to?"

"We are currently enjoying delicious, warm food while we walk back to his apartment. We may or may not watch something on TV, and then...I don't know," I said, shooting Bennett a warning look. After the initial phone call, I hadn't told him too many details. Not because I didn't trust Bennett not to blab to the whole town but because now things between Julian and I had...evolved, it didn't feel right to tell too much of what was his business as well.

Bennett knew enough to know things were going well for us and that I wasn't being used as an experiment. There were still potential problems, like Julian's tendency to lock himself away whenever he felt threatened or the fact that he had a hard time believing in himself. But those were things I was willing to accept and help him work on. Maybe after a little more time, I'd talk to Julian about at least opening up to this group.

"Ooh! I could give you some recommendations," Bennett said, eyes lighting up.

"Your taste in movies is like your taste in music, awful," Chase told him with a smirk.

"It is not!" Bennett protested.

"Babe," Adam said, squeezing Bennett's hand affectionately. "It kind of is."

"You love my taste in movies!"

"Yeah, well, I also love you, so let's not use my taste as a good measure," Adam said with a snort.

"That...is so rude," Bennett whined.

"And true," Chase muttered, earning himself a glare from Bennett.

"This is the part where you're supposed to help me," Bennett told me.

"Sorry, can't talk with my mouth full," I said, shoving a spoonful of hot soup into my mouth. The sudden burn was well worth the look of betrayal on Bennett's face.

Bennett sighed, looking morosely at Julian. "Do you see what I have to put up with? I hope they canonize me after I die."

"Maybe they'll put you on one of the nicer saint medallions," Julian offered quietly from behind me.

I turned, giving him a smirk of appreciation. Seeing his sense of humor was a rare treat, and I was impressed he decided to pull it out in front of people he didn't know. He'd done it a handful of times at the station, which I'd taken to be a good sign of how much he was starting to come out of his shell. I had even spotted him having a few quiet conversations with the guys at the station.

"I can only hope," Bennett said with an indignant sniff I knew he didn't mean. There wasn't a lot that got under his skin, especially a little bit of good-natured teasing. "You guys are free to join us if you want."

No one else could hear it, but I listened to the soft exhale from Julian that signified he wasn't feeling the idea. I didn't know if it was because he was wary about being in a group of people he didn't know or at the inference that we were on a date. Not that we weren't dating, but I knew full well Julian wasn't ready to make that anyone else's business.

"Nah, we're just gonna go veg out in front of the TV," I said with a wave of my hand, pushing aside my disappointment. I understood why Julian was reluctant to make anything known, even if it was to a group of guys who wouldn't have a problem with what we were up to. That didn't change the fact that sometimes I wished we...well, we could be a little more open. As my family could clearly attest, though they never touched the subject, I wasn't one for hiding things.

Bennett cocked his head but kept his smile, and I knew I would get a concerned text later. "No problem. We'll catch you guys another time."

"Yeah," I said, trying not to cringe. Now I had to figure out how much I could tell Bennett and what to keep to myself, which would only invite further concern depending on how vague I was, so that was going to be fun.

The four of them bid farewell and continued walking toward the town center. I smiled as I watched Chase reach out and swat Bennett on the shoulder for something he'd said, only to make Bennett cackle his mad laugh. It was followed by Devin taking Chase's hand in his, and even from a handful of yards away, I could see the lines of Chase's shoulders ease, and I bet he'd squeezed the man's fingers in response.

Turning, I continued walking with Julian, our shoulders no longer bumping together. I could practically feel the gears in Julian's head turning furiously, but as always, I knew it was better to wait until he voiced whatever was going on. To keep myself from fretting too much, I continued working my way through the soup.

It wasn't until I was at the point where I was tearing the bowl apart to start devouring the tasty, soup-soaked bread that Julian finally spoke up. "Sorry."

I chewed furiously, swallowing. "Why?"

"I know you probably wanted to go with them," he said slowly, looking down at the sidewalk rather than at me.

"No, I want to spend time with you," I told him, tearing off another piece of the bread bowl to shove into my mouth.

"Sure. But you wanted to do that with them," he said, shrugging. "You didn't do it because you thought I wouldn't be comfortable."

"You wouldn't be," I pointed out.

"Yeah. So, sorry."

"You don't have to be sorry because you're not comfortable."

"I'm sorry because me being uncomfortable kept you from doing something you wanted to do. Because I'm... because I don't want to have other people know things."

I sighed, tearing another piece away as I neared the bottom of the bowl. "I know how hard it can be, Julian. I struggled through it a bit myself."

"You didn't wait this long."

"True, but everyone's experience is going to be different."

"Sure."

Sighing, I stuffed the last shreds in my mouth, chewing them hurriedly before turning to face him and gripping his upper arms. "Listen to me, Julian. I'm not going to expect you to do things like I did or at the pace I did, okay? Whatever you do, it has to be because you want to do it and when."

"Yeah," Julian said, and even though he didn't shrug his shoulders this time, I could tell he wasn't convinced. "You're still disappointed."

"What I am is happy to have time to spend with you," I told him, skirting around the more forward answer. "C'mon, don't beat yourself up."

The corner of Julian's mouth twitched in what I took as an attempt at a smile. "Bennett knows, doesn't he?"

I hadn't been prepared for the question, and I knew the answer showed on my face, which meant there was no point in trying to hide it. "I, uh, kind of called him after that first night."

"First night?" he wondered, brow creasing. "Oh. The massage."

"Right. That."

"Why?"

"Because, like I told you that day, I was nervous and freaking out a little. I called him up to talk to him," I explained, wincing. "Since he was the only person with any experience with that whole thing, I figured he was the one to call."

"Because of him and Adam?"

"Yeah, because of them."

"Does Adam know?"

"I don't know. Probably. Those two shared everything before they got together, well, almost everything. Pretty sure they fixed the 'almost' part after Bennett fessed up to having a big gay crush on his not-so-straight boyfriend."

Julian chuckled. "You're still having a hard time with that, aren't you?"

"How could you tell?" I asked with a soft laugh. "I guess it's just...with you, I already knew you weren't *totally* straight. At least, during the massage I did because of what you told me. Whereas Adam hadn't had a gay thought in his life until whatever the hell happened that night between him and Bennett."

"You were the one who said that sexuality can be really strange with people," Julian pointed out.

I sighed, drawing my arms away from him and nodding. "I know. It's just weird to think about."

"I get it," Julian said with a small smile. "It's a lot better when things make sense. If there's logic you can recognize, then it's easier."

"Eh, sometimes I'm better about rolling with things. But all that matters is that they're happy. I'll worry about making sense of it later."

"Funny," he said with a light chuckle. "That's what I learned from you to start trying to do. Figured you were the master."

I couldn't help my laugh, fighting the urge to reach down

and twine our fingers together as we approached his apartment building. "I haven't really mastered it."

"Expert then."

"Even experts fail in their specialized field. Look at how you let a whole house fall on you."

Julian snorted, nudging me hard enough that I stumbled. "I seem to recall at least one reason I was in that house. Maybe because another specialist fell through the floor like a real expert?"

I swatted his arm playfully. "Look, there were extenuating circumstances."

"I'm just glad you weren't hurt too badly," he said softly.

"Yeah," I agreed, then glanced at him. "Sorry that you got banged up so bad."

To my surprise, he stopped at the edge of the parking lot, glancing around for a moment before reaching out and taking my hands. It was only then I realized he'd been looking for any potential onlookers. There was still the chance that someone could see since there were plenty of uncovered windows. Still, I wasn't going to remind him when he'd found the courage to do even this much.

"I'm not sorry at all," he said softly. "If it wasn't for that, I wouldn't have had you staying with me, taking care of me. And if that hadn't happened, then we wouldn't be...what we are right now."

It warmed me, and I ducked my head, feeling my face burn. "Yeah, well, hold off on saying that until you've dealt with me long enough."

"Oh yeah?"

"Yeah."

"So what do I have to look forward to?"

"Well, there's my temper," I said with a chuckle.

"Pretty sure you've already managed to chew me out once. So I think we've got that covered."

Well, that hadn't been my true temper, but there wasn't any point in driving it home. "Oh, there's my constant need to keep things clean, my mood swings that come out of nowhere because I start thinking about stupid shit. And the weird way I eat sandwiches."

Julian blinked, shaking his head. "I...the weird way you eat sandwiches?"

"Nibble the corners, then the rest of the crust off. Then work your way in."

"Uh, why?"

"Because I don't like the crust on much of anything."

"Even pizza?"

"Won't eat the crust on pizza. Surprised you didn't notice."

Julian wrinkled his nose. "That's...pie?"

"Nope."

"You're a lost cause."

He said it with such gravity I couldn't help but laugh. "See? You're already learning."

"I think I'll be able to live with it," Julian said, the corners of his eyes crinkling. "Which is...I didn't think I'd ever think that about someone."

"Well," I began, taken off-guard by the heartfelt admission. It wasn't that Julian didn't know how to express himself or hadn't grown comfortable enough to do that lately. It just wasn't usually this...sentimental. "I'm glad that...well—"

The corner of his lips twitched. "I didn't think I'd see the day you'd be at a loss for words."

My nervousness fluttered away as I laughed. "Okay, well, it's not something that happens very often, so I guess you should feel proud of yourself."

"I only feel that way when I make you smile."

That was twice in only a few seconds that he managed to

throw me for a loop, and I was left to stare up at him in wonder. "Oh."

"I know things haven't been what you're used to with other people," he said slowly, a wince flashing across his face. "But things have been better for me being around you, having you around. I-I'm bad at this."

"You're doing amazing so far," I said with a snort. "You've managed to keep me at a loss for words pretty consistently."

He took a deep breath. "Okay. My point is I'm glad everything happened like it did. And I want to make things better for both of us in the future. I know that I-I'm kind of slow at things."

"We talked about this," I said with a smile. "At your own speed."

"I know," he said, trying for a smile. "But I also know you deserve better. And I know it would be better for me too. Not having to look over my shoulder. Being worried all the time."

"It might bring down your stress levels," I admitted with a chuckle.

"Yeah," he said, returning my smile. "It's...different for me. But it's not always a bad different. Sometimes, well, I want to get better about things. I know it'll take me a little while, but—"

"Well, we just reminded you this is about your time, your speed, so there you go."

"Yeah. I just wanted to tell you, is all."

"Well, thank you," I said softly, momentarily pressing my forehead against his chest. "I appreciate it. I'll be here to help, alright?"

"I was hoping you'd say that," he said with a chuckle, squeezing my arms. "Let's get inside."

"Sure," I said quietly, feeling the change in his grip. Julian had gotten a lot better at communicating what was going on in his head, but his main source of communication was his body language and gestures. His boldness in having contact with me in the parking lot said just how serious his words were, and the way he gripped me tighter told me that when we got into the apartment, our planned movie night would be delayed slightly.

Sure enough, the moment we got inside, the door locked behind us, his arms were around my waist. I tilted my head as he buried his face in my neck, kissing it and then nipping precisely where he knew my knees would threaten to buckle. This close, I could smell his spicy cologne, and the lingering smell of his body wash as he brought his hands up to rest on my collarbone.

"Isaiah," he whispered, breath gusting against the spot he'd just been nibbling on, sending another wave of pleasure through me.

I wasn't surprised that we didn't make it to the bedroom, instead stumbling toward the couch. Turning, I fell back onto it, dragging Julian with me. As soon as I settled onto the cushions, I pulled him closer, pushing our mouths together. His larger frame ground against me, pinning me to the couch in a way I couldn't help but savor. Dominance in bed from Julian had come slowly, and he still loved it when I took over, but there was no way in hell I'd complain when he took matters into his own hands.

Sliding my hands through his hair, I gripped the back of his head, throwing one leg around his waist to pull him closer. I sighed in contentment as I felt his hips settle between my legs, his groin pressing against me as I pulled at his clothes. The sooner we got our clothes off, the better, in my opinion.

A sharp knock on his apartment door brought everything to a grinding halt as Julian shot up. His hair stuck out in every direction from my manhandling, and it looked like he'd just woken up from a nap. Frowning at the door, he pushed himself up and adjusted his clothes.

"Who the hell is that?" I grumbled in annoyance. "It better not be one of the guys."

"Your friends?"

"They don't know where you live, except maybe Bennett. I meant the guys at the station."

"They'd text first," Julian muttered, finally walking toward the door. I couldn't see much past his large frame except for a few glimpses of a small woman bundled up for far colder weather than we had. I stood up to discover what was happening when Julian spoke, his words shooting through me like an electric current.

"Mom?"

Ah, well, shit.

JULIAN

It felt like someone had dumped cold water over me and slapped me across the face for good measure. Any residual trace of heat and desire from my attempt at seducing Isaiah was dead and gone, with only the tingle of his kiss left on my lips. I could only stare at the woman who had given me birth as she stood there, eyes darting from side to side and never quite resting on my face.

"What...what are you doing here?" I asked, unable to make sense of what I was seeing. My mother had *never* come to see me, no matter where I lived, even when I'd lived around the block from her years ago. It had always been me who came to her, usually at her behest or less than subtle hinting or out of the obligation I had as her son.

She finally looked up, her lip trembling slightly, whether from nerves or in an attempt to smile, I didn't know. "Well, I haven't seen you in ages. So I figured I would come see you myself."

"You drove out here?" I asked, careful to keep the surprise out of my voice. It was one thing my mother had always refused to do. Which meant Tristan and I were often forced to walk wherever we went, bum a ride, or take whatever public transportation there might be. All it took was for her to *think* about getting behind the wheel, and her blood pressure shot through the roof.

"No, that's...well, I have a surprise," she said, finally turning to smile. I followed her gaze toward the unfamiliar car sitting outside my apartment. Another shock raced through me as I spotted a familiar figure leaning against the car, a cigarette jutting from his mouth.

"Tristan?" I said softly, somehow managing to be even more shocked than before.

"Heya, big brother," he said with his crooked grin aimed toward me.

I was at a loss for words, my brain desperately trying to understand what was happening. My brother had *never* wanted anything to do with me since we were teenagers. Sure, he'd take help when he could get it, but he never went out of his way to deal with me if he could help it. Once he'd hit eighteen, however, he'd become even more distant from my mother and me.

In all honesty, I couldn't remember the last time I'd seen my brother, though it had probably been a holiday and at my mother's insistence. My brother and I could not be more different, and we had never really gotten along growing up. He had always been bold and brash, too impulsive for his own good, and rarely took anything seriously.

He still had the same cocky smirk on his face that I'd seen for years, especially once he'd found his stride in puberty. Tristan had gained our father's red hair as I had, but it was darker, nearly auburn. It also meant he wasn't nearly as fair-skinned as I was, but he'd also gained our father's green eyes. Both features had drawn a lot of attention, especially when he'd grown taller and broader as a teenager, and he hadn't been afraid to use his looks to get what he wanted.

"You don't seem all that happy to see us," Tristan said with a smirk, flicking his cigarette away without bothering to grind it out. "It's not like we haven't seen each other in years."

"You've been busy," I said, intensely aware that our mother was standing right in front of me, listening to every word nervously. I always did my best to keep the awkward animosity between her sons away from her. Much like everything else in his life, Tristan wasn't nearly as conscientious and adored picking at me when he had a chance, whether or not our mother was around.

"True, true," he said, pushing away from the car. "So, are you going to invite us in, or are you going to make our poor mom stand in the cold?"

It wasn't *that* cold, but she had never been one for cold weather. I had once offered to help her move to a warmer climate, somewhere like Arizona, but her panic at leaving the state had been so sudden I'd immediately dropped the subject. It didn't matter that she didn't have any friends to speak of where she was, that her sons had their own lives, or that I offered to help her pay for things while she was there. No, she was staying in Colorado, whether or not she was miserable.

"Sorry, Mom," I told her with a wince, stepping away so she could let herself in.

Turning around, I immediately froze as I spied Isaiah sitting on the couch. His clothes and hair were neat again, and he had his hand clasped between his knees. His eyes swept up to mine, and I knew he saw things in my expression that no one else could read, and I quickly got control of myself, schooling my features.

In my shock at seeing my mother and brother, I had completely forgotten about Isaiah sitting right behind me, hearing every word. I had done my best to keep Isaiah from having anything to do with my family. Some information was bound to come out since, apparently, Isaiah was good at making people want to share.

However, learning some things and seeing them in person were two completely different realities. I could feel the first claws of the beast called panic piercing my chest as I glanced between him and my mother as she entered the living room. She gave a light start when she saw a stranger sitting on the couch. My eyes darted between them, and then I tensed as I heard Tristan come stomping into my apartment.

"Wow, dude, this place is, uh...shit," Tristan muttered, looking around.

I sucked in my bottom lip to bite down on it just enough that the spark of pain reminded me to keep my mouth shut. There was already enough for me to worry about without having Tristan goad me into an argument I didn't want. It wasn't like he had been forking over good chunks of change to help our mother stay afloat while living the good life on a university campus, having an actual life, making friends, and probably partying his cocky ass off in the process.

"Money's been tight," I muttered, closing the door behind them.

"Shit, maybe you should find a better job if this place can't even pay you right for putting out a few fires," he snorted and then cocked his head when he spotted Isaiah. "Who's this?"

I *really* didn't like the way Tristan glanced between the two of us. Panic found another foothold in my head as I turned to find Isaiah gazing at my mother in curiosity, though the look darkened slightly when he turned on Tristan. He was being polite and held back his expressions, but it didn't take an expert in Isaiah to see he was not a fan of my brother.

And it wasn't hard to see the slight grimace on his face as

he bowed his head to push himself upright. I saw all the disappointment and frustration I needed to feel a squirm of guilt in my gut. This was a prime moment for me to follow through on my words to him, but even he could tell I wasn't going to, not with this, not with them.

God, Isaiah, I-I'm so sorry.

"Isaiah Bently," he said, standing up with a brilliant, warm smile as he held his hand out. "Friend of Julian's and a co-worker."

"Huh, I would have guessed a geek who knew where the gym was," Tristan chuckled, taking his hand and giving it a few sharp shakes. "Tristan."

"Be nice, Tristan," our mother chided softly, taking Isaiah's offered hand far more gently and slowly. "I'm Anne, it's nice to meet you, Isaiah."

"A pleasure," Isaiah said. "I've heard a few things about you. It's nice to put a face to the name."

My mother immediately brightened, drawing her hand back to clasp it before her. "Well, aren't you nice? So you work with Julian at the station?"

"I do," Isaiah said with a small smile. "Been there for years, actually."

Tristan snorted as he sidled into the room, taking stock of everything. I could see from his eyes he wasn't impressed by what he saw. Not that I was surprised. My apartment would have seemed pathetic even by the standards of the crappiest dorm he stayed in before joining a fraternity. Not that that was much better, but I couldn't help but wonder if my brother was seeing where I lived and remembering the shitty apartments we'd had as kids.

"Hopefully, you can keep my brother out of trouble," Tristan said, brow rising when he spied the frayed and faded couch. "He's got a habit of attracting it or maybe finding it on his own. Can't quite figure it out."

My mother's eyes widened, darting between Tristan and Isaiah. I knew from previous conversations she didn't necessarily disagree with my brother, but she also didn't like private, family business being broadcast in front of other people. If I were to guess, she was torn between chastising Tristan for the offense and not wanting to make things worse by drawing attention to him.

Isaiah's eyes flicked toward my brother, and I saw his upper lip twitch before his features smoothed out, becoming polite once more. "Oh, I've heard a few things."

"Ooh, your reputation precedes you, Jules."

"It's on record. So it does that," I muttered.

"Funny," Isaiah said with a smile. It was the first time I'd seen that particular forced look on his face. "He's been here for months and hasn't had any trouble with anyone."

Tristan glanced at him, his amusement only half what it had been before. "Maybe it's just a matter of time."

"Or maybe it's just where he was," Isaiah said, and my brow rose as his smile went from fake to razor-sharp. "Or the people he was around."

My brother's eyes narrowed, though he kept the cocky smile on his face. "Maybe he should choose better people to spend his time around."

"And maybe sometimes he can't help the people he's around. You can't choose your coworkers or your family," Isaiah said, his voice still as pleasant as ever. It didn't do an effective job of hiding the sound of the knife twisting, however.

My mother was standing to one side, looking confused and worried. She had no idea what was passing between the two men, but she could clearly sense the growing tension in the room. I knew I should interfere before the situation escalated out of control. Tristan could banter back and forth until he went blue in the face and passed out. Isaiah however…I didn't know how far he could go or how far he *would* go.

This was a side of the man I'd never seen before. Even when he was uncomfortable, he remained perfectly polite, if not his typically sunny self. I had *never* seen him hide daggers behind his smile and words before. It was like watching a train crash. I couldn't pull my eyes away even as I felt horrified by what I was watching.

Although it was fascinating to watch my sharp-tongued brother meet his match.

"Wow, you seem to know a lot about the subject," Tristan said, his smile returning, and I instantly heard alarms in my head. "Personal experience?"

"You could say that," Isaiah said, a glint in his eyes that I didn't like.

"Your last name is Bently, right?"

"It is."

Tristan grinned. "Went to school with one of your cousins. Trina."

"Did you?" Isaiah asked softly, and I felt the urge to reach out and pull him closer. There was a thread of pain in his voice I hadn't heard there before, though it was buried under everything else. "You must have been pretty good friends if you recognized me."

"Not really. We spent some time together," Tristan said, his grin lopsided. It didn't take a genius to understand what he was saying. "She mentioned some family and showed me a few pictures. Talked about you a bit too."

"Sounds about right," Isaiah said, plastering another smile on his face. "Even for someone she…barely knew, she was always pretty big on family."

"Didn't like to talk about you much," Tristan said, picking up an empty beer bottle from the side table and looking it over. "Didn't want to get into the 'drama,' I guess."

"Well, it's always good to recognize when something isn't anyone else's business," Isaiah said sweetly.

Tristan ducked his head with a snort. "Funny, I was thinking the same thing."

"Stop," I said softly, finally finding my voice now things were hitting a little too close to home. The last thing I wanted was for Isaiah to be treated like a pin cushion for my brother's flung barbs.

"Let's not waste our time here...discussing things that shouldn't be discussed," my mother piped up nervously, now wringing her hands. She was the only one in the room with no idea what had just been discussed, but she clearly felt the tension and mutual dislike between them. "We're on vacation, Tristan."

"You're...here on vacation?" I asked, startled.

"Yes," she said with a smile. "Just for a few weeks. Tristan missed Colorado and decided to take a semester off to come back for a little while. And I thought, what better way to make sure you're okay than for us to come visit you."

"Oh, well, that's nice of you," Isaiah said, finally jerking his eyes away from Tristan and giving my mother a gentle smile.

She beamed back at him, apparently at ease. "Thank you. Now, how about I make us a nice pot of coffee? I would love to catch up a little."

"Sure," I grunted, watching Isaiah carefully.

With a shaky smile, she hurried out of the living room and into the kitchen to start fussing with things. Undoubtedly the state of the kitchen would probably come up in conversation later. It was stocked better than ever, with Isaiah having spent so much time here, but it was still run down and stained, and there was more beer in the fridge than she would be comfortable with. Alcohol had always been a touchy subject for her, and no amount of insistence otherwise would get her to understand that my father's alco-holism had not been passed down to her oldest.

"She told me quite a few interesting things," Tristan continued, voice soft enough that it wouldn't carry. He reached into the cushions and plucked out a bottle of lube I hadn't even realized was there. His eyes darted over to Isaiah. "Namely, why you're not a part of the family."

"If this is where you try to threaten to out me, then you're in over your head," Isaiah told him with a snort, his voice full of venom. "There's not a person in this town who doesn't already know, and the ones who might have an issue keep their mouths shut."

"Wasn't what I was thinking."

"What, gay jokes? I've got a few good ones myself. Insults? Heard them all. Do you have anything else in that bag of tricks of yours, you arrogant prick?"

Tristan continued to fiddle with the bottle before bringing his eyes over to me. "I also remember a certain... incident when my big brother was younger."

"You were a kid," I managed, feeling icy fear drop into my stomach.

"Yeah. Funny the things that stick out in your memory," he said, setting the bottle down on the table. "Kind of like how I remember our mother fretting over it afterward. She wasn't as pissed as Dad was, but she was worried. Just imagine—"

"Imagine *what?*" Isaiah snapped.

"Imagine if she had good reason to think Dad's accusa-tions were true," Tristan said slowly, tilting his head to one side. "Hell, just the idea that Julian is spending time with a homo would be enough. Now, what if her favorite son, who she listens to so fervently, were to mention his own suspi-cions about what you two have *obviously* been up to?"

Isaiah went rigid. "Based on what? That you found out

I'm gay? Congratulations, it's something she could figure out on her own while she's staying here. Or on what, the fact that you found lube? Last I checked, it's not the sole province of gay men. Honestly, you should look into getting some for yourself. Any woman who spends five minutes of conversation with you will dry up faster than a puddle in the desert. Could be useful for you."

I stared at Isaiah, taken aback by the sheer vehemence. I had witnessed him deal with cranky people more than once, and he always remained his sunny, friendly self. Maybe there was some grumbling about attitudes, but he'd never taken it out on anyone before. Either he had been hiding this sort of thing all along, or my brother's sparkling personality was bringing out the worst in Isaiah.

Worse yet, Tristan didn't look bothered by Isaiah's comment, and Tristan did *not* like it when someone took a personal swing at him. "It means all I have to do is help confirm our mother's worst fears. Now, Julian, you wouldn't want that, would you? Hasn't she already been through enough?"

"I wouldn't," I admitted through gritted teeth. I refused to look at Isaiah as I spoke, but I could feel his eyes on me.

"Look, personally? I don't give a shit whether you two are making each other bite the pillow," Tristan said with a shrug and a grin that said he understood he had already won.

"But?" I asked in a low voice.

"But, you," he began, pointing to Isaiah. "Will keep your mouth shut about shit that doesn't concern you."

"Ungrateful bastard," Isaiah spat in a low voice.

"As a matter of fact, it's probably better if you keep your little boy toy away from us altogether," Tristan said with a smirk. "He doesn't seem to know how to keep his mouth shut."

"You'd willingly hurt your mother just to stop someone

from hurting your precious little feelings?" Isaiah asked with a sneer. "Christ, when I figured out you were a self-absorbed brat, I didn't think it was that deep."

"Hey, we could start that conversation now," he turned, calling into the kitchen. "Hey, Mom?"

"Yes, sweetheart?" she called back among the clattering. She was undoubtedly scrubbing out the coffee pot first.

"Oh, fuck off," Isaiah grunted, turning his head to the side. "Congratulations, Tristan, you've got what you wanted. You know damn well your brother isn't going to risk it, and unlike you, I care about what he wants, so I'll go."

"Isaiah," I began, heart thudding in my chest.

"It's fine. The longer I stay around him, the more likely I am to say something someone is going to regret," Isaiah said, turning on his heel to find his shoes by the door. "At least we know where all the good genetics went."

I stood there for a few moments, unsure what to do. This was the first time my brother used blackmail to get what he wanted from me, but I desperately wanted to keep Isaiah around. He was easily the best thing to happen to me, and I didn't want to see him march out the door without at least an explanation.

"Oh," my mother said at the sound of the door and appearing in the living room. "Is he not joining us?"

"No," I said before my brother could find a way to color things. "He's got to get home. He's got an overnight shift and needs a nap."

"That's a shame. He seemed lovely," she said before returning to the kitchen.

"Didn't know you were into the sensitive types," Tristan said, as smug as ever.

I held my arms at my side as my hands curled into fists. "Fuck you, Tristan. Fuck you and everything about you."

Not lingering to find out if my brother had more bullets

in the chamber, I shoved my feet into my boots and hurried after Isaiah. "Be right back, Mom!"

I didn't hear her reply as I hurriedly closed the door behind me and jogged after Isaiah, who was already opening the door to his car. I slapped my hand on the top of the door to stop him. Isaiah hesitated, his eyes locked on the ground before he took a deep breath and looked up at me.

"Sorry," he said softly. "But it's probably best if I don't linger. It's obvious your brother really doesn't want me around."

"He's…" I glanced back toward the apartment and grimaced as I saw the curtains twitch. "Why…why did you say something to him?"

Isaiah scoffed. "Are you serious right now? He comes waltzing into *your* apartment, immediately starts talking shit, and suddenly I'm the bad guy? Jesus, Julian."

"That's just…how he is," I said, turning away from the window after the curtains stopped moving. Whoever it was would probably keep glancing out, though whether it was my worried mother or my smug brother was anyone's guess.

"In what world does 'he's always a self-absorbed, selfish asshole' somehow excuse anything anyone does?" Isaiah asked, raising a brow.

"It's…it's different, alright?"

"How is this different from anything else?"

"This is *my* family," I finally ground out at him. Christ, did he not understand? "I know you don't have one anymore, but—"

"The hell I don't," he said, eyes narrowing. "The difference is that I'm not clinging to the toxic one I was born into."

"That's not fair," I snapped. "My mom would…she needs us to be a family, okay? This isn't like your family, where you could just walk away, and everything would be fine."

"Fine?" he asked, his brow shooting upward. "Just fine?

Julian, did you pay attention to a single thing I've said for the past few months, like...at all?"

"I know it was hard."

"No, you clearly don't. I had to give up *everything* I thought was mine, everything my life had been built around. My family had been everything to me, and I had to turn away from that if I wanted to be anything resembling the person I was. If it weren't for Bennett, I would have ended up living under a tarp at the edge of town."

"But you," I began, shaking my head. "You get money from your parents. From working at the station."

"I didn't start off at the station. I was a freaking bagger after they left me behind with *nothing*," he shook his head. "A bag full of things and a 'fuck you, you're dead to me' is all I got when they left. I stayed with Bennett for a little while."

"Then how did you...you know—"

"You weren't here for it, but there was a bad drug problem outside town. Meth isn't exactly known for being stable, and a lab blew sky high. I remember watching the whole station roll out and then a few more from Fovel showing up to help save the town," Isaiah explained, his eyes drifting to the forest around the town. "I ended up riding my bike and going to watch it. Watching them, how hard they worked, how well they worked together, I decided that's what I was going to do. Took me months to get into the right shape to even be considered. I was so freaking nervous going in there to apply. Chief Borton's lived here his whole life, he knew my last name...what it meant. He barely blinked at my last name and put me through the paces."

"Your family?" I asked, feeling like I was missing something.

Something sharp and dark passed over his features when he smirked. "I was tired of working for nothing and barely scraping by, even with help. I decided if they were going to treat me like some dirty little secret to sweep under the rug, then they were going to pay to keep it that way."

It clicked, and I blinked at him. "You…blackmailed them?"

He scoffed, tossing his keys onto the seat with a roll of his eyes. "You could call it that. I told my father he was investing in the continued 'clean' image of our family. That was all I had to say. He understood what I meant and started writing the checks as soon as possible."

"But…" I trailed off, peering at Isaiah. It wasn't like I didn't know the man had a temper and could probably give someone trouble if he was pissed off. But I had been under the belief that his family had chosen to keep paying for his silence. I didn't know how to feel about the fact that he had all but forced their hand in the matter.

"But what?" Isaiah asked, laying a hand on the top of the door.

"After you gave Trist so much shit for blackmail," I said with a frown, trying to wrap my head around this new facet of Isaiah that I had never suspected existed in the first place.

His eyes widened, and there was no missing the shock and hurt in his eyes, and I immediately knew I had made a mistake. "Seriously?"

"Look, I'm just trying to understand," I said hastily.

"Well, here's something for you to understand," he hissed, yanking the door out of my grasp. "My family threw me out, disowned me, and pretended I never existed. They chose their own narrow-minded image over my happiness, willing to stomp me into a box they designed or erase me from the family history. So I decided they were going to pay for the damn privilege. Your brother is willing to sacrifice *your* happiness, again, because he doesn't want to take responsibility for what an irresponsible, brainless twit he is. Are you starting to see the difference yet, Julian? Or are you so hung up on the idea that this is the only family you have that you're going to continue being an ass?"

"I'm not being an ass," I growled back at him, crossing my arms over my chest. "You were the one who provoked him."

"So, what, that means I get to be compared to him?" Isaiah demanded.

"I wasn't," I stopped, shaking my head. "He would have never said anything if you'd just played nice. You can play nice with everyone else, but you couldn't manage to play nice this time?"

"Yeah, fine. I lost my temper because the asshole who's already fucked you over once decided to come back here and start talking shit," Isaiah said with a shrug. "It's almost like I give a shit about what happens to you, that I care."

"I don't need your help with him," I growled.

"No, you're right. You have this situation completely under control right now," Isaiah said with a wave toward the apartment. "They walk back into your life, and you…how can you let them treat you like that?"

"My mom—"

"Fine. How can you let Tristan treat you like that?"

"What am I supposed to do?" I finally demanded, spreading my arms wide. "Tell my mother the truth? Tell her that her favorite child was actually the one who should have had that assault charge? That he's probably been drinking away what money she sends him to help him feed and clothe himself?"

Isaiah stiffened. "Are you telling me that the money you send to her is getting sent to him?"

"Probably," I muttered. "I know she sends him money. So either she's using the money I send or the money the government sends her."

"The end result is the same," Isaiah snorted with a shake

of his head. "In the end, you're going to bend over backward. Let them chip away at you."

"My mother is not 'chipping away' at me," I interrupted.

"Whether she knows it or not, whether she means to or not, that's exactly what she's doing. For fuck's sake, both you and Tristan said that he's the 'favorite' child. Boy, I wonder where that came from? I wonder why you had to take care of the house growing up when she couldn't? Why you sacrifice so much of yourself just to make her happy," Isaiah barreled on.

"Enough!" I barked, slamming my palm down onto the hood of his car, denting it slightly.

Isaiah eyed the dent for several seconds before clicking his tongue. "I don't want to watch you rip yourself apart just to keep them whole, Julian."

"You've seen five minutes of them," I countered.

He pulled his eyes up to meet mine. "I watched you. In just seconds, you were right back to the guy I first met. Locked away, shoving everything deep. The walls went up, and the searchlights were activated. That's all it took for you to retreat, their presence."

"It's...complicated," I said softly, bowing my head.

"I know," he said, letting out a shaky sigh. "I know what it's like to push your feelings, wants, and desires into a little box and pretend like they don't exist. I know what it means to keep sacrificing on the altar of family and getting *nothing* in return. I did it for most of my current life."

"Until you didn't," I said, staring down at the cracked asphalt.

"It was the hardest thing I ever had to do, and I don't regret it for a minute," he told me gently.

"This is...different," I said, shoving my hands into my pockets.

"Sure," he said, and I could see I was already losing him.

"Wait," I said, pushing the door closed before he could get into the driver's seat. "Isaiah. Wait."

For a moment I thought he was going to open the door and swing into the seat to drive off before I could say anything. It wasn't until he stood there, watching me patiently, that I realized this was so much worse. Having him there, knowing we couldn't simply retreat into the safety of my apartment, away from the world like we'd done so many times before, threatened to tear me apart. And even after all this had caused him so much heartache, he was *still* standing there, willing to wait until I found my words.

"It's just until they're gone," I told him. "Okay? I know this is hard, and it's on me. I get that. But it's only—"

"A few weeks?" he asked, interrupting me in a soft voice. "We avoid one another for a few weeks?"

When it was said so plainly, it sounded positively monstrous. "I mean, not completely. Just when they're around."

He looked off to the side, his gaze going distant. "That's not going to work for me, Julian. I'm sorry."

My heart dropped even as my temper flared. "What, just a few weeks? That's too much?"

I expected anger, but I saw only exhaustion. "Two things. First off, it was one thing to hide ourselves from everyone around here because, at the very least, I still had you. But you're asking me to avoid being around you while they're here. Those are two very different states, and...I'm sorry, Julian, but I'm not ready to go back into the closet. Not even for you."

"There...there was another thing?" I asked in a faint voice, not sure if I really wanted to hear the second reason. The first was hard-hitting enough.

He turned his face toward me, and I saw only a deep,

profound sadness that pulled at my chest. "You didn't look in the car when you passed it, did you?"

"I…no?" I answered in confusion.

He smiled sadly. "I did. That's why I wasn't already halfway gone by the time you got out here. You should probably do that, and then you'll have your answer."

"Isaiah," I breathed, watching him pull open the driver's side door and slide in.

"I really am sorry," he said, pulling the door closed after I reluctantly took my hand off it.

I could only stand there helplessly, watching as he turned the car on and backed out of the parking spot. If he glanced back as he pulled out, I didn't see. I didn't know how long I stood there, staring at where his car had last been before he had driven out of sight, but with a heavy sigh, I finally looked away.

Hope wasn't something I regularly indulged in, but with Isaiah, I found a sliver that had been born at some point. I knew he was angry and hurt, and truthfully, I wasn't much better off, but…he had always found a way to bounce back. Maybe once things were settled, we could sit down and figure something out.

I hadn't been able to explain that despite wanting to be less afraid of people knowing about us, I just…couldn't when it came to my family. *Maybe* in the future, but now? God, the thought alone was enough to send me looking for the safest place to hole up and pretend nothing was going on. I understood he was upset and why, but I needed him to understand where I was coming from. Isaiah was good at listening, for understanding. Maybe when he was calmer, we could—

I stopped beside my brother's car and stared, my breath coming out in a soft gasp. The backseat was stuffed with boxes and bags. They were all my mother's clothes and one box with what looked like picture frames, lamps, and other odds and ends. I couldn't help but glance toward the trunk and wonder what was in there.

Standing there, I felt alternating waves of confusion and horror washing through me. If my mother was just coming for a visit, why did she need so many of her things? It wasn't as though she owned a lot in the first place, but I knew a good deal of it could have fit into the back of the car without much trouble.

With an overwhelming sense of dread, I understood what Isaiah had said.

JULIAN

"Hey, Julian!"

Snapping out of my fugue, I turned to find Zach struggling with a large box. "Oh, sorry."

Pushing myself up from the table, I grabbed the other side, helping him carry it to the back where it would be broken down and the supplies unpacked. The deliveries came at least once a week and could cover anything from cleaning supplies, equipment that needed replacing, or food for us. The food usually came from the townspeople who liked to put together whatever they felt was best for the station, which is how we ended up with things like fresh instead of canned veggies and sometimes whole birds or hunks of meat.

"Thanks," Zach said once we got it settled. He snatched the inventory form off the wall and looked it over. "Didn't realize it was so heavy."

"Right," I said, looking it over and wondering how he couldn't see the thing was monstrous and would have been awkward to carry by himself even if it had been light.

"Then again, I was calling you the whole time," he said, looking up from the clipboard.

"Oh," I said, looking down at the box. I couldn't remember what I'd been thinking about when his calls finally got to me. Then again, I probably didn't need to think that hard. All I'd need to do was go into the break room, where Isaiah most certainly was not avoiding being around me while I sat out in the garage bay.

"I see you've gone back to simple sentences," Zach said quietly.

I shrugged in response, not sure what he wanted me to say. Truth be told, I didn't have a whole lot to say to people as it was. There were too many things going on in my head to put energy into trying to talk to other people.

It had been just over a week since my brother and mother had arrived in Fairlake to 'visit.' My mother hadn't delivered the news, but Veronica Jones, one of three real estate agents in town, had caught me while I was grocery shopping. The woman, as bubbly and engaging as ever, had been effusive in her happiness for me that my mother had decided to find a property in Fairlake. It was only to rent one of the few houses under Veronica's company's ownership, but it still confirmed what I had suspected all along.

That had been earlier today, and the thought was still in the back of my head. My mother knew my schedule, so she would be waiting for me when I got off my shift. I was pretty sure Tristan would also be there because he was *always* there. Always around me, a slight smile on his face whenever I caught his eye as if he were mocking me for the position he'd put me in.

"Right," Zach grunted once he realized I wasn't going to say anything more. "I should probably get through this shit. Do you wanna go scrub down the break room?"

Alarm shot through me, and I reached my hand out. "I'll do this."

"You sure? It's mind-numbing."

"It's fine."

"You won't hear me arguing," Zach chuckled, handing over the clipboard and a pen. "Cleaning the break room will take half the time getting this shit out of here will."

I nodded, turning to look down at the clipboard instead of watching him. Everyone at the station had been curious about me for the past week, and I would take any excuse to escape their gazes. None of them had pushed too hard when it became obvious I didn't want to talk. I tried to remind myself they were probably asking out of some misplaced concern, but that didn't change my aversion to wanting to be around them while they were still sniffing around.

Taking a deep breath, I looked over the list before opening the container and peering through everything. There was a certain kind of Zen to sorting through the box, marking off the item and its quantity. The room was at the back of the building, where it was quietest. Even if sound could have made it back to me from somewhere in the building, it would have been drowned out by the heating unit rumbling away, working overtime to heat the building.

Which was precisely why I didn't hear the footsteps coming down the hallway until Isaiah appeared in the doorway. "Hey, Zach, I needed…oh. You…are not Zach."

"No," I said, straightening. "He went to clean the break room. Thought you were in there."

"Uh, no, I was out back," he said, an inexplicable blush rising to his cheeks.

"Oh," I said, a little confused. That was until the air in the room brought the familiar smell of fresh smoke to my nostrils. "Oh."

Isaiah hunched his shoulders slightly, shoving his hands into his pockets. "It's not a big deal."

"No, it isn't," I said, setting the clipboard down. "Were you looking for Zach for a reason?"

"He was just bitching earlier that with all the climbing I do on the roof, the least I could do was help him clean out the gutters before it gets cold enough that everything freezes," Isaiah said with a smirk. "Which, I think, is just his way of trying to get me to do most of the work on the roof."

"Why?"

"He's scared of heights."

"Wait, really?"

"Well, ladders specifically. And even more specifically, not the ladders we use for work. He hates the aluminum ones you buy at the hardware store. Says they feel like they're going to throw him off."

I couldn't help but raise my brow. "Throw him...they're not horses."

Isaiah snickered. "That's what I tried to tell him, but then he threw his gloves at me, and I had to run away before he found something harder."

"He wouldn't," I said with a small smile.

"Probably not, but you can never take any chances."

"He cares about you."

"Yeah," he said with a shake of his head. "They all do, but he gets tired of dealing with me sometimes. Pretty sure Laurence has even contemplated throwing me in one of those boxes and sending me to who knows where."

"I think it's funny seeing you guys."

"Yeah, well, that's...that's family for you."

That was all it took for the slight warmth in the conversation to cool in an instant. Isaiah's eyes dropped to the floor, his thumbs sticking out of his pockets and softly beating a rhythm against his jeans. I wished I could say something to bring the moment back, that little piece of what I'd had just over a week ago, but I knew the moment had passed.

"I should probably go find Zach before the sun goes down," Isaiah muttered to his feet.

"Uh, Isaiah," I said quickly as he went to turn away.

Isaiah hesitated before coming to a stop but didn't turn back toward me. "Julian, I'm really not ready for another round, okay?"

"It's not…I'm sorry," I managed to get out, feeling helpless. "I'm sorry all this is happening."

"Happened," he corrected in a flat voice.

I swallowed hard. "Happened. I'm sorry it happened."

"That makes two of us," he said, and I could see him once more try to leave.

"And," I added hurriedly, "you…you were right."

He glanced toward me, an unreadable expression on his face. "About?"

I bowed my head. "Ran into Veronica earlier today."

"Veronica…oh, Jones. Right."

"Her company does rentals too. She was…really excited for me because it looks like my mom is renting a place not too far from me."

I heard him make a soft noise, and I desperately did not want to pick my head up and see the expression on his face. There was no other choice, however, and I forced myself to look him in the eye. My chest tightened as I saw the tightened jaw and the glassy-eyed stare of unshed tears.

"Right," he got out in a tight voice.

"Isaiah," I said, taking a step toward him.

"Don't," he said, turning away. "Just…don't."

"Sure," I muttered.

He grunted. "Goddammit."

Then he was gone, leaving me to stare at where he'd just been standing. The bubbling sense of urgency and need I'd felt just moments before deflated with his absence, leaving me with an empty feeling in my gut and an ache in my chest. I had no idea what I'd been trying to achieve by talking to him so urgently, but I had clearly got nowhere.

With a heavy sigh, I returned to the inventory, picking up the clipboard and sorting through the box again. The sense of calm Zen from earlier was utterly absent. Instead of a serene emptiness in my thoughts, there was only misery and the realization that no matter what I tried to do, I was bound to fall flat on my face.

More footsteps brought my head up, and I frowned when I saw Chief Borton standing in the doorway. The frown on his face wasn't strictly out of place. I was pretty sure that was his usual expression. This time, however, there was something about the look in his eye that told me this was something else entirely.

"So," he grunted, and I sighed, hearing an annoyance in his voice I only heard when he was well and truly mad.

Sighing, I set the clipboard down and turned to face him. At this rate, I might be able to finish unpacking and putting everything away by the time my shift was over. It probably came as no surprise to him that I said nothing, only raising my brow slightly to show him I was waiting. On my end, I wasn't surprised when he crossed his arms over his chest and eyed me carefully for several seconds before deciding to speak.

"When we spoke before, I thought I was pretty clear," Borton said with a scowl.

"About?" I grunted.

"Isaiah."

"What about?"

His scowl only deepened. "I'm pretty sure I told your ass that you weren't supposed to do anything that would screw with him."

It was my turn to scowl and feel a little defensive. "What are you talking about?"

He scoffed. "Boy, do you think I'm blind, deaf, and stupid?"

I blinked at him, unsure if he wanted an answer or if it was rhetorical, and instead chose to simply stare.

"That boy ain't exactly hard to read," he finally growled. "Wears his heart on his sleeve and ain't afraid to show what he's feeling. But suddenly, I've got him walking around, barely saying a word, lost in his own world, and just looking at him hurts."

"I don't know what that—"

"And then we've got you, wandering around like it's the first few months you worked here. Right back to communicating in grunts, stares, and those shrugs of yours."

Unable to help myself, I shrugged. "Okay."

He rolled his eyes. "God save me from stubborn idiots."

I turned away from him, snatching up the clipboard. Nothing I could say to the man would make him feel better or fix my current problem, so there was no point in saying anything. I knew he was doing it from a place of caring, but I simply didn't want to talk about it.

The whole situation was too large, too heavy even to begin to find a starting place to talk about what was going on. There were too many little moments that were far bigger than they appeared. Too many things that had a nuance and meaning I wouldn't be able to find a way to describe. On top of all that, there was the clear understanding that at the end of the day, it had been me and my choices that had brought Isaiah and me to this point.

My sincerest hope was that if I busied myself with the work, he would eventually give up on his little crusade and leave me in peace. Of course, after working under the man for a year, I should have known better. There were few people as stubborn and determined as Borton.

"I know you two were an item," he said softly.

Okay. I hadn't been expecting *that*.

Slowly, I set the small box of dish soap back into the crate, carefully setting the clipboard to the side. I turned on my heel to face him, surprised to see the frown on his face gone and replaced by something gentler, almost understanding.

He snorted softly, looking me over. "Yeah, that got your attention, didn't it? And don't think I'm the only one around here who figured it out."

"Did..." I began and then frowned. No, Isaiah wouldn't have said anything. It was one thing for him to tell Bennett, he was a close friend who didn't have a connection to me. Telling everyone at the station was something else entirely.

"I don't need Isaiah to say anything, and I'm betting a few other people around here didn't need it either."

"H-how?"

"You."

"Me?"

"Well, and so you know, I sometimes review security footage from overnight. Just to make sure things are running like they should."

"Okay?" I asked, and he waited, raising a brow. Suddenly I understood what he was saying, and my face burned.

"Yeah," he said dryly. "Can't imagine what you two could have been doing for up to thirty minutes when you both disappeared into the locker room when you were on shift together overnight."

I ducked my head, intent on staring at my boots. "Right."

"I knew before that, though. Isaiah was a little harder to read, but you were pretty easy."

I picked my head up, confused. "Me?"

"Yeah, I know," he said, leaning against the doorway with a smirk. "You're not used to being easily read, huh?"

"No," I admitted, still confused.

"Isaiah, and I'm sure this will come as a shock to you," he said, sarcasm lacing his words. "Is generally a happy and talkative sort of guy. So if he's a little more chatty than usual and laughs a little more, no one's going to notice."

"Right," I said with a frown as he stepped closer and snatched up the box of soap.

"But when someone like you, who expresses his emotions in the way a statue does," he said, dropping the box into the right receptacle. "It starts to become pretty obvious when something big is going on...something good. Suddenly you're smiling more than once a month, you actually laugh, and funnily, you're always around Isaiah when it's happening."

"So? That's what happens when you have friends," I argued, though I wasn't quite sure why. It was clear Borton already had my number. Any argument on my part was just a vain attempt to keep a secret I had once promised to share with the people around us.

"Most of that smiling and laughing is when he's around."

"Friends."

"Not to mention, you go out of your way not to touch anyone unless it's for work. Except Isaiah, you don't seem too shy about putting your hand on his shoulder or back or letting him touch you."

I scowled. "I'm just going to keep repeating myself."

"Did you already forget about your little visits to the locker room with him? I've only seen it happen twice, but I bet it was much more than that. You wanna tell me it's all about having a nice friendly chat?" he asked, his brow raised at such an angle I wondered how his whole face didn't twist.

I had forgotten about that or tried to push the memory

out of my head. Then, feeling my face warm again, I grabbed a bag full of gummy treats. Borton marked it off the list before grabbing it and tossing it into the food box against the wall.

I glanced at him for a moment before reaching in and taking the next item. Without saying anything else, I began digging through the box, only for him to take the item from me to place it where it went. After a few minutes, I allowed myself to get into the shared task, letting my mind drift off again. Borton wasn't grilling me any longer, and I took that as an opportunity to shut my brain down for a while and give myself a break.

"Are you in love with him?" Borton asked once I handed him a box of deodorant.

My fingers nearly lost their hold on the box before I righted it and shoved it into his arms. I flipped the crate over with a huff and began undoing the flaps to break it down. They were thick plastic, and with every delivery, we would send them back to the company to be used again. It also meant there was enough sound from the heavy creaking and cracking that I could pretend he wasn't waiting for an answer.

With a grunt, I slapped it against the wall so it would be easy to get to later. Glancing over my shoulder, I found him standing in the doorway, apparently willing to block my way out of the room.

"I...don't know," I finally admitted, busying myself by crouching to ensure everything was in its proper box ready to be wheeled out on a dolly.

"How don't you know?" Borton asked, and I didn't have to look up to know he was frowning at me again. "Either you're in love with him or not."

"I don't know. I've never—" I stopped there, shaking my head.

"Been in love?"

"No."

"It's not too hard to figure out. I mean, you've loved people you weren't dating, right?"

"Right."

"Well, then, you've got a place to start."

"It's…not the same," I muttered, shuffling things around unnecessarily to make everything neat and orderly in the boxes rather than simply tossed in.

"Yeah, well, loving your boyfriend ain't gonna be the same as loving your momma," he snorted.

"No," I said, struggling to pull a bag out without sending the boxes it sat on tumbling all over the place. "*He's* different. It's different with him."

"Boy," he growled in clear frustration. "Just what kinda screwed up home life did you have that you can't even tell if something is love or not?"

Startled, I looked up at him, my mouth moving uselessly. I remembered my father, always angry and usually drunk, whose idea of caring for his family was cursing them out, threatening them, and sometimes following up with a fist or belt. I could see my mother, always frail and fragile, terrified of the world around her and leaving it up to other people to care for her and her children. Then there was Tristan, who, for most of his life, had looked at people through the lens of what he could gain from them or what he could use them for.

Borton blinked, and his face softened immediately. "Oh."

"No," I grumbled, turning back to the bag and, with a low growl, yanked it out with more force than necessary. Not only did I send the boxes flying, spilling their contents all over the floor, but the bag ripped and sent two dozen individually wrapped toothbrushes flying in every direction. "Motherfucker!"

A strong hand came down on my shoulder, making me

flinch. The grip didn't bite but curled gently, holding me in place not by force but through calm. "Son—"

"I'll clean it," I muttered, hating the stinging I felt in the back of my eyes.

"Worry about it later," Borton said softly. "I'm more worried about whatever mess you just discovered in your own head than anything else."

"I'm fine," I said, wanting to pull away but finding myself stuck, trapped by the hand that held me not by force but by something far gentler and warmer.

"I think you haven't been fine for a long while," Borton said, his voice gentle. "I think the first time you were okay was when you were spending time with Isaiah."

"Yeah," I agreed, bowing my head as I felt my throat tighten. "Yeah."

"Now, I don't know if you two were actually at the point of love yet, but from what I've been seein' lately, you were damn close."

I swallowed hard. "Maybe."

"And I'm not gonna ask what happened to change things. That's none of my business, honestly."

"And this is?" I asked with a thick laugh.

"Maybe not, but I'm guessin' this is the most I'm going to get out of you. I don't know what got between you two."

"Family," I whispered.

I felt his fingers flex, and he let out a low breath. "Same kind he had?"

"A little," I admitted, unsure of myself.

"Tell me one more thing."

"Maybe."

He chuckled, the sound deep and rich. "Alright, that's fair. Did he make you happy?"

"Yeah."

"Make you feel special? Like you had someone in your corner who would root for you no matter what?"

"Yeah."

"Did he make you feel like you never wanted anyone else at your side and that maybe you could get through anything between the two of you?"

My throat tightened further, so the best I could do was nod. I hadn't given it much thought while it was happening, I had been content to simply bask in the warmth of being around Isaiah. He was a bright spot in my life, and I had never known someone like him could exist, let alone want to be around someone like me. For the first time in my life, I understood what it meant to have something to look forward to and hope for.

"I can't speak for what you're going through, son," he finally said, giving my shoulder another squeeze before pulling his hand away. "Any more than I can say what that boy went through in his life. But if I've got the basic idea of things, then it's looking like you'll have to choose."

"Him or my family?" I guessed.

"The type of love you want in your life," he corrected. "Do you want the kind that made you give me that damned look that damn near broke my heart to see? Or do you want the one that made you happy?"

I hung my head, once more unable to answer him as I stared at the floor. I knew what he was trying to say. It was so similar to what Isaiah had tried to tell me repeatedly. Both of them made complete sense, and I was sure if I were someone else hearing this same problem, I would be in complete agreement. But I wasn't on the outside. I was living it, and every time I tried to come to some conclusion, I couldn't.

Even the idea of putting my head down and rolling with the punches made my stomach squirm and shift uncomfortably as I tried to make sense of everything. Giving up my family meant giving up everything I'd ever known, even if it was often messy and ugly. Giving up Isaiah meant going right back to where I was and losing the one thing in my life that had been beautiful and wonderful.

"Give that some thought," he said softly. "And while you do that, get your ass moving. This place looks like a bomb went off."

I blinked at him and couldn't help the snort of barely contained laughter as I looked around at the mess I'd made. He sounded like his old self before disappearing back into the hallway, but I caught a glimpse of what Isaiah had been saying the whole time. For all his apparent disinterest and grumpiness, Borton did care about the guys, even me. Hell, all the guys at the station had taken more of an interest in me since the accident, and I couldn't put that all on Isaiah's influence.

Maybe, without me noticing, I had found a place to call home.

ISAIAH

"Are you serious?" I growled at the machine, smacking it with the palm of my hand.

To my growing annoyance, the candy bar remained, barely hanging on by the small coil that *should* have dumped it to the bottom where I could retrieve it. But no, it had to hang on tight, mocking me as it kept the delicious mixture of chocolate and coconut out of my grasp.

I reached out, gripping each side of the machine and shaking it, punctuating my words. "Give. Me. My. Fucking. Candy. Bar!"

"Woah!" Bennett's voice barked from behind me. "You know, thirty-seven people a year are killed by falling vending machines, right?"

"Well that would fit. This fucker is greedy. Why not bloodthirsty as well?" I growled, slamming my palm against it again. "And that was thirty-seven people over several years, not per year."

"Oh. Well, shit. How'd you know that?"

I grit my teeth against the answer because it had come from Julian. Along with his historical obsession over time periods, he was also a fount of information for random trivia. One of my favorite things to do had been to sit down and watch game shows like Jeopardy and see how much he knew. I would rarely get half a dozen questions right during the show, while he could knock out ones I was sure he would get wrong.

"Fucker," I grumbled, giving the machine a swift kick for good measure. I blinked when the machine rattled and finally dropped the candy bar. "Damn right."

"Wow, that was three 'fucks' in only a couple of minutes," Bennett said with a whistle, walking over to the pot bubbling away on the stove. "That's impressive for you."

"I wanted my candy," I grumbled as I ripped open the packaging and took a bite. "Blech, I think it's stale. Goddammit."

"Oh, God," he muttered, backing away from the pot. "Is that Laurence's chili? Or Zach's?"

"Laurence," I told him, spitting the chewed candy into the trash can, followed by the bar.

"Oh, hell no," he said with a shake of his head. "The last time I tried some of that, it was dragon fire coming out of my ass for two days."

"Thanks for that information," I muttered, then narrowed my eyes. "What are you doing in here anyway? Last I checked, you worked for the cops."

"Chief let me off early," he said, beaming. "Said he was happy for me to leave for the day."

"Right," I said, clicking my tongue. "Was that happy to give you the extra time off or happy to see you go so he wouldn't get any more gray hairs?"

Bennett chuckled, hopping up onto the counter and kicking his feet. "Same thing, really."

I opened my mouth to reply and stopped when Julian walked in. He stopped when he spotted me, his eyes going warily to

Bennett. When Bennett only waved merrily at him, I saw Julian's shoulders ease before shuffling forward to grab a bowl and fill it with chili. Two weeks of awkward silence and avoiding one another filled the room, and I tried to look anywhere but at him.

Easier said than done, considering how much attention his presence demanded. Even before we'd become involved, I had always found his presence distracting. Now there was so much hanging between us, I found it even more difficult. Gone were the days when I could content myself by watching him move around, utterly oblivious to how good a sight he was for my not-so-sore eyes.

"Excuse me," he muttered as he slipped past me and out into the hallway. He would undoubtedly eat his meal in the garage bay. It was usually the least populated part of the station, so he'd be left in peace.

Bennett waited a few seconds before letting out a low whistle. "Wow."

"Don't," I muttered, opening the fridge to grab a can of Coke from the top shelf. "Just…don't."

"I mean, I knew you guys were going to be awkward around one another, but whew, that is a level of awkward I haven't seen since Devin accidentally announced that Chase is hung like a horse at the bar," Bennett said.

Coke sprayed out of my mouth and nose as I choked on the drink. "*What?*"

"Oh yeah, it was hilarious," Bennett said with a chuckle. "Last weekend. We were sitting there talking with a couple of farmhands who decided to come out and gay it up away from their families. They were making jokes about feeling inadequate whenever they breed horses. Devin had one too many that night, I'd warned Chase to moderate him, but you know Chase, 'he's not a kid, Bennett, he's a full-grown fucking adult.' Well, he regretted that when Devin snickered at the guys and said to take Chase with them, then the horses would feel inadequate."

"Oh, good God," I said, letting out a bark of laughter. "I can't imagine Chase's reaction."

"I swear," Bennett snickered, "I've never seen him turn *that* particular shade of red before. It was almost purple. One of those moments where you wish you could take pictures with your eyes and show everyone later."

I wiped my face with a paper towel. "First, I really wish you wouldn't tell me those things when I'm drinking. Second, is he right?"

"You're such a gossip," Bennett teased.

"Hey, you had a thing with him in the past. You would know."

"And I'm sure he'd be so happy to know you're asking after his dick."

"Consider it...professional interest," I said slowly.

"Right," he snorted. "Professional what? Dick measurer?"

"Fine, it's blatant curiosity," I admitted.

"Well," he drew out, grinning slowly. "I wouldn't say it would put a horse to shame, but let's just say it's impressive that someone like Devin manages to walk."

I scrunched my nose as the mental image rose. Devin was noticeably smaller than all of us, which wasn't saying much, considering the rest of us were above average height. Julian was the only one noticeably bigger than us, but I had always joked that he had some giant blood in him somewhere. Chase was slightly larger than I was, which meant he towered over Devin. I could easily picture how that would equal a lot of manhandling and dominance from what I'd learned about Chase from Bennett in the past.

"Kinda hot to think about, isn't it?" Bennett asked with a wicked grin.

"Don't let your boyfriend hear you say that," I told him, raising a brow.

"My boyfriend knows full well I get turned on by the idea of other people having sex and will always want him more than anything or anyone else in the world," Bennett said with a wink. "And if me getting turned on by something else means he gets to reap the benefits, all the better for him, wouldn't you say?"

"I'm glad you've given this so much thought," I snorted, turning away to bag up the trash. I just wanted a moment to recover from the sudden stab of pain in the chest. I was happy for Bennett. His lifelong dream had come true, and he was living in his own personal heaven. I could be happy for him and sad for myself at the same time, but I'd prefer he didn't equate his happiness with my sorrow.

"Oh, what the hell is this?" I heard Chief Borton bark. I looked up from the garbage bag to find him standing in the doorway, glaring at Bennett.

"Heya, Chief Borton," Bennett said, looking him over. "You're looking quite strapping today."

Chief Borton scowled at him. "Hell no. You are not coming in here and starting your bullshit, Livington. Trevor might be willing to deal with you, but I'm not having any of that shit in here. I deal with enough with these idiots around here."

"Thanks, Chief," I muttered, yanking the bag out of the can to tie it.

"You're the one who keeps bringing this menace around," Chief growled at me. "*And* leaving him unsupervised."

"I'm just here to hang out with him until his shift is over," Bennett said innocently. The problem with Bennett's innocent demeanor was that anyone who'd dealt with him didn't believe it for a minute. Even Adam didn't believe it. He just so happened to be a sucker for it and tended to give in.

"Guess what? Bently?"

"Yes, Chief?"

"Your shift is over. Get you and your little troublemaker out of here. Stat."

"Got it. I'll take the trash out, and then I'll clock out."

"Good, you're going with him, Livington."

"Alright," Bennett said brightly, hopping down from the counter and following me out. The chief continued muttering as he went to the bubbling pot and sniffed it.

"He still hasn't let go of that little accident with the hose, has he?" Bennett asked me.

"Little accident?" I scoffed, booting the bar to unlatch the back door. "Bennett, you flooded the entire truck bay and the hallway. We practically had to swim to get to the break room."

"I misjudged the power on the hoses, alright?"

"They're fire hoses, Bennett. Of *course* they're high pressure."

"And the instructions on clamping it down, so it doesn't fly off the water source were unclear."

"Probably because we're trained to do it, not reading a sticker on the side of the truck," I said, chucking the bag into the dumpster. "You never told me what you were trying to do with it in the first place."

"I was testing to see how far the water would go, and I was going to see if I could spray someone coming out of my station without causing damage."

"Right. That makes sense."

"See?"

"I meant it makes sense for *you*. Not for an average, functioning human being."

"Rude."

I snorted, opening the back door and walking in to find a computer to clock out. I could already feel the tension I'd

265

been feeling earlier bleeding out of me, and I was glad Bennett had come to see me. In truth, most of my time had been spent at home when I wasn't working. Dealing with the rest of the world had seemed too monumental a task, and being at home seemed the safer option.

There had only been last weekend when Bennett had come over, a fifth of whiskey in his hand, that I'd dealt with anyone else. After working our way through half the bottle, I finally started to tell him everything. The bottle and a few of the beers in my fridge were gone by the time I got to the end, a soggy, crying mess. Then, after proclaiming he was the best friend in the world, I promptly passed out on the floor. Hours later I woke up on the couch instead, with a humming Bennett whipping up food for a cranky, hungover stomach.

Not my finest moment.

"So, I had a thought," Bennett began as we walked out.

"Didn't we just have a conversation about how that's a real thing?" I quipped.

"Har har, God, you and Chase, you're both just so witty," Bennett said dryly, hopping into my passenger seat.

I opened the driver's side, bending down to peer at him. "What are you doing?"

"Oh, Adam dropped me off this morning before he went into the shop to start fixing things up," Bennett said with unmistakable pride. Adam was exceptionally handy from his years of learning and practice. And after a little push from Bennett and working freelance in the town for months, he had decided to open his own handyman business. It was just him, but he was pretty popular in Fairlake, so it was inevitable he would one day bring in someone else. "I texted him that I was going to harass you today, so he's gonna head home once he's done."

"I don't recall agreeing to this plan," I said dryly.

"I didn't ask," Bennett said brightly.

Rolling my eyes, I slid into the driver's seat and turned the engine over. I frowned when it took a moment before kicking on. "I'm going to need Chase to look this over soon. I think something's wrong with the starter."

"Eh," Bennett said, leaning on the seat back as I left the parking spot. "Just have him start the thing. He'll probably figure out what's going on long before that fancy computer he has to use at work."

"You realize those computers make it easier to diagnose problems, right?" I asked, pulling out onto the street.

"Do yourself a *huge* favor and never say those words around Chase. Otherwise, you're going to have to listen to a bunch of grumbling about how everything's getting stuck on computers and how it completely ruins the work of people who know what they're doing," Bennett said with a chuckle. "He sounds like a cranky boomer who's mad that the internet proved gum doesn't stay in your system for seven years if you swallow it."

"Sometimes I wonder why he stays friends with you," I smirked, turning onto his street. "You give him so much shit."

"Probably because he needs to get shit sometimes," Bennett said. "Otherwise, he'd lapse into being a grumpy ass. Someone needs to drag him out of that pit or give him a target to grump at."

"I'm familiar with the idea," I said quietly, thinking of Julian. Not that he needed a target for his grumpiness, but more the need to have someone willing to shine a light into his mental pit and give him a reason to climb out eventually. At times it had been easier said than done, but I had always thought it was worth it. "Guess you're pretty good at it."

"Hey," he said softly, bumping my shoulder. "Don't do that to yourself."

"Do what? Feel sorry for myself? I know."

"Nah," he said as we stopped in his driveway. "You're entitled to feel sorry for yourself. You were falling in love with the guy, and he dropped you like a hot potato because he's scared shitless of changing his life in an obvious, public way. That's a pretty good reason to feel sorry for yourself."

"I know why he did it. Unfortunately, that doesn't make it any easier," I said softly, then frowned. "Wait, I never said anything about falling in love with him."

"Look, from what I saw last weekend, that was clearly falling in love, if not already in love's zip code."

"I was drunk."

"So?"

"Drunk people are always more emotional."

"True, but you forget, we've been friends for years now, bud. I've seen you with other guys. But I've *never* seen you so patient and understanding with someone's nonsense like you've been with Julian."

"I put up with you," I said with a smirk. "That's pretty patient and understanding."

Bennett beamed, hopping out of the car. "Come on, let's have a couple of beers while I put some food in the oven."

"Fine," I said, not bothering to argue what I knew was a lost fight.

"Yeah," I muttered. "Since I know I'm going to see him before I can escape, just how much does Adam know? At least that way I can gauge how awkward it will be."

"Well, you *were* drunk, so maybe I shouldn't have taken you at face value, but you did tell me I could tell him."

"Lovely."

"I told him the facts, but I didn't go into how you were that night if that helps."

"A little," I said with a smile. "It's nice to know he didn't have to face the mental image of snot and tears on my face."

"Aww, but you've never been more attractive," Bennett said, ruffling my hair.

"Ass," I snorted, swatting him away.

"See, this is why you and I were never going to work out," Bennett said with a shake of his head. "Because you don't appreciate my humor."

"We weren't going to work out because you were madly in love with your supposedly straight best friend for most of your life," I snorted.

"Shh, not too loud. I have a reputation to uphold," Bennett said as he led me into his and now Adam's house.

"In this town? I'm surprised you haven't had people asking when one of you is going to propose," I said, closing the front door behind me and kicking off my shoes.

"Oh, we have," Bennett snorted. "But he's being Mr. Practical about the whole thing. Even if we're great together, he wants to make sure our lives mesh as well as adults and lovers as they did when we were younger and just friends."

I knew how much having Adam meant to Bennett and chewed my bottom lip. "How's that make you feel?"

"I mean, it stings a little, you know? But I realize it's not personal. It's not just him being practical by nature. I have to remember he's been badly burned by marriage," Bennett explained, cracking open two bottles and handing me one. "Just so long as I have him, that's what matters for now. I think he's the one stressing about whether or not it should happen."

Right, the ex-wife, the ugly divorce, and then the showing up a few weeks before giving birth to their son that Adam didn't even know about. "So, how are things between Bri and Adam?"

"Well," Bennett said thoughtfully, bouncing forward without warning to turn the oven on. "It's tricky for both of them. They've still got a lot of unresolved shit to sort through. That and Bri was kinda intent on trying to make things work out between them, what with Colin on the way.

But for Colin's sake, they're going slow and trying to find an amicable friendship."

"I haven't seen Colin yet," I said, wrinkling my nose. "Does Adam get time with him?"

"Are you kidding? Adam is positively *greedy* when it comes to spending time with him."

I hadn't seen much of that, but then again, I'd spent the past few months wrapped up in Julian and staying with him. "And Bri?"

"For all they did to one another while they were going through their separation, she's never once shown signs of using Colin against him," Bennett said with a shrug. "They're both trying, so that's what matters."

"And you?" I asked slowly. "How do you feel about them mending bridges?"

He gave me a soft smile. "I'm happy for both of them. Bri's looking like she's letting go, especially now they're officially divorced. And I've never worried about Adam catching any feelings. The man's madly in love with me, which sounds cocky, but I'm just as crazy about him, so it's fair."

"That's fair," I said, feeling an unhappy squeeze in my chest.

"Hey, I don't mean to rub your nose in things," Bennett said with a frown that looked out of place on his face.

"You're *not*," I insisted, shaking my head. "You being happy isn't something you should be worried about. And as your friend, you should be able to tell me things without feeling bad."

"Yeah, I just…I know this is a hard time for you right now," Bennett said softly.

"Me having a hard time doesn't mean you should stop having a good time," I told him, narrowing my eyes. "Don't you dare stop telling me all this goofy, lovey-dovey shit, okay? You deserve it. God knows how long you were hung up on him. Enjoy having it."

"And to think, it all got kickstarted because you got a little too drunk and told him I had a big ol' crush on someone and then ran away," Bennett snickered.

That made me smile. "I was so freaked out that I'd nearly given away your big secret."

"And then he *totally* got jealous because he was having big gay feels for me but didn't realize it. Then boom! Next thing you know, we're arguing. I punch him, kiss him, and then he's getting a blowjob," Bennett said with a chuckle. "Life is weird."

"Your life, maybe," I said with a snort. "Only you would find yourself in a situation like that."

"True," he said with a pleased sigh.

We were interrupted by the sound of the front door opening and Adam's voice calling out, "You guys decent?"

"Nope," I called back. "We're balls deep. Mind coming back in like two minutes? That's all it'll take him."

Adam entered, running a hand through his dark hair as he chuckled. "I guess that means you must know what you're doing."

"I might," I said, taking a drink.

"Hey," Adam said softly, bending to catch a quick kiss from Bennett.

"Hey yourself," Bennett said, and there was no mistaking the pleased smile on his face. I was pretty sure he was squealing on the inside.

"Bri called. She's bringing Colin by if that's alright," Adam said as he dropped a bag of tools beside the wall in the dining room.

Bennett's eyes sparkled. "Like I'm going to say no. I've almost got him to fist-bump me. I'm sure I can succeed by tomorrow."

"Nice to know you have your priorities straight," Adam snorted, taking off his jacket.

"Babe, you should know by now, there's *nothing* straight about me," Bennett said, waggling his eyebrows ridiculously.

Adam rolled his eyes, smiling at me. "Hey, Isaiah, doing alright?"

"Alright, just so long as you don't ask me if that's a lie or not," I replied.

"I've been acquainted with the feeling," Adam said gravely. "Saw that guy you were talking about."

"Which one?"

"Julian's brother."

"Oh God, why?" I asked, wrinkling my nose.

"He was walking with Julian. There was enough resemblance that I could tell it was him. They were walking down the street with some groceries, it looked like. I might've been tempted to jump the curb with my truck, but I didn't wanna risk breaking Julian's arms again."

"But not Tristan?" I asked wryly.

"Beep beep motherfucker," Adam said, twirling his finger to show his dismissal at the idea of hurting him.

I snickered. "I appreciate the thought, but I don't think you going to prison for vehicular manslaughter is going to fix things."

"Manslaughter? Nah, just a little…maiming," Adam said with a wink. "I'm going to take a shower."

"Rude!" Bennett grumbled at him as he pulled a foil-wrapped baking dish out of the freezer, probably a gift from Adam's mother.

"I can go so you can join him," I said lightly.

"You stay put," Bennett said, pointing a finger at me.

I sighed. "Damn it. I knew this was an intervention."

"Play nice, boys," Adam said before closing himself in the bathroom.

"Not an intervention, just trying to pick your brain," Bennett said as if that was somehow better.

I sighed. "Okay, fine, what?"

"Well, I was originally going to ask if you two had talked, but it's clear from what I saw today that you haven't," Bennett said, sliding the dish into the oven.

"Not about non-work stuff," I said, shrugging sullenly. "There's not a whole lot either of us can say to the other, you know? Especially after him telling me his mother is officially moving here. What can I say to that?"

"A big ol' 'I'm sorry' sounds about right," Bennett snorted, leaning back against the stove and taking a drink thoughtfully. "His mom sounds like a basket case. Having her around all the time and worrying about her sounds like a full-time job, and one he's not even getting hazard pay for."

"I feel bad," I said, deflating. "He's going to be stuck right back where he was before. But now he's going to be smothered by his mom, and since she's here, his brother will be hanging around while he's not at school."

"That's the little fucker that blackmailed Julian into petrified silence, right?" Bennett asked.

I scowled. "Not *so* little, but a big fucker, fucking prick."

"I'll take that as a yes."

"Yes, Tristan."

"Sounds like a real piece of work. Kind of a shame he got involved. It might have been easier for you both. You can't help that."

"I can...a little," I said, draining my bottle. "Literally moments before we knew they were there, I was telling him we would go at his speed. That I wasn't going to rush things."

"All good things to tell someone in his position," Bennett said with a nod. "But there has to be a speed in the first place. If he doesn't want his mom to know, that's out of the window the minute she decided to live here."

"And I think he understood that. Otherwise, why let me walk away like I did?"

"I don't know. Maybe he was too scared to pull you back to him."

"That's...an awful thought."

Bennett sighed. "Look, I only know what you've told me about the guy. I don't know him personally, so I can only guess what motivates or pushes him. Maybe he would have still found the courage to come out with her here, maybe not."

"And if he did? Then what does that say about me?"

"It says that you saw it would take a long ass time for him to do that, and that would mean constantly hiding. It'd be like being a teenager all over again as you tried to hide it from your family, or going back a few decades when people like us were terrified for even their friends to know. It would mean going against everything you ever believed. Maybe it was unfair for you to walk away, but it would have been equally unfair for him to expect you to stick around during that."

"So, damned if I did, damned if I didn't?"

Bennett bit his bottom lip. "Life doesn't usually have simple or easy answers."

"So I'm learning," I said, taking a bottle of liquor out of his freezer. Seeing his smirk, I rolled my eyes. "I'm not getting shitfaced. But I'd like to clear my head a little and not have it bogged down by my personal bullshit if I'm going to be hanging out."

"Hey," Bennett said, holding up his hands. "Drink as much as you want. You're free to crash on the couch, or one of us can take you home."

"Your support for my emotionally charged binge drinking is appreciated," I muttered as I poured, then took a shot. After a moment's thought, I took another for good measure and tucked the bottle back in the freezer in case I wanted some later.

The bathroom door creaked open, and Adam walked out, still damp from his shower and wearing a pair of loose pants slung low on his hips. He had a towel on his head, vigorously rubbing his hair. I could objectively see what Bennett found attractive about Adam, especially when he inadvertently made a spectacle of himself. However, Bennett was finding himself incredibly distracted by the accidental show, and I had to cover my mouth with a fist to stop laughing.

Adam sighed and dropped the towel, stopping in his tracks when he spotted us staring at him. "What?"

"Nothing," I said, glancing between him and Bennett, who was doing a poor job of hiding his ogling. "Am I expected to tip you for the show, or is this pro bono?"

"Hey!" Bennett protested, punching me in the shoulder. "That's mine."

I laughed, rubbing my arm. "Do you want me to get you a bucket, or would you prefer to drool on the floor?"

"If I have a choice, I would prefer to drool on his—"

"Alright," Adam said, clearing his throat. "I think we all know how that sentence was going to end. No need to finish it."

"What?" Bennett asked innocently. "I was only going to say your dick."

I snorted at the exasperated expression on Adam's face as he went to find a shirt. "He puts up with your shit so well."

"Doesn't he?" Bennett asked with a snicker. "But he knew what he was getting into long before he decided he was a little gay for me."

"True," I said, watching Bennett as he pretended he was looking at his phone but kept glancing toward the bedroom.

"You know you want to go molest him," I muttered with a smirk.

"Maybe."

"And what's stopping you?"

"I have a guest."

"A little groping out of sight isn't loud fucking, now is it?"

"You are a terrible influence, Isaiah."

I grinned. "That's me."

It turned out my being a bad influence wasn't going to stop Bennett from taking my advice and quickly scuttling off. It only took a few seconds until I heard Adam yelp. "Cold hands! Cold hands!"

I chuckled, stepping closer to the back door to give them some privacy while I stared at their backyard. There was still a heaviness in my chest that I couldn't shake, but at the very least, between being around my friends and perhaps a little help from the alcohol, it was a bearable weight.

It was criminal that somewhere in Fairlake, Julian was going through his own pain and didn't have people to lean on. I wasn't so blind to think that he didn't care about me or perhaps love me in his own slow, careful, and slightly fearful way. I had never questioned whether or not he felt for me, but in the end, I knew his fear of his family would ultimately win over whatever he did feel.

Our time together had been wonderful, and as much as it pained me, I wasn't going to let the bitterness and pain eclipse the great times we'd had together. Perhaps one day, I'd be able to think about him and not feel like the oxygen was being squeezed out of my lungs, but that would take time.

Not for the first time, I cursed the very existence of his brother. I had disliked him from the moment Julian had told me about what he'd done for his brother, and it had only grown with time. He had been every bit as arrogant and dickish as I'd imagined, and then some. It was clear he was a manipulative dick who would blackmail, steal, and lie to get whatever he wanted.

Wait a minute…

"Uh, Isaiah?" I heard Bennett ask from behind me.

I turned to see him standing in the kitchen, holding a bottle of beer out. "What? Oh, thanks. How long have you been standing there?"

"Long enough to see you were deep in thought," he said, raising a brow. "Want to share with the class?"

I thought about it before digging my phone out of my pocket. "In a second. I need to make a call."

"You're not calling Julian after only a few drinks, are you?" Bennett asked in a wary voice.

"Nope. I'm going to call one of the only people in my family who I know will still talk to me," I said with a snort, scrolling through the list. "Not that she'd tell anyone and risk losing financial support for school."

"Ouch," Bennett said, wrinkling his nose.

"I don't blame her," I said. "You do what you have to in order to survive in this world."

"I meant, ouch, it's fucked up she even has to make that choice in the first place."

"Yeah, well, welcome to the Bentlys."

"But—"

The ringing stopped, and a familiar voice answered, making me smile. "Hey, Trina? Yeah, it's me. I know it's been a little while since we talked. Uh, yeah, actually, something is up, and I wondered if you could help me. Do you know someone named Tristan Maccomb? You do? Yeah, it is a small world, but do you happen to have any good dirt on him?"

I turned, meeting Bennett's eyes as I heard her reply, and I grinned. "Oh, well then, we have some things to talk about."

JULIAN

A little over two weeks later, I was beginning to wonder if my brother would ever leave. I knew he was taking a semester off, according to my mother, but I had no idea why he was staying with her in the meantime. With a whole semester at his disposal, he should have been more than ready to do anything but hang around Fairlake. It wasn't like him to spend this much time with the family, and I couldn't figure out what his game was.

It was obvious why he spent so much time around me. Tristan had made it very clear that so long as he was around, it meant Isaiah and I had to stay apart. It delighted him to cause so much trouble for me, and I knew he knew that I knew what he was doing, which probably added another layer of delight for him.

"I always knew you were a prick," I muttered to him as I separated the ground beef for the three of us to have burgers. "But I didn't know you were a sadist too."

He looked up from his phone, raising a brow. "Oh, it speaks. And not only that, but it makes accusations. What did I do this time, bro?"

"You know what I'm fucking talking about."

"Let's pretend I don't."

"And we can also pretend you're not doing this to intentionally make it harder on me by making me say it out loud."

"Your pretty boy decided to run his mouth," Tristan said, plucking a pretzel out of the bag and biting it noisily. "In this world, actions have consequences. I suppose it was time he learned that."

"You wouldn't know the consequence of your actions if they bit you in the ass," I grumbled, rolling the meat into equal-sized balls.

"Careful," he warned.

"Or what? You'll tell Mom my secret? Then what ammunition will you use against me to keep me away from Isaiah?" I snapped at him, careful to keep my voice low. My mother's hearing wasn't the best, especially when watching TV, but she was sensitive to tone, and if she heard anger, she'd be in the kitchen in an instant.

He chuckled. "You'd still stay away from him because then Mom would know your secret. You'd have to spend so much time trying to convince her it wasn't true, so you didn't break her poor heart."

"You'd be the one breaking it, not me," I reminded him.

"I'm not the one who has the hots for the muscley-looking geek."

"He's not a geek."

"Guy looks like he works at a library and lifts weights at home."

"So?"

"So, that's an observation. Oh hey, which one of you is the pillow biter? I'd place money on you. There's just something about you, like you just let people do whatever they want, that tells me you bend over real nice for him."

"Listen to me," I said, slowly placing the last ball of meat down. "You can say whatever the fuck you want to taunt me, but you don't get to know *shit* about him and me, alright? And while you're at it, stop talking about hearts because yours withered and died years ago, if you ever had one to begin with."

Tristan blinked. "Wow. When did you find your spine? Well, spine for you anyway. How long's it going to last?"

"Blow me, Tristan," I snarled, returning to the food prep.

"I'm pretty sure it's not me you wish was the one blowing you right now," Tristan chuckled.

My temper flared, an inferno that curled and tightened in my chest. I whirled on Tristan, taking a step toward him. As I saw his eyes widen in sudden understanding, I was snapped out of it by a sharp knock on the door.

"Better get that," he said with a smirk, though I was sure I saw it wobble slightly.

Taking a deep breath, I stepped around him, avoiding looking at my mother and risking her seeing my face. I opened the door and felt the hot balloon of anger in me pop suddenly as I found Isaiah standing there. He was wrapped in a thick coat against the chilly weather and held a folder in his hand.

"What...what are you doing here?" I asked softly, even as my heart squeezed at seeing him outside my door. For a moment, I could almost imagine it was like things had been before my family showed up.

"You and I need to talk," he said, glancing over my shoulder. I knew the moment he spotted my brother by the tightening in his jaw. To my surprise, he smiled brightly and waved with his free hand. "Alone."

"Sure," I said, turning to find Tristan already stalking toward us. I smiled and lightened my voice. "Hey, Trist?"

He stopped, watching us. "What?"

"Could you get dinner cooking for us? They're just burgers. I'll do the veggies when I come back in. It would be a big help," I called, and my mother perked up, glancing at Tristan with a smile.

I could tell my brother wanted to scowl but shrank back toward the kitchen. "Sure."

I stepped outside, closing the door behind me. "We won't have long before he finds an excuse to come out here."

"Here," he said, shoving the folder toward me.

"What's this?" I asked.

"Something you can use," he told me mysteriously. "And no, this isn't me trying to…it's ammunition you need. Something you could use if you so choose."

"What does that mean?" I asked, taking the folder and peering at it.

"It means there's stuff in there you should know. Stuff you might want to use as a weapon, show your mom, or keep to yourself. It's my way of helping in the only way I can right now," he said, taking a step back.

"You're still trying to help," I said softly, looking down at the folder and wondering what was in it that was so important. "Why?"

"Because even if I can't be with you, Julian, I still care about you, maybe even love you."

"What?" I asked, looking up, eyes wide.

He smiled sadly. "So yeah, I still want to help. It's up to you what you do with it."

"Stay," I told him gently, swallowing hard and opening the folder.

There were printouts of news articles and a couple from a website. I scanned everything and felt a surge of heat shoot through me. Jaw tight, I read through the articles. The information sank into my brain, and I felt it whirling around, becoming a screaming dirge.

I raised my head and met Isaiah's eyes filled with compassion and understanding. "I'm sorry, Julian. I really am."

"Don't be," I said between gritted teeth. "Not you."

"I know this hurts, even if it might not be a surprise," he said softly.

I heard the door open. "Well, well, look who decided not to listen."

Clenching the folder, I turned to face my brother. Tristan smirked in absolute delight at Isaiah, taking a second before he looked at me. Whatever he'd seen in the kitchen was nothing compared to whatever was on my face now as he shrank away from me.

"What?" he asked, a frown creasing his brow.

"You *son of a bitch*," I hissed, stepping closer.

"Uh, Julian?" he began, stepping back into the apartment. "Mom is right there."

I barely registered his words as I stepped closer. "You lying, backstabbing, hypocritical fuck!"

"Julian? Tristan?" my mother called out worriedly. "What's going on?"

"Yeah, Tristan," I growled, throwing the folder at him. It hit his chest and exploded in a flurry of papers. "What could be going on?"

Tristan scrambled, not managing to catch any of the papers as they floated to the ground. His eyes shot to the ground, widening as he saw the headline of one of the articles. "That...where the fuck did you get that?"

"What is that? What's going on?" my mother asked, getting up from the couch.

"It's nothing," Tristan snapped.

My mother's eyes widened, having never heard Tristan talk to her like that. "Tristan?"

"You," I seethed, stepping closer. "This whole time, you were what, taking us for a ride? How much have you lied? *How much?*"

The last came out in a roar I had never before used, sending Tristan shrinking away from me and making my mother call out in alarm. I advanced on him, only to feel a hand on my arm, holding me back. I turned to find Isaiah at my side, his fingers squeezing my arm. I hesitated and then faltered at his soft smile.

"Someone, please, tell me what's going on," my mother called, practically on the verge of tears.

"I..." but the words wouldn't come as I stared down at the papers. "Isaiah?"

"Are you sure?" Isaiah asked, bending down to pick up the papers.

"*Yes.*"

Isaiah cleared his throat. "Your son, Tristan, has been lying to you, Mrs. Maccomb. For at least a year now."

Tristan's eyes widened, and he opened his mouth, only for me to step forward. Isaiah waited until he saw Tristan shrink back before stepping behind me with the papers in hand, meeting my mother's eyes.

"He hasn't been in school for over a year," he told her softly.

"He's only out for a semester," she protested, glancing at Tristan, then at me.

"He was kicked out last fall semester," Isaiah said, still speaking gently and holding out a few sheets of paper. "He got into a drunken brawl on campus with another fraternity member. Broke his nose and his jaw and dislocated a shoulder. Not only that, but when the frat brother's girlfriend tried to intervene, Tristan turned on her and broke her jaw as well."

My mother reached out, taking the paper hesitantly. "No, no, not...no."

Still gentle but persistent, Isaiah continued. "Not only that, but they found drugs in his room, cocaine mostly, but pills as well. After all that, he was arrested, and the school booted him out since he was already on academic probation. He served a few months but hasn't been at school since."

"I guess the money Mom sent you that came from *me* wasn't going toward food, huh?" I grumbled at my brother. "Bet you were feeling real fucking stupid when I wasn't there to take the fall for you, *again*."

"W-what?" my mother breathed, her voice shaking as she clenched the pages, her eyes darting over them.

I felt for her, but the anger, betrayal, and rage were too much to contain. "Remember when I got that felony assault charge from that party?"

She reached out, gripping the back of the chair she had shrunk behind. "Y-yes."

"That wasn't me," I said, turning my eyes on my brother, who looked too stunned to so much as twitch. "That was *him*. I took the fall for him. I was there to pick him up but wasn't quick enough to stop the fight. He did that. He beat that poor bastard, but I took it because he was my brother. After all, he was the one with the bright future."

"No," my mother insisted, shaking her head. "He's shown me pictures of him on campus. There's...I haven't been sending him enough money to live off."

I met Isaiah's eyes and nodded. "Because he's been making money on the side."

She turned to him, tears finally leaving her eyes to track down her cheeks. "Drugs?"

"No," Isaiah said grimly. "But it's where the hypocrisy comes in."

"I don't understand," she said, voice wobbling further.

"Tristan's been blackmailing me and Isaiah," I said. "All because he didn't like that Isaiah knew about me taking the fall for him and because he's a dick."

It was the oddest thing, getting the truth out there for

everyone to see. Even though I could see my mother's fragile heart breaking at everything she learned, I no longer had this secret beating away inside me. Even as the truth beat at my mother's chest, I could feel it loosening a weight that had pressed against my own.

"Blackmail for *what?*" she demanded.

"Well," Isaiah began, looking at me uncertainly.

I opened my mouth and couldn't find the words, clamping it shut. Desperation clawed at me as I watched the soft pain but understanding cross Isaiah's face. Even now, when it counted the most, I couldn't find the words to tell my mother the truth.

"It's okay," Isaiah said, gently reaching out to squeeze my arm.

"No," I grunted, pulling him toward me. I heard his gasp as I bent down and caught his lips with mine. I could feel the pull to deepen the kiss, to taste him completely as I hadn't done in weeks, but I pushed it aside, content to have the tingle of his lips against mine before I broke apart.

"Okay," Isaiah said with a nervous laugh. "That's one way of doing it."

"Don't always need words," I said, pressing our foreheads together. "I'm sorry."

"Don't be," he said softly, running his fingers through my hair. "We'll talk, okay?"

"Sure," I said and was met with a delighted smile.

Taking a deep breath, I leaned away, turning to face my brother and mother. Tristan somehow managed to look even more stunned than before as he stood against the wall, staring at us. My mother's tears had stopped as she stared at me with wide, still watery eyes.

"I'm in love with Isaiah," I said, feeling Isaiah straighten next to me but keeping my eyes on my mother. "He treats me better than anyone I've known. He takes care of me, and I take care of him. He makes me happier than anything in my life ever has, and I know he's got my back. Tristan figured it out and threatened to tell you about it if Isaiah and I didn't stay away from each other. That's why he's been around me so much. It wasn't bonding. He wanted to make sure Isaiah stayed away so he could taunt me about it."

My mother glanced between us, eyes sweeping side to side in long, slow movements. "I...you're...your father—"

My expression hardened. "Was an abusive bastard who would rather beat his son and wife than deal with his own problems. Whatever he had to say about me doesn't matter."

"No," she breathed, shaking her head. "You...not you. No."

It hurt a lot more than I thought it would, but I sucked the pain down and frowned at her. "Yes, me."

I could sense Isaiah growing annoyed. "If that's what really breaks your heart, might as well make it double."

"No!" Tristan hissed, coming to life finally.

"What is this?" she asked, staring down at the pages but not approaching them as Isaiah threw them at her feet.

"Turns out, after getting out of jail, your youngest decided to make an OnlyFans page. From your expression, you don't know what that is. It's a website where people can post whatever they want, but it's usually amateur pornography. Some people post naked pictures of themselves, and some post pictures and videos of them having sex with other people. Turns out Tristan is part of the latter group, where he posts videos of him having sex with both women and men," Isaiah said, turning a cold glare on Tristan. "Hence, hypocrite."

"W-what?" my mother breathed, her hand coming to her chest.

"Both of your children are bi, Mrs. Maccomb. The difference is one is a conniving, backstabbing, lying asshole who's been taking you for a ride, probably for years. While the other one has bent over backward his whole life to try to take care of you and a brother who didn't deserve it," Isaiah said, crossing his arms.

"You motherfucker!" Tristan shrieked, barreling toward Isaiah.

I stepped forward, intent on plowing my fist into his face like he deserved, only for Isaiah to step between us. "Hey, hey, Julian! Don't, okay, don't. He's not worth the trouble. You know he'd call the cops, and then your prior would catch up with you. You can't hit him."

I snarled, bunching my fists at my side. Isaiah was right, but that didn't mean I had to like it. "Fine."

"Good," Isaiah said gently. I let out an annoyed huff, crossing my arms over my chest as Isaiah turned to Tristan.

Before anyone could blink, I watched as Isaiah reached back and, in a flash, lashed out to hit my brother once, then twice in the face, once in the nose, and another in the jaw. Tristan stumbled backward, taken completely off-guard and slumping to the ground with a groan, blood spurting between his fingers.

My mother shrieked with dismay and darted toward Tristan as Isaiah turned around to face me. He blinked up at me, looking as innocent as the day I'd first met him. "What? I said *you* couldn't hit him. I don't have a record."

I couldn't help but reach out and kiss him as I'd wanted to the first time. It didn't matter that my mother was practically wailing as she tried to help Tristan up or that my brother was muttering curses under his breath as he got to his feet. All that mattered was the man in my arms, pressed against me as I kissed him with every bit of passion and intent I could manage.

"Don't," I growled at Tristan as he moved closer. "Just don't. Get the fuck out of my apartment, and do not *ever* come near me again. As far as I'm concerned, I don't have a brother."

He looked between the two of us, his mouth opening. To my surprise, Isaiah turned to smirk at him, his brow shooting up as if daring him to say something stupid. With a hiss, my brother yanked away from our mother and stomped toward the door, slamming it behind him.

My mother glanced between the door and me and then back to Isaiah. "You...you really feel this way?"

"I do," I said softly, taking Isaiah's hand in mine. My heart beat furiously in my chest as my worst nightmare unfolded around me, even as the man of my dreams stood next to me. "And I might not have a brother anymore, but whether I have a mother is up to you now, not me."

"I..." she glanced between us again. "I don't...I don't know, Julian."

"You don't have to know right now," I said, even as the words sunk the blade deeper into my chest. "Figure it out when you can. Take your time. Just know that no matter what, the truth isn't going to change. I'm still going to be bi, and I'm still going to want to be with Isaiah."

Her bottom lip trembled, and she jerked when a sharp horn interrupted the silence. Taking a shaky breath, she nodded at us and hurried out of the house. She stopped in the doorway to give us one last lingering look but then disappeared, closing the door more softly behind her than her youngest had.

"Oh shit," I breathed, stumbling back to sit on the arm of the couch and taking a deep breath. "Holy fuck."

"Woah," Isaiah said, steadying me before kneeling so he could peer up into my face. "Hey there, hey."

I peered into his face, reaching down to run my fingers along his jaw. "Hey."

"Hi," he said with a warm smile.

"I'm okay," I assured him.

"For the moment," he said with a knowing look. "And in

another moment, you'll be freaking out and wondering if you can't get the cat in the bag again. Then you'll be mad that you waited so long, then you'll be mad at them for making it this way, then you'll want to cry because it's all so pointless and stupid and heartbreaking. Then you'll be something else."

"Got it all figured out, huh?" I asked softly.

"Might have been there a few times in my life," he said with a chuckle, laying his head on my thigh.

"Yeah, I guess you probably have," I said, cupping his face. "But right now, I'm just a little overwhelmed by everything that's happened. But I'm glad it happened."

"We'll see how you feel about that later." He laughed, looking bashful.

I frowned, pulling him closer to me. "I know it's selfish, but…will you be there? To help."

"Do you want me to be?" he asked softly. "I didn't give you that folder so this would happen."

"You didn't?" I raised a brow, feeling a little disappointed.

"Well, a part of me hoped. But in the end, it was to help you," he said with a sigh. "You deserved to know the truth, the whole truth. And well, maybe I was hoping it would result in Tristan finally getting what he deserved."

I glanced toward the door. "I don't know if my mother is really going to…care. Tristan's always been her favorite. She's not going to be able to handle losing him after losing our dad."

"Then that's *her* loss, not yours," he said softly. "And I know that's easier to say than do, but it's the truth. If she can't see the gift she's had in you all along, then that's her failing, not yours."

"Yeah, I guess," I muttered.

He peered at me knowingly. "You're still going to take care of her financially, no matter what she does, aren't you?"

Sometimes it amazed me just how well he knew me. "Someone has to take care of her. She can't take care of herself, and I've always known Tristan was never going to do it."

He sighed heavily. "Oh, Julian."

"Sorry."

"Don't be. As much as I believe she doesn't deserve it, I'm not going to get in the way unless it affects you more than it already does. I'm just going to sit by and marvel at how big your heart is."

"Mine? What about yours?"

He laughed, wrapping his arms around my neck. "It's yours."

"Really?" I asked in surprise. "Even after everything?"

A crease formed on his brow. "It hurt, I won't lie. It hurt so much sometimes that it was all I could think about."

"I'm sorry," I said softly, reaching down to squeeze his sides gently. "I never...I hated it. I hated every second of it. I felt trapped. I wanted out, but—"

"You got out," he told me gently. "You did that."

"You did most of it," I said, disappointed in myself. "You found it. You said it all."

"You said plenty," he chuckled. "And none of that would have happened if you hadn't started off by confronting Tristan. Well, and then you went and kissed me in front of them. Christ, I thought Tristan was going to have kittens on the spot when you did that."

"Hypocrite," I growled.

"Indeed."

"Wait," I said in realization. "If you were on his OnlyFans, that means...you paid for it."

"Ugh, as *if*," he said with a snort. "Do you know how many forums there are to access the content on someone's

OnlyFans without paying a dime? I mean, I would have if I needed to, but thankfully I didn't."

"You watched him," I said, wrinkling my nose.

"Sweetheart, I would desperately like not to think about that too much if you don't mind," he said, sticking his tongue out in disgust. "I've never been so soft in my life, trust me."

"Well, that's good," I mumbled, pulling him closer. "But otherwise, I like you hard."

"Are you trying to seduce me right now?" he asked with a laugh.

"Watching you punch Tristan was hot. That's going to be mental porn for weeks."

"Wow, that's kinda kinky...I think."

"Where'd you learn to hit like that?"

"I took boxing lessons with Chase a couple of years ago. He still does it for exercise, but I lost interest."

"Oh."

He sidled closer to me, kissing me gently. "Look, I...oh, who the fuck is that?"

I raised a brow as he yanked his incessantly buzzing phone out of his pocket. When he saw the caller ID, he let out a groan. Sighing, he swiped the screen and answered it. "Bennett, can this wait? I'm having a moment while you blow up my...what? Are you shitting me?" Isaiah let out an ugly snort. "Of *course* he fucking did, the absolute wuss. So are you showing up to arrest me, or is it someone else?"

"What?" I straightened with a growl.

Isaiah shook his head as he listened. "Okay, well, you come up here and take my statement, but do you think you could hold off for, like, twenty minutes? Actually, hold on. How long is this going to take? Because if you can make it quick, I wanna borrow your handcuffs. What? That's a perfectly reasonable...and he hung up."

"Handcuffs?" I asked, blinking.

"Sure, I was thinking of handcuffing you to the bed and riding you until you lost your mind, or you could handcuff me and have your way with me." He shrugged. "But from how hard Bennett just laughed at me, I don't think that's going to happen."

"We'll buy some," I muttered, heart fluttering at the thought of being helpless while I watched Isaiah perched above me, doing whatever he wanted.

"He's going to show up to take my statement over the supposed assault," Isaiah said, scooting close again.

"I don't want you to get in trouble."

"Eh. Twice to the face is a misdemeanor. I'll probably end up with a fine and some community service."

"Borton—"

"Will yell at me for losing my temper and probably buy us pizza once he learns why."

"I guess you have it all figured out," I said softly.

"Most of it," he said, wrapping his arms around my waist. "But while we wait for the men in uniform to show up, how about we make up for a little lost time?"

"Cuddling," I said firmly. "I want everything else to last."

His expression softened as he pushed me back onto the couch, following after me and curling up by my side. "Now that's something I can get behind."

"Good," I said, holding him tight as I tried not to fall off the couch. "I'm glad you're going to be here with me. For all of this."

"I'm glad you chose yourself instead of them," he said softly, nuzzling into my chest.

"I chose us too," I said, breathing in the scent of his hair.

"Us," he said with a smile. "I like the sound of that."

"Me too."

EPILOGUE

Three Years Later

With a heavy yawn, I rolled over, only to be met by a blockage. Vaguely I remembered I was on an overnight shift at the station. That usually meant curling up in one of the bunks in the sleep room and not running into something that wasn't the wall when rolling over. That was until I remembered we had pushed a couple of the cots together before falling asleep while Zach had kept an ear on the radio for us.

Julian stirred beside me after my graceless splat into his back. "You up?"

"Mmph," I muttered, wrapping an arm around his chest and pulling myself closer. "No, I'm sleeping."

"No, you're not."

"Am too."

"You're not snoring anymore."

"I don't snore!"

"Sure," he chuckled, rolling to wrap his arms around me and pull me closer to him. "Whatever makes you feel better."

I could tell from his voice that he hadn't just woken up. "Have you slept at all?"

"No, just laying here."

"Thinking again?"

"Some."

"Bad?"

He reached behind him and plucked his phone up to show me the screen. I laughed as I caught a few of the words on the page. "Wow, you're expanding closer to modern history. Bold move."

"Hush," he muttered, locking his phone and pulling me close. "Couldn't sleep. Figured I should do something with myself."

"You could have got up and done something. Reading in a chair is probably more comfortable than in these damn cots."

"Yeah. But you wouldn't be there."

I smiled, scooting closer so I could stick my head under his chin and burrow into his chest. Communication still wasn't his strongest suit, but that didn't mean he didn't know how to get his point across. Emotions were still occasionally tricky for him, but he had got quite good at knowing the right thing to say to ensure I knew I was still important to him.

"Sometimes I suspect you might be in love with me or something," I mumbled against his chest.

"Or something," he said, and I could hear the smile in his voice.

The cots in the station were some of the most ungodly uncomfortable things mankind had ever created, but I wouldn't trade them for the world's comfiest mattress if I didn't get to have moments like this. Sure, we would get up, and both grumble about our backs and bitch about needing to get something better than slabs of concrete disguised as mattresses, but those rare moments we shared overnight at the station were some of my favorites.

"Hey! Lovebirds!" Zach barked into the room. "You decent?"

"Nope, he's currently choking on my dick," I called back, sitting upright now the moment was ruined.

Julian chuckled even as his face warmed a little. It had taken him a couple of months after the incident with his family to warm to the idea of some people knowing. It started with the guys at the station, with only the twins genuinely surprised when they found out. After that, it was pretty much accepted that we were a couple, even if the chief liked to grumble about workplace-appropriate behavior even though he had no proof to the contrary, as far as I knew anyway. That didn't mean he was quite as comfortable making lewd jokes about us as around other people, though he eventually started finding the humor in it.

From how Zach rolled his eyes as he entered, he clearly wasn't finding the humor. "Well, get up, get moving. Shifts over in a couple of hours, and you two are going to help me clean rather than make my teeth ache."

"Aw, he thinks we're cute," I told Julian, who ducked his head, avoiding Zach's gaze.

"Him maybe, you? Not so much," Zach shot back.

"Wow, my man's so hot he turns straight, married men curious," I said, cackling when both Julian and Zach groaned in dismay. "You two are too easy."

"Just get up," he grumbled, giving me a wary look. "I'm going back to the radio. You've got half an hour."

I smirked. "Yeah, yeah, I'll get caffeinated by then."

"Right," he said, rolling his eyes as he walked out. I would also bet my next paycheck that he smiled as he walked away.

"You're awful," Julian muttered beside me, getting off the cot and stretching.

"Probably," I said, leaping up to slip my hand up his shirt. I ran my fingers along the flat plane of his stomach and squeezed his chest. "But you like me awful."

"What are you doing?" he asked in a low growl that told me he knew exactly what I was doing.

To answer his question, I reached down past the band of his sleep pants. Finding his dick wasn't difficult, considering the size of the thing, especially since it was already half hard. I wrapped my hand around it, giving it a gentle squeeze.

"I'm about to take a shower," I told him lightly. "Perhaps you could join me?"

"Seriously?"

"We've got half an hour. I'm sure we can get clean in that time. And if we find a way to wake me up faster than coffee, who am I to complain?"

"Awful," he repeated before wrapping an arm around my waist and dragging me out of the room.

* * *

AFTER OUR SHIFT, we elected to walk around the town center for a while, stopping by Grant's Bakery the moment it opened. The quiet and somewhat distant man might have been hard to relate to at times, but there was no denying the brilliance of his baking.

"God," I muttered as I bit into the warm croissant. "How do you do it?"

"Very carefully," Grant said with a smile.

It was the sort of answer I expected from him, but the smile was nice to see. Once upon a time, he was almost as serious as Julian, albeit with the skill of making people happy with his baked goods. Things had changed, though, after he'd discovered that being in love was pretty damn sweet.

"Oh," I said before leaving with Julian, who was nibbling at a muffin like a chipmunk. "I forgot to ask, how's the boyfriend?"

Grant ducked his head, holding up his left hand to show a twinkling band. It was simple, a little at odds with the fact that his boyfriend was stupidly rich and the famous brother of a star.

"Ah!" I barked, giving him a big grin. "Congrats! When's the date?"

"Next June," he said, smiling as he bent to knead some dough. "We're doing it here."

"Oh, that's great," I said with a smile. It made sense. The two had been dating for a couple of years now. Adam and Bennett were already long since married, which made sense for the two of them. There was also a rumor that Chase was getting ready to ask Devin, but the guy kept waiting for the perfect moment, as if the moment wouldn't automatically be perfect for Devin just because Chase asked.

"A lot of people are getting an invite. You two will get one," he said, inspecting his dough with sudden intensity. "Have a good morning."

I snorted at the sudden dismissal. "Yeah, you too, Grant, and congrats again!"

Beaming at his news, I walked out with Julian, humming a little tune. It wasn't until almost a block of walking that I realized he had grown quieter than usual. Glancing at him, I found him frowning at his muffin.

"Something wrong with it?" I asked.

"No," he said quickly. "I just...do you—?"

"Uh, do I what?" I asked in confusion. After three and a half years, I was the leading expert on speaking Julian, but that didn't make me a flawless translator.

"Get married."

"Oh…are you proposing?"

His eyes widened to an almost comical level as he turned toward me. "No!"

I tried not to let his sudden denial sting, but it still did…a little. "Um, okay."

"No, I mean," he let out a huff of frustration, and I saw the muscles in his jaw tighten. I immediately recognized the signs of frustration with himself and his inability to communicate the words and feelings in his head. It generally wasn't a problem, but every once in a while, it would catch up with both of us.

The worst had been after a year together when I'd asked him to move in with me. It made sense to me at the time, I had more space, and technically it was easier to move out of an apartment you rented rather than moving out of the house I owned. The problem was that Julian had been intent on covering half the living costs. He quickly realized it wasn't possible with his income being bled away by his mother.

I had innocently said it didn't matter to me if he couldn't pay half, just so long as he was there. In doing so, I had accidentally trodden on his pride and independence. From there, the argument boiled forth as he refused to move unless he could pay half, and I was hurt and angry that he didn't want to live with me and accept that being unable to make bills didn't make him less than me.

Those had been a quiet couple of days for us until he'd pulled me aside while we were working the same shift. He'd told me he'd talked to his mom, and he was going to be giving her less money so he could meet me halfway on the bills. It pained him, but he'd told me he was okay if I spent the majority on extra stuff, but he wanted to help give us a home and food.

Needless to say, I felt like an ass, and we talked more over several days. The reality of our situation had to be addressed, and we came to an understanding eventually. It meant more bickering and occasional arguments, but we'd finally found peace. He'd still stuck with giving her less, forcing her to be careful with her government aid money and get a part time job, but he was able to do his part for the house on his terms.

"Hey," I said, taking his free hand in mine. "Take your time. I'm okay. I can wait."

"I meant...does being married...is that something you'd want?" he asked, then scowled. Clearly, that wasn't what he meant to say, but I thought I understood.

"Being married to you would be great, and I'd be more than happy. But it's *not* a requirement," I told him quickly. I didn't want him to think he had to be married to me for us to be happy.

"But..." he began, frowning.

"Our lives? I love our lives," I told him softly. "You , me, the guys at the station, our friends. I love every moment of it."

It had taken him time to adjust to the idea that his world wasn't just him and his shitty family anymore. His mom still talked to him occasionally, though nowhere near as often as she did before. I hadn't been surprised when she'd refused to see the truth and continued supporting Tristan and involving herself in his life.

The asshole had disappeared from Fairlake after his attempt to get me arrested. I honestly didn't know what Bennett had done, though he insisted it wasn't him, but Tristan had dropped the charges a few days after trying to sic the cops on me. If he ever showed up to visit his mother, then he did so quietly and without fanfare. I suspected the dickhead was content to soak up his mother's attention and her money from a distance. I wasn't heartbroken over that development, and if it bothered Julian, he never said.

So now he had a real family, admittedly the same one I had, but hey, it's a good family. The guys at the station, Bennett, Adam and even Chase and Devin, were all we needed in our lives. Sure, it had taken Julian a little while to warm up and accept them in his life. It had started with cooking with Zach, talking cars with Chase, and learning to laugh at Bennett's shenanigans rather than be confused by them. Yeah, it was slow, but it had happened, and I didn't think he'd ever been as happy and comfortable in his own skin as he was now.

"You want to get married?" He frowned, pulling me back into the moment.

"I'd be happy to," I said, not pointing out that it sounded like a really weird proposal. "But again, not required."

"Okay," he said with a resolute nod. "Okay."

"What…what does that mean?" I asked warily.

He gave me the little crooked grin that always shot straight to my heart and groin. "Don't worry about it."

Julian left me standing there, blinking after him as he continued walking, now merrily eating his muffin once again. I stared after him, heart beating a little faster at the implication of his words. Julian wasn't always the best at explaining himself, but somehow he always found a way to get his meaning across. Maybe it was just because I was so used to him, but I was almost sure I knew what he was insinuating.

"Julian?" I called. "What does that mean?"

He just smirked at me over his shoulder and continued walking. I narrowed my eyes at this infuriating man who was both enigma and answer all in one. With a growl I jogged after him, launching myself onto his back.

"Tell me!" I yelled dramatically, not caring that people were laughing at me.

"You'll see," he said, now smugger than anyone had a right to be.

"You're going to drive me crazy," I accused, wiggling as I held on tight.

"Maybe till death do us part?" he asked cryptically, and I could hear he was trying not to laugh.

"You are an evil bastard!"

"An evil bastard who loves you."

I sighed, sagging against his shoulder, still wrapped around him as he walked as if he didn't have a full-grown man clinging to his back. "I love you too. You know that?"

He hummed. "Sure."

I smiled at that one simple word that meant so much more than the sum of its letters. A word I recognized in all its little intricacies and meanings. It had become as potent as 'I love you' between us, and I felt myself turn to mush on the inside as I kissed the back of his neck, enjoying the rumble of pleasure that came out of him.

So yeah, sure.

Made in United States
North Haven, CT
01 December 2023

44857571R00166